The Lost Son

A KAREN BLACKSTONE THRILLER - VOLUME III

NINO S. THEVENY

SÉBASTIEN THEVENY

Nino, my son, of course.
Someone far from being lost!

∽

"Une fille attend au firmament du Septième Art"
Une star pleure dans une Roll's sur Hollywood
Boulevard.

Mais, dans la vallée,
Tournent les poupées,

Dans cette vallée profonde
Où des starlettes blondes

Meurent d'un somnifère en trop."

Michel SARDOU, La vallée des poupées, 1976
[Valley of the Dolls]

Prologue

THE YOUNG LADY was running desperately, as if fleeing Death itself.

WHICH FOR HER actually was the case.

Nikki was running as fast as her legs could carry her. As fast as her lungs would allow. She could feel them tearing apart, burning. Her irregular panting betrayed how close she was to abandoning.

Soon she would no longer be able to escape that person pursuing her.

She didn't even know where she was running to. Just why she was fleeing. The young lady had no idea where she was heading in that dense and moist forest. A rainforest. Trees and gigantic vines towered towards the jet-black sky, one that barely let beams from the reddish harvest moon that could have belonged in a horror movie come through.

Surrounding her, Nikki could hear the terrifying noises of the Amazonian jungle mixed in with her own throaty, dry breathing. Wild animals growling in the shadows, reptiles she couldn't even see hissing eerily, constantly fearing to put one of her feet down on the cold and sticky skin of a snake with a deadly venin. Shrill shrieks from nocturnal birds with yellow eyes cut through the darkness between the huge bleeding leaves from the myriads of poisonous plants surrounding her.

Her pulse was pounding in her head like the bass notes of drums in the Bronx, where she had been born twenty-eight years ago and lived until that fatal day when she decided to go to Brazil with Jason. What had brought her here, lost and alone in the middle of the Amazon?

Why was she fleeing, her bloody bare feet full of wounds, attacked by deadly roots in the arch of each foot, fearing she'd twist an ankle because she was running so fast that she'd trip over one of those roots, slip and fall on the muddy, spongy and hostile ground in that hostile forest?

Nikki knew that should she trip and fall, that would be the end. The man would pounce on her just like a vulture on its prey, and she would be a goner.

While drawing on the last bit of her resources left, the young lady thought once again of Jason.

Her boyfriend hadn't been able to escape their aggressor a bit earlier in the cabin they'd rented. What an idiot he was, such a dumb idea! "A long weekend for us two lovebirds, far from everything," was what he'd proudly told her, showing her the reservation he'd made in the isolated cabin in the middle of the rainforest. Just the two of them, making love day and night, with no one to bother them, no one to prevent them from joining together.

Just the two of them?

Too alone, too isolated... faced with that surprise guest who broke into the cabin in the middle of the night, a brightly colored wrestler's mask on his face, shirtless, just his oversized muscles, pecs, biceps, and deltoids tight with wrath and fury. And above all, that curved machete he was waving in front of them. The ideal wilderness survival tool. Advancing through the forest, cutting vines, cutting down leaves that were just as long as hammocks.

As well as being the perfect instrument to cut Jason into bits.

Nikki had succeeded in escaping the blind wrath of their aggressor by jumping out of the back window of their cabin, scratching her thighs through the nearly transparent nightgown that barely covered her intimacy. It was so hot and humid in the rainforest that Jason and she had spent most of their time as wannabe Robinsons, nearly nude. Now the silk was stuck to her skin, almost like a snake that was molting.

Her nightie, from fleeing that horrible, hooded man, was now in shreds, and you could now easily imagine Nikki's generous and firm shapes, her ebony color standing out in the cold and pale moonlight.

She suddenly heard the footsteps more distinctly of that evil man hunting her down. She was exhausted. Her legs could no longer hold her up, her feet were bloody stumps, her lungs had been ripped open, her eyes were filled with tears.

She collapsed, panting, her face against the spongy, muddy ground.

Her heart was pounding. Nikki thought for a fleeting moment that maybe she'd die right then from a heart attack.

A death that would probably be preferable to the one she'd soon have.

Above her, she could feel the heavy presence of the assailant.

"Turn around," hissed the man through his rubber mask. "Look at the face of Death."

The young lady mentally refused to obey that atrocious order. Nonetheless, her head turned slightly.

Behind the round holes of the mask, two yellow eyes were shining, just like those of the caiman lizards here in South America's brownish waters.

The man raised his machete above her head, Jason's fresh red blood still dripping from it.

Nikki's eyes opened with horror, and she screamed, breaking the noisy silence of the Amazon rain forest.

Moonlight reflected itself on the curved blade right before it reached her neck.

. . .

"Cut!" shouted Brad Purcell, the movie director, with satisfaction. "We're rolling with this one. Thanks guys, you were just perfect."

CHAPTER 1
That star that went out before shining

Los Angeles, June 6, 2024

I pressed the stop button on the remote control when the background faded to black, signaling the end for Nikki LaToya, the character that actress Shondra Wallace was playing in the highly successful movie, *The Bloody Machete 2*.

Highly successful, you have to understand me here, for what it was, B series – or Z as it is also called– a horror flick that well represented this successful genre in the 80s. The ingredients were simple and mixed together with limited resources: a handful of principal performers, an oppressive and isolated venue, dangerous situations, a hint of nudity, dialogs written on napkins in cheap restaurants, and a plot that would fit on a stamp. As for the actors, you just needed a very Machiavellian and evil one, who met a naive and nice but above all innocent young lady, but one whose plastic would drive even saints to hell. Plastic that hands down compensated her artistic talents and filled the seats in movies, but not large complexes, rather underground venues, with an audience composed of a cohort of sixteen-year-old teens and young adult males with capricious hormones.

These were the reasons why *The Bloody Machete 2* was a successful film. Undoubtedly shot in about two weeks, the movie had turned a profit by being shown in secondary venues but especially in its second life, in video club and streaming circuits.

Had someone told me that over the age of 40, I'd still be watching a flop like this, as I did when I was still in high school, I never would have believed them.

Yet I had to watch them to understand their mechanics and immerse myself in their atmosphere as Myrtille Fairbanks, my dear and unique Big Boss, would be sending me to Los Angeles on another investigation. I had to admit that this was something I'd asked her to do, a couple of months ago, and she'd found something to keep me busy in California as my personal investigation seemed to be pointing me in that direction. While I was there, I was hoping to do both my job and make progress in my private case.

But I was far from imagining that I'd have to glue myself to the screen for dozens of hours watching two-bit horror movies just because the apparently naive Shondra Wallace was starring in them.

. . .

But who the heck is Shondra Wallace you must be wondering.

Just like you, that was the question I asked when Myrtille phoned me a couple of days ago, explaining what my next investigation would entail.

"My little chickadee, you won first prize!" she said, overjoyed. "You're going to L.A."

"Fantastic!" I thanked her even before knowing what I'd be doing there.

"Imagine that it's the thirty-fifth anniversary, perhaps that's not the right word, of Shondra Wallace's disappearance."

I tried to make my brain cells work but I still hadn't had my first cup of coffee of the day, and believe me, it was tough. Despite my efforts though, the name didn't ring a bell.

"Shondra who? Who is she?"

"What, Karen? You're pulling my leg... You've never heard of the buxom – yet talented – Hollywood actress Shondra Wallace?"

"Nope, never heard of her! What about you?"

The shrill and contagious laughter of my boss was loud in my ear.

"Me neither, hun. At least not before I stumbled upon an article in an underground cinema magazine about how she mysteriously disappeared in 1988 while shooting a movie entitled, and I hope you're sitting down here, *The Coyote-Woman of the Desert*."

"Oh Homie!" I replied, awkwardly imitating Marge Simson's voice. "Sounds promising. A Hollywood actress who disappeared while shooting a movie and that no one noticed till now?"

"I mean, and here you have to understand, that this Shondra lady wasn't really number one on the billboards. She wasn't Sharon Stone. I even have the impression that she wasn't even mentioned because the movies she starred in were never even shown in the movie circuit but went directly to the VHS one. See what I mean?"

"A B-series actress who's totally unknown?"

"Except for those who like movies like that, which is not my case."

"Myrtille, it's not my case either."

"But that's no big deal, Karen! That's not what's important here. I'm not asking you to write an article about third-class movies in the 80s. Rather I'm counting on you to shed light on this incredible disappearance. Think of it this way. Had it been a huge star who suddenly disappeared smack in the middle of shooting a movie and was never heard of again, would that case have remained unsolved? No, it would have been in all the tabloids, magazines, on each and every TV channel. The other stars would have sobbed and praised her on all the talk shows, like Johnny Carson's *Tonight Show*, or David Letterman's *Late Show*, or on Oprah Winfrey's show, especially as she's an Afro-American like Shondra. Instead of that, that unfortunate actress must not have been important in the Californian movie industry, because when she disappeared, no one ever heard a word about it. A couple of lines in local papers for two or three days, and she was quickly forgotten. Except for her unconditional fans, of course, for whom she was an icon in second or third level movies. See what I'm getting at? You're going to bring justice to that poor star, that star that went out before shining."

And so that's how I found myself watching improbable movies – *The Bloody Machete 2*, who could dream up a title like that? – on my laptop sitting cross-legged on the bed of my hotel here in California.

Trying to shed light on whatever became of Shondra Wallace, the actress who mysteriously went missing in 1984 and that no one had bothered to look for over three decades.

Till today.

OR MORE PRECISELY, up until the troubling disappearance, thirty-five years later, *on the exact date*, – let me repeat myself here, *on the exact date* – in nearly similar conditions, of a young actor on the Hollywood beat, the very well-known child-star Jabaree Smith, Hollywood's favorite, who hadn't yet blown out his ten candles on his birthday cake, and also disappeared mysteriously...

CHAPTER 2
The camera's range

I FELT like I was an orphan.

Without my 1967 Ford Ranchero, I felt like a part of myself had been amputated. Usually my investigations don't take me to the West Coast, and this time, I reluctantly had to resign myself to flying to California, and not driving there with my usual travel agency, meaning my Ford, parked in the street in front of my house.

I also must confess that I'm afraid of flying. I luckily didn't have to cross the ocean to fly from the east to the west. But that wouldn't have changed anything, would it? A plane crashing on the ground or in the sea is the same thing, you still die.

When I finally landed at Los Angeles International Airport, the sun was setting over the Pacific. Used to living on the east coast, I basked in the sunset over the horizon, something that we didn't have, living on the Atlantic. I couldn't wait to discover this huge Californian city, one I'd never yet set foot in. A population of nearly four million, making it the second largest city in the United States, after New York. Plus, icing on the cake, the movie capital of the entire world!

I walked out of the terminal and gazed at the Theme Building, a futuristic one that looked like a flying saucer. That UFO immediately made me think of those made out of cardboard, in low-budget movies of the 50s and 60s, those where it was easy to guess, in the camera's range, that there were strings holding up the flying saucers, made from simple plates to cardboard layouts that were supposed to represent unidentified flying objects.

I went to the taxi line. When my turn came, I got into the back seat of a yellow and blue Ford and asked the chauffeur to take me downtown, where my boss's secretary had reserved a hotel room for me.

As THE TAXI pulled into the lane with countless other cars, the preferred way of getting around by the Angelinos, I thought back on the conversation I'd had with Myrtille right before leaving for California.

Rewind. *Replay.*

"Jabaree Smith, that kid who everyone who's anyone in Hollywood and fans from all over the world are in love with?" I asked. "Is that the Jabaree we're talking about?"

"Well, I only know one," replied my dear boss smugly.

"Okay, hey! Miss-I-know-everything," I joked. "That kid who disappeared a couple of days ago when he was shooting his latest movie?"

"Himself."

"How come you want me to investigate that?" I asked, astonished. "As far as I know, I'm specialized in cold cases. If the kid vanished only a couple of days ago, it's up to the cops to find him, not me. I only deal in cold cases, not boiling hot ones."

"Exactly. We'll let the cops do their job. But if I'm sending you to L.A., it's because I've got a good reason. As you know, I pride myself on having a good flair for unearthing interesting subjects…"

"Yeah, *you pride yourself*… And who gave you your legendary flair?"

Myrtille waited for a moment before answering, as if getting ready to pull an ace from her sleeve.

"Can you believe it, but when I heard that news, on a site that I scroll through regularly, I suddenly had a flash. That info reminded me of an old case dating back to the 80s, when an actress, a *famous unknown* one, named Shondra Wallace, went missing."

"Okay, two missing people from the Hollywood movie industry, with a gap of about forty years, I'd say that it's not something to write home about. Not as if an actor went missing once a week. Then we would think of a serial killer, maybe someone who hated strass and flashing lights, indecent money or Hollywood's depraved and decadent parties. But here, a case in the 80s and another one in 2024, if we're talking about a serial killer here, I'd say he's a pretty lazy one, don't you agree?"

Myrtille burst out laughing.

"Totally Karen. But a little birdie told me there's something to investigate here. Because there's this detail, one that I do admit could be a coincidence, but I've got a hunch that it represents something. My little chickadee, can you believe that those two disappearances took place *on the exact same date*? Shondra Wallace, a B-series actress and Jabaree Smith, a popular child-star, both went missing on June 1st, one in 1988 and the other in 2024. Curious, isn't it?"

I sighed so loudly in front of that insignificant coincidence that Myrtille jumped back at me.

"Go ahead, make fun of me while you're at it."

"Okay, don't get mad, I just meant on the first of June, both of them. So what? In terms of probabilities, that's one chance out of three hundred and sixty-five. Much easier to get that than winning the Lottery, don't you think? First prize is what? One chance out of a ten million, or even more? But you're the boss. If you want me to exhume a cold case from the eighties, no problemo, it'll be a pleasure. Especially as, thanks to you, I'll be able to go to Los Angeles as I'd asked."

"There you go! You just study up on the subject and then you contact the local authorities who are already working on the Smith case. The cops for the current case, you in the past, that's something that worked in Long Island, didn't it?"

I smiled thinking of my little Kathy that my investigation in Montauk, one that was complementary to the one the Missouri police did, and that had a happy ending*. Before I heard the click of a phone being hung up without anyone saying goodbye, my dear boss had another question.

"Now that I think of it. Do you like series-B horror movies?"

Click. She'd hung up.

AND THAT'S how I found myself watching terrible movies in my hotel room in downtown L.A., trying to understand what could link two similar cases that took place forty years apart.

I suddenly had an idea.

Maybe it was a copycat?

---

* *I Want Mommy*, Nino S. Theveny, independently published, 2023.

Taken

I finally found you!

I've been looking for so many years that I can't even remember how many, I wanted to see you again so much. Or should I say to be honest, meet you?

As you had been taken from me so quickly, so young.

Here I am, standing in front of your house, I got the address.

We're in June, this is a month where anything can happen, one where everything will be decided.

It's already hot out. Los Angeles has been the victim of increasingly frequent extreme weather events during the past years. Both El Niño and La Niña have been the cause of early and increasingly hot summers here in California.

I'm waiting for you to come out, sitting in a cafe that's across from the building where I think you live. I have no idea when you work, I'll just have to wait with hope in my body, my heart and my soul. You'll end up coming out sooner or later.

How will I be able to recognize you then? Instinct? A mother's instinct?

That's life, it reminds me of a movie.

A movie... Here in the spotlight of world cinema, in this artificial, superficial animated fiction universe, how can we separate what is real and what is fake?

Beforehand, I began looking for pictures of you on the internet. Nowadays it's so easy to track someone, learn more about their life, their relationships, their hobbies, their love life and friends. Social networks, what a goldmine! A paradise for stalkers sitting behind their computers or phones: private lives served to you on a silver platter, right in your pocket!

Three cups of coffee later, your front door opens.

You leave. At this moment, I'm sure: it's you, otherwise it wouldn't be possible. You are just like I imagined you'd be, quite logically.

It's still early in the morning. You rush down the steps and turn left, walking quickly. I immediately put ten dollars on the table to pay for my coffee, leaving a generous tip, and rush into the street to follow you.

Watching you without being seen, the slogan that stalkers, peeping Tom's, perverts, coy lovers, obsessed fans, and private eyes or spies all prefer.

I remain discreetly about a hundred steps behind you, trying to match your rhythm. As we walk north, the sidewalks begin to fill with more people. Will this enable me to remain unnoticed, or will this be a handicap, allowing you to outdistance me?

Where are you going? Will you be using public transportation? A bus, tram of subway?

What scares me the most is the fear of not making the right decision, not choosing the right moment to talk to you. What should I say? How should I say it? What should I do?

In front of others, or alone with you?

My entire body is trembling, that moment seems so intense, so hoped for that it has become taboo, impossible, unthinkable.

Yet, it will happen.

I'm going to do this.
  I have to do this, I can't back down.
  I can't give up.
  Not now.

CHAPTER 3
Top of the bill

A *COPYCAT*.

A small number of Americans who love local mysteries and solved or unsolved criminal cases immoderately worship the macabre work of former serial killers. Such fascination is hard for me to understand even though I do work for a crime and tabloid magazine.

And *True Crime Mysteries* is one of the leaders in publishing articles on these kinds of murders and wrongdoings, whether they're real or imaginary. I remember something that took place in London in 2008 where a criminal confessed to having killed two people precisely in the Whitechapel district, to pay tribute to Jack the Ripper, someone he admired. Seriously though, how can people worship fictive characters as if they were fans of a singer or an actor?

I also remember that guy in Belgium who stabbed and killed a fifteen-year-old, camouflaged in a costume that anyone could recognize from the *Scream* series.

And getting closer to home in Los Angeles, another mentally ill person, John Hinckley Jr., who tried to assassinate Ronald Reagan in 1981, and who was directly inspired by the *Taxi Driver* movie, where Robert de Niro played the role of a war veteran who wanted to kill a presidential candidate... Here his imitation of fiction shifting to real action was proved when he confessed having done that just to be noticed by young Jodie Foster who had a role in Scorsese's motion picture. He was so obsessed with that actress that he collected things linked to her.

So I was asking myself lots of questions.

A fanatic, or should I say a fine connoisseur of B-series horror flicks from the 80s, obsessed with Shondra Wallace, maybe wanted to attract media attention by kidnapping Jabaree Smith, someone who was now much more in the limelight than Shondra? The same day of June 1st, the same Hollywood cinema universe, the same disappearance, one without a trace...

A DOUBLE KIDNAPPING? Double disappearance? Or a double crime?

THAT'S what I'd be talking about in person with Inspector Jonas Crimson of the LAPD[*], Hollywood

---

[*] Los Angeles Police Department: The Los Angeles police force

division, who had agreed to meet me despite his heavy workload, caused, amongst others, by the Jabaree Smith affair, something all the movie world was talking about.

When I walked into the Hollywood police station, a red brick building on Wilcox Avenue, near Sunset Boulevard, I could tell that the front desk agent wasn't exactly thrilled by my presence. That surly lady wearing civilian clothing just looked at me when I asked her if I could see Inspector Crimson after I'd introduced myself as an investigative journalist.

"Can I see your press card?"

I handed her the priceless sesame that I hoped would open many doors, including ones that harpies like her were jealously keeping closed. She gave it a cursory glance while staring at me with her other eye – I had no idea how she could look in two opposite directions without ripping her optical nerves... And then at the end of what seemed an eternity to me, she pressed a button on her switchboard and told the inspector I was there.

"Sit down over there," she said, pointing at a couple of plastic chairs against the wall. "Inspector Crimson will come out."

She handed my press card back to me and then

---

employs nearly 10,000 agents and 3,000 civilians and is the third largest police force in the United States after New York (NYPD) and Chicago (CPD).

ignored me, concentrating on intensely chewing her gum.

Five or so minutes later, a tall man with broad shoulders, short blond hair, blue eyes and a Crest toothpaste smile on his pearly whites, walked up to me.

"Inspector Jonas Crimson," he said in a deep Barry White type of voice.

I put my little hand out to shake the inspector's powerful one.

"Karen Blackstone, a journalist for *True Crime Mysteries*. Thank you for granting me a bit of your precious time, Inspector."

"That's for sure," he replied, sighing.

His tired eyes and dark circles below confirmed his words.

The policeman escorted me to his office and invited me to sit down. He sat across from me in an armchair that groaned under his weight. I wouldn't say that Crimson was fat, not at all, but sturdy and hefty, with movers' shoulders and an ice-box type chest. I wouldn't have liked to be a delinquent that he arrested, pushed down on the hood of a patrol car, with his arms handcuffed behind him... Or maybe, depends on the handcuffs and venue... *No, Karen, calm down now, get a grip.*

"What did you want to talk to me about Mrs. Blackstone?"

"Miss... I wanted to run a theory through you about the recent disappearance of Jabaree Smith, which I imagine that you're now investigating."

"You seem well informed, Miss. You interest me, I mean your theory interests me. Tell me more."

"Where are you in the investigation, Detective?"

My journalistic background habits were immediately blocked by Crimson.

"In rooms like this, I'm usually the one asking questions. And I'm not supposed to be giving out any details about on-going cases. I'm listening though," the policeman said, sitting back in his chair, with his hands on the desk.

"Did you ever hear of anyone named Shondra Wallace?"

"Never. I should have?"

"Well, according to what I know, she was a minor actress here in Hollywood, someone that only a selected few appreciated, and she starred in B-series movies. But she's not only known for her roles, but she's known for having vanished during her last movie."

Crimson's eyes popped wide open with surprise and interest.

"Like Jabaree Smith…"

"That's right. And even better than that, she disappeared on June 1st, just like the child-actor. A coincidence or not, but you must admit it's food for thought."

"I do. And I'm also wondering why I never heard of that case."

"Probably for two reasons. The first one is that Shondra Wallace was far from being number one on the bill, meaning that nearly no one ever heard of her. Her disappearance quickly no longer interested either the media or the investigators. The second one is that this took place in 1988."

"Now I understand, I was only four then. But how did you know that?"

"I've got a really curious boss, and her memory is always in fifth gear. Always ready to rumble. She's the one who assigned me to this cold case, and that makes another reason why it was forgotten as it was never solved. Fell through the cracks."

Crimson nodded pensively while mechanically rubbing his hands together.

"And your theory believes that these two cases could be linked? If so, I'd like to know how. Because frankly, a difference of over three decades..."

I bit my lip feeling the detective's irony mixed with skepticism. Did he think I'd lost my marbles?

"I know that it seems difficult to believe if you persist in thinking that the same person was behind both cases. On the other hand, maybe you could think of the second case as a copycat one."

"I'm listening."

I expanded my theory, gave him examples, and little by little I could see a glint of interest on Jonas Crimson's square face.

"Could be," he said when I'd finished my argument. "We could explore that line of thought. Even though it's not really solid, at least it is something in the quagmire of unknowns in this case."

"I'd say that at least we won't lose anything by considering it, and that's where I'd step in. I'm a specialist in unsolved cold cases. I've got my own methods, ways of working, let's say my bag of tricks. And I'd like to support you in the Shondra Wallace case. To do that, I'd like to access the case's archives, as I'm sure that the LAPD covered it then."

The inspector burst out laughing.

"What? You gotta be kidding! That's the same thing as asking me to fly to the moon. At that time, nothing was digitalized like it is today, unfortunately. So there's no digital traces of it."

"A paper copy then, like back in the day. You must have that somewhere!"

Crimson shook his head.

"I'm afraid that for cold cases, files are destroyed after several years when there's nothing new. Did you know that over a third of the annual fifteen thousand or so criminal cases are never solved? Meaning that five thousand cases are closed each year, becoming cold cases if there's nothing new. And here I'm just talking about criminal affairs. And when it *only* – if I can use that word here – concerns someone who's gone missing with no body, someone who ran away or something, the files are closed ever more quickly. So, I'm sure you'll understand that for a case that's thirty-five years old... Sorry. I can try – and I promise you I will – to contact our cold case department, but I'm not going to guarantee anything."

"I understand," I said, though I was not really

surprised here. I'm used to working with nearly nothing. A simple testimonial, a letter, a rumor... But here, things happened quite a while ago and I was afraid that most witnesses would no longer be alive to speak to me. But I'd do my best. Especially if the two cases were linked, like my dear Big Boss thought.

"That'll take that monkey off my back, I do admit," sighed Crimson. "So, here's what I propose, Miss Blackstone. You take care of the 1988 case, and me and my department, we'll continue our investigations on the Jabaree Smith case."

"Consider it a done deal!"

"Hopin' the good Lord heard that," concluded the policeman.

CHAPTER 4
Vip

BEFORE LEAVING THE POLICEMAN, I decided to ask him one more thing.

"Detective Crimson, as I'm going to have to try to figure out what happened to Shondra Wallace maybe from a copycat point of view, don't you think it would be useful for me to know how Jabaree Smith disappeared? If that case actually is the *bis repetita* of that other one..."

The policeman, used to my questions now, smiled, nodding his head and looked me straight in the eyes.

"You got a one-track mind, lady!"

"What do you mean?"

"As you well know, I'm not supposed to give journals elements of on-going investigations. But, as we'll be working together, I will, though reluctantly and outside of a legal framework. Seeing as how my teams and myself can't take care of both cases at the same time, and maybe your background investigation could be useful to us,"

"Why do you think so?"

"An intuition. Just looking at you. Your communicative determination. I don't precisely know why, but I'm going to trust you. To come back to my investigation, like I said, it's the kid's mother who alerted us. That's about all we know right now, meaning not much, as you'll see."

∼

Audition of Miss Janice Lovelace by Inspector Jonas Crimson, Hollywood Station, Los Angeles, June 2, 2024

"Miss Lovelace, Inspector Jonas Crimson, in charge of the investigation about the possible disappearance of the child, Jabaree Smith, following your alert."

Though he knew she was married, the policeman well understood Hollywood cinema codes, thus addressing her as *Miss*, rather than *Mrs.* Lovelace. He continued.

"I'd like to go over with you the circumstances that led you to worry about the disappearance of your aforementioned son."

Janice Lovelace, languidly sitting on the leather couch overlooking a huge picture window that dominated Hollywood from their Bel Air mansion, was holding her hands together and bending her fingers, a sign of despair. On the other side of the window, the lights of the city were twinkling like hundreds of stars, attracting the policeman's eyes.

The young lady, pushing forty or so with artificially blond hair, just as artificial as the roles she played in the few films she starred in, began to speak with a shaky voice, holding back her sobs.

"INSPECTOR, I don't understand how that could have happened. My poor little Jabaree, my sweetie. You have no idea how much I regret having urged him to star in movies. He's so young, so fragile."

"How old is he?" asked Crimson, opening his notebook and taking out a pen.

"Not quite ten! He'll be ten in August. He's like a baby to me."

The policeman, just like everyone in Los Angeles, in the United States, or even in the whole world, could not ignore who Jabaree Smith was. For several months now the photo of the young lad had been posted on the backs of buses, on buildings under construction, on the front page of magazines specialized in the seventh art, and soon on the countries' papers and on the web. No other kid-stars had received so much attention since Shirley Temple in the 30s or Macaulay Culkin in the 90s. His chubby little face, tender round eyes with their penetrating glaze, brown curls on his *café au lait* colored face, his slightly lopsided smile that everyone loved, and of course the way he was able to act, something that seemed to be innate to him, when you put all those ingredients together, how could you not melt under that charm?

In just two movies, spectators and the paparazzi were crazy about him. His third movie's shooting had just been terminated and his fans couldn't wait to see this new and final opus of the *Daddy, Mommy* trilogy. Inspector Crimson remembered having taken his own kids to the movies last year where they saw *Daddy, Mommy and Company*, which was the second movie, just as hilarious and moving as *Daddy, Mommy and Me*, the first one. All of that due to Jabaree's talent as an actor.

"Miss Lovelace, could we go over the circumstances in which your son disappeared?"

The young lady squirmed on the couch, as if she were uncomfortable.

"Last night we wrapped the movie up. The producers had organized a little reception for this, right at the studios. Of course, Jabaree as well as the other stars were all invited."

Crimson, disdainful, frowned, thinking that long and rebarbative parties like that certainly weren't for kids, especially those not even ten years old.

"I'm not judging you here, but was it a good idea for a child that young to be staying up so late for a party? Wouldn't he have been better off in the comfort and calm of his own home, his own room?"

"I can assure you that something like this is rare. It was exceptional. Plus it was Saturday."

"Now it's Sunday," said the policeman, looking at his watch. "Were you also at the party?"

Janice bit her lower lip.

"Unfortunately, no. I sometimes suffer from terrible ophthalmic migraines and last night, I think it was worse than ever. The only thing I can do when something like that hits me is to lie down in bed, with all the lights off. And wait until it gets better."

"Is it better?"

"Thank the Lord, yes. But when I woke up, in those circumstances, believe me it was worse than my migraine... My son..."

Miss Lovelace began to sob again. Crimson nodded his head, compassionately, leaving her time to calm down, softly repeating, "It's going to be okay," regularly.

"Would you be able to tell me how many people were there?"

"I have no idea. Generally, there are the movie directors, most of the actors, the editor, his assistants, some members of the crew and some VIPs they invited. Plus a handful of carefully selected journalists. And everyone can come with a plus one, making it hard to give you an exact list of who was there."

The policeman shook his head, bothered by the idea that the multitude of guests would be increasing the number of suspects in a case like this, where everyone would be observing everyone else, but where no one – something even more flagrant in Hollywood – would be paying attention to anyone but themselves. Yet the young Jabaree Smith must have been in the heart of all the discussions and attention. Maybe too much? The policeman had another idea.

"Your husband, Jabaree's father..." Crimson began.

"My husband isn't Jabaree's father," Janice Lovelace said, cutting him off. "He's my second husband."

Crimson wrote this down in his notebook.

"You're married to Ruppert Magloire, who directed the *Daddy, Mommy* trilogy, is that right?"

"That's correct. So you see that Jabaree's success concerns a stepfamily. We're so proud of him. Ruppert, though he's *only* my son's stepfather, took charge of him as soon as he understood that with his innate talent, he could become an exceptional actor. Exceptional maturity for someone so young."

Deep down inside Crimson was thinking *or a circus animal* but didn't want to hurt the love that mother had for her son. A mother who, dazzled by the limelight, seemed to have forgotten that her son, before being an actor, was merely a child.

"So Ruppert was at this party then?"

"Of course."

"And he couldn't have prevented Jabaree from disappearing? I would imagine that he's the one who told you what happened?"

"That's right. When my phone rang, like I told you, I was sleeping in my bedroom with all the lights off and it woke me with a jolt. My migraine came back as soon as I heard his first words on the phone. Ruppert had panicked, he couldn't even utter two sentences. He finally told me he couldn't find Jabaree anywhere, that he'd looked everywhere for him in the building where the party was, then in the studios, on the movie sets, in the halls. Ruppert was frantic, he was talking faster and faster. I wanted to join him to look for my son, but he told me that it wouldn't do any good, that everyone there was already looking for him and that the best thing to do would be for me to stay home, if Jabaree came back, and call the police. So, that's what I did, and here I am, Inspector. Praying that you'll do everything to find my son, my little baby."

And once again, the kid-star's mother burst into tears.

"Please find him, Inspector. Otherwise I'll die."

"Miss Lovelace, I promise I'll do everything I can to find him. The first thing I have to do is call your husband. Can you give me his number? I'd like to call him immediately."

The policeman jotted down the numbers Janice gave him in his omnipresent notebook.

"I hope you'll be luckier than me, because I've been trying to reach him for two hours now, but he's not picking up... Almost like he disappeared too."

CHAPTER 5
Front row seats

When Inspector Crimson mentioned this new disappearance – one that took place the same day in his investigation, which was already three days old –, Ruppert Magloire's disappearance, I nearly jumped and began shouting.

"Inspector, you're telling me that Jabaree's stepfather also disappeared?"

The policeman cleared his throat.

"Had disappeared, to be correct. Because he came back."

"Dead or alive?"

"Alive, because I met him when he came back, three days after Jabaree's disappearance. He spontaneously came to the station."

I mentally counted the days.

"The day before yesterday then?"

"That's right. A completely distraught, totally

overwhelmed man. Had someone told me he was Jabaree's real dad, I wouldn't have been surprised..."

∽

AUDITION OF MR. RUPPERT MAGLOIRE BY INSPECTOR JONAS CRIMSON, HOLLYWOOD STATION, LOS ANGELES, JUNE 4, 2024

"MR. Magloire, thank you for coming to the Los Angeles police station. Please know that we're doing everything we can to try to find Jabaree Smith, who's your step-son, if I'm correct. The son of your second wife, Miss Janice Lovelace. From what she told me, you had front row seats when Jabaree went missing."

The man sitting across from Inspector Jonas Crimson in his office was but a mere shadow of himself. The policeman, though he's seen him dozens of times in the papers, on the web, or on TV shows, was unable to recognize that tall brown-haired man who generally had a princelike posture and a smile as large as an interstate highway when being filmed by TV's cameramen. This movie producer had had an enormous success with his hilarious yet moving comedies – as was the case for his *Daddy, Mommy* series – and was normally quite jovial, funny and the life of the party. But there, talking to the policeman, his shoulders were slumped and there was no smile on his face.

His pasty white cheeks competed with his sunken eyes in sadness, and his reddish pupils as if he'd already cried out all the tears in his body since Jabaree had gone missing. He was beating himself, his voice strangled by pain.

"If something happened to my son, as I consider him as my son, I'll never be able to live with myself again. Never. I was taking care of him that evening because my wife wasn't feeling well, she was in bed. He was my responsibility, only mine, and I failed her, I failed him. It's unacceptable."

"I understand," replied Crimson, trying to calm him. "But I'd imagine that during parties like the one you threw, everyone must be wanting to talk to you, interview you, as well as Jabaree. A toast here, a discussion there, a quicky interview. People left, right and center, so many you can't take care of them all. Or at least that's how I imagine a party like that, I don't do social niceties myself. Maybe it's just an idea, I don't know. What happens with the movers and shakers in Hollywood studios seems totally inaccessible, far, I could even say factitious... So I can understand that a moment of inattention, and..."

"That's exactly what happened, Inspector. A fatal moment of inattention. One second Jabaree was next to me and the next one, I couldn't find him in the middle of the crowd. I thought he went to the bathroom or maybe went to get himself another glass of soda or something. Then after about ten minutes, I started to seriously get worried. He was supposed to be giving an interview to *People Weekly* in about ten minutes and both the journalist and I went looking for him. Unsuccessfully. I searched all the rooms in the studio, plus outside, but it was dark out. He'd vanished!"

Regularly nodding, now Inspector Crimson was astonished.

"And you didn't think of calling us right then? Why?"

"Because... because I was too busy trying to find our little Jabaree. I thought I'd be more useful looking for him. But I did call my wife, his mother, and she called you."

As the producer told the story, Crimson was writing everything down in his notebook. Had you been following the movements of the pen, you'd easily be able to imagine the number of question marks on the sheet of paper. He looked at him, innocently.

"Mr. Magloire, did you drink any alcoholic beverages that evening?"

Ruppert's eyes shrunk.

"Inspector, I'm afraid to interpret your question. Are you insinuating that I wasn't lucid enough to watch over Jabaree? Is that it? You're accusing me?"

"It's just a simple question," the inspector replied. "Just give me a simple answer, please."

"Of course I had something to drink! Like everyone else! Is that what you wanted to hear?"

"Not everyone drinks alcohol..."

"Well, I do. But it was just a glass of champagne and then a cocktail that the barman prepared for the event. I wasn't drunk!"

"I believe you, Mr. Magloire, though I never touch a drop of alcohol. So, you had all your wits about you, and you began to look for Jabaree after having called your wife. But there's still something I don't understand. The party took place on Saturday, June 1st, and today we're June 4th. That makes nearly seventy-two hours between the two dates. When I auditioned your wife, during the night of June 1st to June 2nd, she affirmed that she couldn't reach you. So here's my question: where were you between the time that Jabaree disappeared and right now? What did you do during that time?"

Ruppert Magloire squirmed around in his chair, biting his lip. He took a while before answering the question.

"I do understand why this may seem suspicious to you, Inspector. I was overwhelmed, do you understand?"

"It is understandable, yes."

"I suppose that each person reacts differently when they're stressed. As for me, I spent hours going to each place where I thought I maybe would be able to find our child. We've got a house in Pasadena and a villa in Malibu too. So I went to both places, hoping..."

"Hoping what?" Crimson interrupted him. "Hoping that Jabaree, a kid not even ten, had run away to hide in one of your homes miles away from the studio where the party was held? I don't think so."

"I know," Ruppert sighed, "it seems crazy, but I don't have any other explanation."

"We're going to have to find one," warned Crimson.

CHAPTER 6
Just smoke and mirrors

I AGREED with the policeman in charge of the investigation.

"There must be an explanation for this disappearance. Just like you, I can't imagine Jabaree running away, at his age, and then walking up and down the streets in Los Angeles in the middle of the night. To go where?"

"Right. The sixty-four-thousand-dollar question Miss Blackstone! We started viewing all the CCTV footage in the street where the studio entrance is, as well as the underground parking lot, but didn't find anything. A kid like that, late at night, that's something that would have stuck out like a sore thumb. Plus my team questioned most of the guests who were present at the reception, but no one had seen a thing. Like I think deep down inside, people from that line of work, they're all busy navel-gazing."

"Yup, navel-gazing, Hollywood's favorite activity. A microcosm where people only look out for number one, hoping to be known and famous in the entire world. Paradoxical."

"But all so true. Hollywood is a separate world, a world of false pretenses, just smoke and mirrors."

"Something that seduces you then fools you, is that what you're saying?"

Crimson nodded.

"Exactly. That's why movies were invented: showing things that are false and pretending that they're true. Filming reality and affirming that it's fiction. So where can we place the cursor between what's true and what's false in this case? Except for our questions, my team and I don't have many certitudes here. If we start from the principle that the child didn't run away, what can we conclude, in your opinion?"

I could see what Crimson was getting at.

"You think he was kidnapped."

"Totally. That was my preliminary hypothesis, but three days after, you'd be expecting a ransom demand. But nothing. Kidnapping a child-star that the whole world knows, they must have had some precise goal? Either to vindicate some cause they think is just, or maybe to benefit financially? Everyone knows that little Jabaree has a fortune, thanks to his actor's paychecks, and the huge success of the series of movies produced by Ruppert Magloire. And that wasn't his first blockbuster. Money's not a problem for the

Magloire-Smith couple. And it could be tempting to try to relieve them from part of it."

"But I don't think that he was an easy target. On the contrary, despite how young he is, Jabaree is a public figure, and in that case, he's incapable of walking around without being noticed."

"I don't think stardom prevents kidnappings," the officer disagreed. "There are loads of cases of kidnappings of famous people just to get a ransom. Frank Sinatra Junior, who was kidnapped in his dressing room before going on stage. Baron Empain, who was abducted right in Paris. Just like the CEO of the Fiat automobile group. Or going back farther, Charles Lindberg's son! Or Josephine, the daughter of Frederic Dard, the famous French author of thrillers. Ironic, isn't it? He was someone who'd written, and brilliantly so, about all the facets of crimes, and he was now a victim... So anyway, there are tons of examples and when a kidnapping concerns a child, the outreach of the event is increased tenfold. Even more so when the child is himself a star, just like both of his parents are."

I agreed with Crimson's analysis and nodded slowly. But couldn't help but saying what was on my mind.

"Inspector, I'm sure you'll agree to admitting the theory I expressed upon arriving, that strange coincidence between this case and the one where Shondra Wallace went missing, on the same day, also on a June first. I mean, it seems to me that all these elements converge towards a premeditated act. And I wouldn't be surprised if we soon had new and unexpected developments..."

Right then, I was far from imagining that my intuition would be right.

CHAPTER 7
Churned Out

AFTER HAVING LEFT Inspector Jonas Crimson and of course thanking him for trusting me, I left the Hollywood Police Station in the unseasonable scorching heat of that month of June. We agreed that I'd focus on what happened back in 1988. And of course, something I couldn't forget, that was also what Myrtille wanted me to do.

But how to begin when you've never even heard of the person concerned? Like I'd told my dear boss, Shondra Wallace didn't ring a bell for me at all. And anyway, was this her real name or just her stage name?

The first reflex investigators have nowadays, both amateurs and professionals, consists in focusing on new technologies. What can be more automatic than wandering around in the internet's magical meanders? Just ask a question, you'll get a million answers!

Well, believe it or not, for the first time in ages, I didn't find much on the web. Mundane things, a few lines about the insignificant career of the actress and a few slim articles about her disappearance that didn't seem to have stirred those in Hollywood. Nor anyone else, real people I mean!

I found the longest article in a digital copy of the *Los Angeles Time*s, dating back to June 5, 1988. Just a couple of paragraphs though.

```
Our correspondent from the Hollywood
Studios has just informed us that
Shondra Wallace, an African-American
actress from Watts, disappeared while
shooting a new movie. Shondra, prob-
ably unknown to most of our readers,
is 28 years old and is said to have
taken part in over thirty B-series
motion pictures. Nothing but low
budget horror films, comedies or
action movies without any preten-
sions. Most of these features were
produced by Brad Purcell, a movie
director specialized in this type of
films churned out for a niche audi-
ence. To date, she has not yet been
found. The police investigation is
ongoing and no stones are being left
unturned. We'll inform our readers
about any subsequent developments in
this case.
```

. . .

Ain't that great! I hadn't made a lot of progress, except for learning how old Shondra was and for some reason the journalist informed us that she had African-American origins. I also noted she'd mentioned the Watts district, as if that meant something.

Watts, Watts, Watts... What's? Why point that out?

I suddenly had a flash. My memories, probably when I was still at school, or what I'd read, made me associate the name of Watts with riots. I quickly googled the two words together and this time had a host of results, including a Wikipedia page called "Watts Riots."

Without writing everything down, I remembered the most important data, which was that the riots took place in the summer of 1965, from August 11 to 17, after white policemen had pulled over a young Afro-American man for drunken driving, and a physical confrontation had ensued. In those few words I recognized the permanent tension between the Los Angeles police force and the city's black community from the 60s to the 80s, something leading to those types of tragic events. Tragic, because, according to the article, there were over a thousand people wounded and thirty-one deaths in the rioters and three in the police. Violence was so strong, with the *"Burn, baby, burn"* slogan, that the army was required to intervene. Nearly a thousand buildings were burned to the ground – often shops owned by white people – as well as the luxury cars they owned. The chief of police made mass arrestations, nearly three thousand five hundred people and the army imposed a curfew.

I realized that Los Angeles had been the theater for civil war scenes, of course only for a week, but extremely violent ones.

On the other hand, what relationship was there between the Watts riots and Shondra Wallace's disappearance, over twenty years later? I could not for the life of me understand. And why did the reporter mention her geographical origins? Unless, as I know what sometimes goes on behind the scenes, it was to give rise to a type of suspicion, questions, or tension for their readers?

As I couldn't find any links in this field, I decided to focus on her career as a second zone B-series actress. I found the site that seemed to be the most complete for data on the seventh art, IMDb[*]. In this very complete database, I found a file on her.

My enthusiasm unfortunately quickly collapsed when I read her nearly inexistant biography. Though her date of birth was mentioned, the date she'd disappeared was not. For that site, Shondra Wallace was not dead. Though I had to say, nothing proved that she was. The young lady had never been found, neither her nor... her eventual cadaver.

However, her filmography included about thirty

---

[*] Internet Movie Database.
A database for movies, television, and celebrities.

titles, as the Wikipedia page said, and ended in 1988 with *The Coyote-Woman of the Desert*, noted as uncompleted. I also noted as the article in the *L.A. Times* said, that she'd done twenty-five movies with the same director, Brad Purcell. Often in motion pictures, directors like to use their favorite actors or actresses in movie after movie. For example I thought of Robert de Niro with Martin Scorsese, Tom Hanks with Spielberg, or even Johnny Depp with Tim Burton. But twenty-five movies? That was an addiction! And I'd also heard that sometimes the movie director and his favorite actress are also a couple in real life, as they say. What if Wallace and Purcell...? A hypothesis I couldn't ignore.

I immediately clicked on the director's page and began reading it. With much more information than the actress's, I learned that he had directed nearly a hundred and fifty feature films! Including the last one, dating back five years. Born in 1954, he now would be seventy. If he'd shot twenty-five movies with Shondra Wallace, he must have known her pretty well. Maybe I finally had a direction I could take.

How to find him though?

At the bottom of his page I found "Contact Information," then "Agent." I clicked on it, but a pop-up forcing me to pay for the pro version of the site prevented me from continuing. Okay, I did understand that it would have been much too easy for any old person to get the contact details of Robert de Niro or even Brad Purcell! I had to give my credit card information, decided on a monthly or yearly adhesion, though I did have a thirty-day free-of-charge option. But what the hell! After the various steps required to create my professional account, I finally arrived at Purcell's complete page, with, and there my mouth dropped open, with a list of phone numbers, email addresses and names of the production companies he was working with, as well as his legal representative - meaning lawyers, and last but not least, his agent. I had my work cut out for me.

I grabbed my cell phone, crossed my fingers, and dialed a number.

Shondra Wallace, here I come!

Delivery

You disappeared from my life as quickly as you'd come.

I remember a frigid day, during a winter that seemed to be never-ending for my tired soul – also for my body – by months of singular heaviness.

I think I also was still a child. I'd just become a young adult if I believed my parents who undoubtedly refused to see me grow up. I was still their baby and what happened to me... couldn't have happened.

But it was too late!

I was too ashamed to talk to my mother. As for my father, it was completely unthinkable, he would have shouted at me, insulted me, maybe even beaten me until I asked for mercy. Or until his blows ended up solving the problem that was growing inside me. A problem that I hadn't been aware of quickly enough.

Yes, it was too late!

At the beginning, it wasn't evident. Just a bit of

nausea that I attributed to my shame, ignorance, and fear.

Then little by little my silhouette began to change, at first imperceptibly, then visibly as the weeks went by. I wasn't eating more than I usually did and was going to the gym as often as in the previous months. I finally understood that my hips weren't surrounded with muscles and fat, but by someone else, a creature growing inside me. A little human who was there, without me having asked for his presence.

Neither desire nor pleasure.
Hatred and pain.
Cries and tears.
Violence and fear.
But it was too late!

I was living in Massachusetts, a place where young girls like me were protected by the law, innocent ones, ones who wanted to put an... end to what had happened to them. Up until a certain date though, one that unfortunately had gone by.

I no longer had a choice, I had to keep it, waiting for... delivery.

That was how, at the break of dawn one frigid winter morning, with nurses, midwives and anesthesiologists around me, your fate was sealed.

You were born in suffering, fear, shame, and anger.
Suffering and pain for me.
Shame and anger for my parents.
And what will you remember about this event that

concerned you, but that you had no idea of its importance?

The main character here wasn't me. I was just eighteen years old and still living at home, the head of the family was my father and no one else. A descendent from a conservative Irish family, no one gave me a voice.

My father decided.
My mother agreed.
And I had to concede.

You appeared from nowhere.

Someone put you on my stomach. Just a few minutes. Just time for me, for us, to meet each other. I looked into your dark eyes.

We both fell asleep.

When I woke up, two hours later, in an impersonal room, I looked all over for you, even behind the frost covered windows looking out of the gray hospital parking lot, gray like my morale.

You had disappeared to an unknown place.

Today, I'm coming back to get you.

My lost son.

CHAPTER 8
A fictional character

I WAS SUBJUGATED by the delicious smell and the myriads of different kinds of pancakes that The Griddle Cafe on Sunset Boulevard had on its menu, where I was to meet up with Brad Purcell.

"One of the best places in Hollywood," he'd told me proudly on the phone, after I'd left my contact info with his agent, and he'd called me back. Though his agent was astonished that someone would still be asking about the movie director. And even more so, that someone wanted to meet him.

Anyway though, when I walked into the cafe with its magical fragrances of melted chocolate, caramel, and maple syrup, I thought I recognized some of the stars sitting there but couldn't associate their names with the faces I'd seen on TV or at the movies. Purcell hadn't been pulling my leg then.

I hoped I'd recognize him when he walked in. His

portraits on the web were still of a man far from being seventy years old. I had the feeling that his heyday, if he had actually had one, was long past. I'd told him what I'd be wearing today: a blue dress with white polka dots, easy to spot. I was sitting at a table at an angle of the cafe, about half an hour before our rendezvous.

I finally saw a man, easily seventy, who was weaving his way through the customers in my direction. When he caught my eye, he gave me a wide smile on his craggy face, with gray eyes looking out through white bushy eyebrows, sort of like his hair which was an unnatural shade of blond. He raised a hand, looking at my dress.

"Miss Blackstone?"

"Mr. Purcell. Pleased to meet you."

"I'm sure I'm the most pleased of us two," he said flirtingly. "Can I sit down?"

"Of course, sorry. Thanks so much for having accepted to see me."

"Have you seen my movies?" he blurted out.

"I must admit... I don't think I've seen any of them. I don't watch movies like that, but I bet you have a whole community of fans."

"Bah! Don't bother trying to give me empty compliments, Miss. My days of glory are past. And to be frank with you, glory has always run faster than me and now, I've stopped trying to catch up with it."

"Don't be modest. I did some research on you, and you produced over a hundred and fifty movies. That's incredible!"

The old man burst out laughing, showing a dentition that tobacco had probably spoiled.

"Do you think quantity is a criterion of quality? Take a look at Casanova or the Marquis de Sade, with their impressive number of mistresses. Did that make them happier? Don't be fooled, Miss Blackstone. Just think that producing that many movies in fifty years was more of a way to fill my plate than trying to snag an Oscar! So, what would you like to eat? I think I'm going to let myself be tempted by some *Mounds of Pleasure* pancakes, just because of their name. What about you?"

The menu looked so delicious I had no idea what to choose. I finally decided on their *Teacher's Pet*, a buttermilk pancake stuffed with apples and sprinkled with cinnamon, accompanied by tea for me and a beer for Purcell.

"So you wanted to talk to me about one of the actresses I worked a lot with?"

"That's right. A certain Shondra Wallace, whose destiny was quite unique."

The old Brad Purcell's facial features tensed up. A painful recollection?

"You're right there! Had that kid not had a tragic accident because she was so young and so lively when that happened, who knows how many more movies we would have shot together! We really got along well, both of us. Good Lord, that really did something to me."

"You said she had an accident? What do you mean by that? Do you know what happened?"

"Not at all! I have no idea. But a lady who vanishes into thin air just like that, right in the middle of a movie, and you never hear about her again, you must admit that something like that isn't logical."

"Were you two working together then?"

The movie director frowned, pushing his lower lip out.

"No, we didn't always work together. She had to put food on her plate too. So she worked with me, with others too, a small role here, an apparition there, a voice-over for someone else, to make enough money. But she was never on top of the bill, even though I certainly believed she had the potential. When we worked together, she was usually the star in my movies... but they weren't worth much! We didn't have the budget, my own producer either, he was independent, and I'm sure you can easily imagine what that means in a world dominated by huge Hollywood studios."

I confessed my ignorance, raising an eyebrow.

"I don't know all the ins and outs, Mr. Purcell. If stuff like that can help me understand the context in which Shondra went missing, please explain it to me."

The old movie director smiled, delighted to talk about his job, while the server brought us our orders.

"I don't know if that could explain the tragedy, but it will certainly help you undoubtedly understand why no one cared about her disappearance... Neither the media, the movers and shakers in Hollywood, nor even the police. It didn't make all that noise the disappearance of that kid is making, that little fart who was born with a silver spoon in his mouth..."

"Jabaree Smith?"

"Yup, Hollywood's new darling! And for Shondra, it's as if she never even existed! Like she was a mere fictional character... A lady on a roll of film, reproduced with twenty-four images per second on reels that you put end to end to create an hour and a half story. Shit! Shondra was real, you can believe me. A very beautiful woman to boot, with her black skin, her hair like a lion's mane, her dark eyes like two brilliant onyx stones. I never understood why she didn't have the success she deserved. Maybe I wasn't able to make her shine like she should have... *Mea maxima culpa*! Maybe it was my fault. So in a nutshell, she never took off. That's the drama of independent B-series movie makers faced with giants and their blockbusters. Us guys, we made two-bit movies, we designed our own special effects with string, cardboard and elbow grease. We created factitious monsters like crocodiles using resin and plastic iguanodons. We wrote our scenarios on a paper tablecloth, ten pages long at the most and we filmed all that in a couple of weeks, edited it in a week, and then it came out in a handful of independent movie theaters that only a few fans of stuff like that went to... That's why Shondra went unnoticed, both during her life as well as after her death."

I jumped when hearing Brad Purcell say that last word between his teeth, his eyes still moist by his story.

"You think she'd dead then?"

The fake blond man put his hands apart in a sign of his helplessness.

"Don't you think that's the only explanation? When we know that she mysteriously disappeared right in the middle of a film we were shooting in Lone Pine in June."

"Lone Pine?"

"That's right, Lone Pine! The Mecca of Hollywood westerns! A village three or four hours north of Los Angeles, in the middle of the Californian desert, in Alabama Hills, the perfect backdrop for cowboy and Indian movies or the type of movies we shot. Hundreds of feature films were shot there for decades. So when in the 80s you disappeared smack in the middle of that magnificent but hostile landscape, with its arid and dramatic mountains, you'd probably stumble upon some crotals or other friendly animals like that. And if you did survive all those dangers, the hot sun on your skull in the month of June would probably finish off the job. In that part of the desert, the days are scorching and the nights, well, if you don't have any shelter, you'll freeze. And then if you're still alive, you'll hear nocturnal animals barking, howling, hooting, you'll feel the hyenas wandering around, searching for carrion to chew on. If you've already seen pictures of skeletons of animals with their sun-bleached bones, you'll understand what it looks like around Lone Pine. And then to top it all off, if you head west, you'll find huge forests in Yosemite, Inyo, Sequoia and Sierra parks, and if you head east, you'll end up in Nevada. That's where you'll stumble upon Death Valley Salt Flats, just as hospitable as the Californian desert..."

"Death Valley," I repeated, horrified. "Death Valley..."

CHAPTER 9
Golden Globes

I MUST ADMIT that I had trouble swallowing my last mouthful of buttermilk pancakes when I thought about the image of Death Valley, Shondra Wallace's last stop. Was that where the twenty-eight-year-old actress died?

"No one found any trace of her from Lone Pine? No one knew how she vanished from the film sets? And, ever since then, you never tried to find out either?"

"My dear Karen, like I told you before, when it happened I wasn't there. Shondra unfortunately wasn't working for me at that time. You know, I've felt guilty for years."

"How come?"

Brad Purcell hesitated.

"Because I had the vanity to believe that I was like a big brother for her. Yeah, I always vaguely considered Shondra as a little sister, someone I had to protect. I couldn't actually tell you why, but when I first saw her, something about her moved me. She seemed to have a very strong character but deep down inside, somehow seemed to be broken, a scar that had never healed. Fragile. I was five years older than she was, and because of that, I felt like I had to protect her. Like a big brother would do."

I could hear the producer's voice break when he said that. He seemed to sincerely be affected by the painful souvenir of his pseudo little sister. We remained silent for a moment while the customers at Griddle Cafe were coming and going. All of a sudden people began turning around and taking out their phones. I looked up and saw one of my favorite actors, Leonardo Di Caprio, walking in. Purcell had told me that a lot of stars came to this place, but still... I felt like a little kid in Santa's lap on Christmas. My youth! I can still remember how jealous I was of Kate Winslet when she was hugging the bow of the ship in *Titanic*.

"It's..." I whispered with a movement of my chin in the direction of the actor who'd won Oscars, Golden Globes, and the BAFTA[*] Film Awards.

"It is," Purcell confirmed. "He comes here often. Want me to introduce you to him? I know him well."

My eyes popped wide open, and I shook my head.

"No, no, no!"

But it was too late, Purcell had already gotten up. I watched him sashay over to the table where the wolf of

---

[*] BAFTA: British Academy Film and Television Arts Awards

Wall Street was sitting. The old producer walked right up to the famous actor, but he seemed to be ignoring him. He even put one of his hands up, clearly showing him he wanted to enjoy his pancakes and coffee alone. I could hear snippets of sentences. *"Brad Purcell, producer." "I don't know you, just leave me alone." "Come on, Leonardo!" "Who the hell are you?" "Scram..."*

I chuckled to myself while Purcell was turning around to come back to our table.

"He was happy to see me again, but you understand, he just wanted to have a bite to eat without being disturbed."

"No problem, I understand. Should we continue? As you two weren't working together that time, would you be able to tell who she was working for when she went missing?"

Old Brad took a couple of seconds to regain his calm after having been politely slapped in the face by Di Caprio.

"Yes, I can because I was also at Lone Pine then."

"Yet, you weren't able to protect her... is that what is weighing down your conscience now?"

"Now and like each and every day for the last thirty-five years that she's been gone. Yes, I was at Lone Pine on June 1st, 1988. You gotta understand that this little town, in the middle of the arid mountains in the desert, is like an extension of Hollywood. There are often several movies being shot at the same time, nearly in the same place, and for similar scenes. And sometimes we even shared technical crews, and little directors like me, we used accessories or scenes that larger studios had used a bit earlier. And as there are hardly any hotels there, you always saw the same people that you see here in Hollywood. At that time I remember that Shondra was working for Peter Lundgren, and his movie was backed by the same producer I have, old David Apfenstein. So I was somewhere around there, but didn't see a thing..."

His voice went down as he ended his sentence and Purcell remained pensive, his eyes brilliant.

"Did you try to find her?"

"Of course! The next day when I woke up and learned that she hadn't showed up for Lundgren's shooting, so that was on June second, I looked all over Lone Pine just like a lost dog looking for its master. I also looked in the outskirts of the town, went up the hills, the same hills where a couple of years ago *The Hills Have Eyes*, by Wes Craven, was shot. I questioned everyone I met, but to no avail. No one knew a thing. On the other hand, I can guarantee you that Apfenstein was royally pissed! The whole movie was shot, and he'd be losing big bucks. As for Lundgren, he just gave up and wanted to go back to Los Angeles. It wasn't much of a loss for him.

"You don't really seem to appreciate that Lundgren guy very much," I insinuated.

"I'm going to be frank with you, Miss Blackstone. I could never stand him."

Right then there was a sudden commotion in the

Griddle Cafe, and I recognized Di Caprio's voice, calling out to the owner.

"Hey, Janet! Turn up the volume, they're talking about Jabaree Smith on the news!"

And it was true, on the TV screen on the cafe's back wall, there was a closeup of the young actor's face and the journalist was speaking in an emotional tone.

CHAPTER 10
Without makeup

"BREAKING NEWS.

An unexpected rebound in the case of the young ten-year-old Hollywood actor, Jabaree Smith, well known to fans for his role in the Daddy, Mommy, etc. series. His parents have had no news of their missing child since he vanished during a party organized by the producers of the third movie in the trilogy on June 1st, but we have just received an email here at the studios. Malcom, can you read us this message?

"So, Jodie, like you can see on the screen, all the message had was a photo of Jabaree, one where we can perfectly recognize the actor, but without any makeup. He seems to be natural, but with a sad little smile. He's holding his little stuffed rabbit, the one that fans of the actor and trilogy know well, tight up against him, with both hands on the stuffed animal's mouth, as if he were forbidding it to speak... A powerful picture, Jodie. And the email is accompanied by a couple of words: NEVER FORGET!"

"What do you think they meant by that?"

"For the moment, it's not clear at all. Our investigators are working on that, examining the past of the child and his family. But what's the most mysterious in that email is the subject line, and here I'm quoting 'June 1st, 1988.'"

"Something that dates way back, and that can't concern little Jabaree, who was born in 2014..."

"That's right. The person who sent the anonymous message is asking us not to forget something, but what? Jabaree Smith's disappearance? Or something that happened on June 1st 1988, thirty-five years ago? And if so, what links those two events? Or is it a simple coincidence that the kidnapper noted?"

"Just a sec, Malcom! You used the word *kidnapper*, does that mean that Jabaree was kidnapped? Was there a demand for ransom or were the child or his family threatened?"

"Nothing like that, Jodie. But it certainly looks like that type of crime, don't you agree?"

"And do we know who wrote the email or where it was sent from?"

"Unfortunately, not yet. From what I was told, it was LOCKED AND encrypted to make its traceability more difficult. Of course, our experts are working on it and I'm sure I don't even need to tell you this, but we also gave the police this message for their investigation."

"Thank you, Malcom. If there's anything new, we'll get back to you. We can see the photo of Jabaree Smith on the screen and we'd like to invite all of our TV spectators to contact us, if they know anything at all in this case of a missing child. Now, turning to what's new in the economy..."

. . .

THE REST of the news didn't interest me, and anyway, we'd be seeing Jabaree's picture for the entire day, either during replays of Malcom intervention, their expert, or other specialists, policemen, or if there was anything new. Either with pictures or in the ticker at the bottom of the screen.

In the meanwhile, I looked at the movie director, sitting across from me at the Griddle Café, who was staring at the TV.

"Mr. Purcell?"

"June 1st, 1988," he replied with a hollow voice.

He didn't need to say anything else. I took my phone out and called Inspector Jonas Crimson.

CHAPTER 11
Heads on the movie sets

"Miss Blackstone, I must tell you that your intuition seems to be true."

Detective Jonas made amends on the other end of the line.

But the one who really had the intuition to begin with was my dear boss, Myrtille Fairbanks, who I must admit, sometimes is like a soothsayer at the head of *True Crime Mysteries*. That's what I told the detective, who, like us, was listening to the non-stop news channel. He continued.

"And seeing as how the date of June 1st seems to be the key here, both in 1988 and today, maybe it's someone – the kidnapper or someone else – who wants us to reopen the Shondra Wallace investigation. A true or false clue? In either case, why? Whatever, but I have to admit that your copycat hypothesis can't be excluded."

"A copycat who's a tease too," I added.

"A tease, okay. But a kid's life is at stake here! And is he still alive? The email they sent to the TV channel neither confirms nor denies it. Just a photo and a few words. The clock is ticking, and I don't have enough time to earmark men for the Wallace case too. While I was at it, I checked the archives, and as I had feared, they'd been destroyed. So Miss Blackstone, my teams can only take care of the Jabaree case, meaning that you'll be my backup for Shondra."

"Hope so, Detective. Right now, I'm with Brad Purcell, the movie director, the one who worked with Shondra Wallace the most. I'll update you as soon as I make any progress here."

"I'm counting on you."

I hung up.

"Mr. Purcell, could you tell me how I could get in touch with the people you talked about, your former producer, David Apfenstein, and that other director you really don't like, Peter Lundgren?"

"For Lundgren, I have no idea and could care even less. What he's doing now doesn't interest me, but I'd imagine he's still directing total duds, we're about the same age. As for Apfenstein, ever since I hung up my gloves, he doesn't speak to me anymore. You know, Hollywood is a world of sharks. As soon as one is bleeding, the others rush to devour it. No pity behind the scenes! I actually don't even know if he's still alive. If he is, he must be about ninety, that old dude. Back in the day, he had a villa in Bel-Air and regularly threw crazy parties there. Crazy Hollywood nights, like those that Errol Flynn had, they were something... If Apfenstein is still alive, he must not be quite the talk of the town like he used to be, if you see what I mean."

"You don't have to describe it for me Mr. Purcell, suggestions are just fine here. Do you remember the address?"

He raised his eyes towards his bushy eyebrows, trying to remember.

"No, not his exact address but I remember that his property was located above the Bel-Air Country Club, where he was a member. Maybe on Bellagio Road."

"Thanks, that's already something. And thank you for your time. Could I ask you to contact me if you remember anything else that could help me with my investigation, Mr. Purcell?"

"As long as it concerns rehabilitating Shondra's memory, I certainly will, you can trust me. You have no idea how much I regret her. She was my sunshine. A black sun, but for me she was brilliant, shiny. Maybe others burned their eyes in her light?"

The old man's last words left me with a feeling that our conversation was unfinished, while Di Caprio left the cafe, and I stuck a handful of dollars on the Griddle Cafe's table.

"What do you mean by that?"

"Nothing precise. I'm just saying that for me, Shondra always stole the show because of her beauty, her charism, her charm. I don't understand why she didn't have the success she deserved. All I know is that heads turned towards her on the movie sets. All the guys literally devoured with their eyes, especially when we were shooting scenes that were a little... bare skinned, you could say, as all our B-series fans wanted to be scared, to laugh, and to be titillated. And Shondra knew how to do all three... And she did titillate a lot of men."

"Got any names for me?"

"The list would be too long. Without considering the many – or sorry, maybe I should say the few – fans of her movies. Sometimes beautiful actresses trigger feelings for their spectators that near idolatry."

"And could that idolatry lead them to commit a criminal act?"

"Like harassment? Kidnapping? Murder? John Lennon was assassinated by an overly jealous fan. You're right Karen, we can't exclude an act by one of her secret admirers."

CHAPTER 12
The supreme art of illusion

BEL-AIR COUNTRY CLUB GOLF COURSE is a very private social club with a mind-blowing clubhouse. To be allowed to enter, you have to show a clean bill of health – meaning you've got a membership card, or you're well known in the jet set – to join all the movers and shakers of L.A., businessmen, politicians, TV and movie stars, as well as the ultrarich whose villas overlook those eighteen holes. Up on the hills, between palm trees and softwood, you'll have a fantastic view of downtown L.A. And above you, the iconic white letters of the *Hollywood* sign make this venue one of the most unforgettable ones in the city.

Yet I was allowed into the sacrosanct venue where the old – or maybe I should say ancient as the he must have been at least ninety – producer, David Apfenstein, had granted me an interview arranged by his agent. He preferred to meet me in the clubhouse rather than at his home, his assistant said, as he never invited anyone in. His invitation was an incontestable sesame for me, and the hostess escorted me to the main room. In the rules and regulations, it was stipulated that all visitors must be accompanied by a member of the Country Club.

Serious stuff!

When I arrived, I was asked to turn off my phone, as cell phones were prohibited inside the clubhouse as well as on the golf course. Text messages were however allowed, but the phone had to remain silent.

Apfenstein's agent had also advised me to consult and comply with the strict dress code that was imposed, and I couldn't resist quoting it here, as it seemed too excessive to me. For women, *Shirts, skirts, culottes, knickers, tailored slacks and bermuda shorts (no shorter than 5 1/4" above the knee) are permitted. Jeans, denims, abbreviated tops, tank tops, cutoffs, swimwear, football jerseys, or any type of shirt with printed phrases and warm-up suits are not permitted. Bermuda shorts are not permitted in the Bel-Air Room except during lunch on Tuesdays.*

As for men, they were invited to wear *golf shirts with collars, golf slacks and knickers. Turtlenecks and mock-turtlenecks are also allowed. Shirts must be tucked in at all times. Bermuda or walking shorts, jeans or denims of any color, tank tops, cutoffs, swimwear, football jerseys, any type of shirt with printed phrases and warm-up suits are not permitted. Hats must be worn brim forward at all times and may not be worn inside the Grill Room, Top of the Tee or Bel-Air Room. No metal spikes, soft spikes only.*

So I put a skirt and a plain blouse on. I sure didn't want any problems with the country club management!

"The Country Club is a home away from home for me," David Apfenstein told me right off the bat with a metallic voice, one broken by decades of smoking.

And *metallic* was the right term, as the old man spoke by using a device that looked like a mic which he put in front of his throat and when he spoke it was with a robotized synthetic voice. I understood that it was an artificial larynx, one that was a substitution for his natural voice as his original larynx had been ablated.

"Damn cancer, Miss. I hope you don't smoke. That's the worst thing you can do in your life. When I think of all those cigarette makers who grow rich by selling what we now know are chemical weapons..."

"I luckily don't have that vice. I've certainly got other ones. Thank you so much for seeing me Mr. Apfenstein. I certainly would have understood, that in these circumstances, you would have refused to see me."

The old man moved back, not in one of the club house's comfortable armchairs, but in his electric wheelchair. That old producer didn't seem to have too much going for him anymore. I certainly hoped that his neurons were still functioning otherwise I'd end up empty-handed when I asked him to tell me about memories that were over thirty-five years old.

"Bah! For the few years – or months – that I've got left, might as well make good use of them. So, my agent told me that you wanted to talk about the dearly departed Shondra Wallace?"

"That's right, and I know that she starred in several of your productions, and I was hoping that you'd be able to tell me more about her and her... disappearance at Lone Pine as I was told you were also there when that took place."

"You've got good information, Miss. You're a journalist, aren't you? All that is ancient history now. I don't know with my memory..."

Was that a ruse or the sad reality? Had he sincerely forgotten or was he faking amnesia? I hoped the upcoming minutes would be fruitful.

"I'll try to help you," I said with a friendly smile, just like a nurse to a bedridden patient. "You must remember Peter Lundgren's name."

"Lundgren? He wasn't a bad apple. Not very gifted, but a hard worker. He never disappointed me. Except that one time."

"What one time?"

Apfenstein's eyelids closed for a moment, antique double parchment wrinkled by the years. He opened them and his electronic larynx began to cackle.

"Even though that happened decades ago, I'll never forget that shoot and its consequences. When Shondra went missing, of course, we were all shaken. At first we thought she'd run away, an abandonment of post, if you want to use the term they employ in the workplace. She wasn't the first nor the last to have whims of a star, to leave the set right in the middle of a shooting for some reason or another, a valid one or not. But the more we thought about it, no one who knew Shondra was able to find a plausible explanation for a voluntary disappearance. She loved her job as an actress, though the success or reputation that all actors strive for were never there. No one knew of any boyfriends, no one had heard of any enemies. Or maybe she hid that stuff well. No, really, no one understood what happened, almost under our eyes."

"No witnesses?"

The movie producer shook his head, his artificial larynx against his throat whistled, seemingly saying no. I went back to what he'd insinuated a couple of minutes ago.

"You said that Peter Lundgren had disappointed you that time. Why?"

"That's true. I did say that" he replied, seemingly lost in his thoughts. "I wonder what I meant by it. Got it! He disappointed me because he left the set to hightail it back to Los Angeles. He abandoned all of us in Lone Pine, the other actors, the technicians, and me. As if he was fleeing something too. Maybe his responsibilities. Whatever, but you can believe me, ever since that day we never worked together again. And I didn't produce any others of his movies."

An idea suddenly popped up in my cinema-lover's brain.

"I think that sometimes, some movies that a director started – and maybe he died before they were finished for example – were taken over by another film director. Could that have been the case here?"

"Of course," nodded Apfenstein. "A famous example is *Spartacus*, that Anthony Mann begun, and that Stanley Kubrick finished. Or sometimes there are bones of contention between a movie producer and the director. But the problem in *The Coyote-Woman of the Desert* was that our main actress went missing. Nonetheless, most of the closeups had already been finalized and it's true, we could have maybe cheated, like it sometimes happens, using a standby to shoot the reverse shots or wide shots. All cinema lovers would have been thrilled to find our mistakes! Cinema is the supreme art of illusion, Miss Blackstone, never forget that..."

While old Apfenstein nodded off in his wheelchair, the words reality, *fiction, false pretenses, cheating*, and *illusion* were dancing around in my head.

In the next few days my investigation would prove how much cinema was merely a factitious world...

CHAPTER 13
Things are moving in Hollywood

My interview with David Apfenstein, the former producer, ended on a bitter note. The ninety-year-old, visibly exhausted by the heat and efforts he'd made to remember, asked me to let him rest. He did add though that he'd be available should I have any more questions about the Shondra Wallace case. Though he had no idea what he'd be able to add. I nonetheless gave him my business card and left the Bel-Air Country Club, switching my phone back on. It immediately began to beep, informing me I had several messages and missed calls.

Beneath the shade of a sycamore tree near the entrance to the Bel-Air Golf, I listened to Myrtille's high debit message.

"Hey! My little chickadee, what's up? I've been

trying to reach you for an hour, and you haven't deigned to pick up your phone when your dear boss is calling, that's totally unacceptable! You see the news? Tell me, you are in Los Angeles? Or at the North Pole? Call me back ASAP."

And after a message like that, how could I not call my dear boss?

"Mrs. Fairbanks," I said in a sickly-sweet voice, "you wanted to speak to me? How can I be of use to you or agreeable?"

"Don't bother looking, useful and agreeable, you never got the recipe for that... Come on, I was only kidding. You see the news? Were you hiding in a cave? In the Californian desert?"

"Nearly. Lone Pine, you ever heard of it?"

A lone pine? Never, why?"

"I'll explain but prepare yourself for expense slips from there. Tell me what I missed."

"You can zap on CNN, they'll be replaying it all day. Anyway, Jabaree Smith's parents, or should I say his mother and stepfather, called a press conference after having seen the photo of their son yesterday. You know that at least?"

"The photo, yes. But not the press conference. What did they say?"

"I'll let you watch it yourself. All I can say though is that things are moving in Hollywood! And you, my little chickadee, you're smack in the middle of the circus! *Ciao, Bella!*"

And as usual she hung up without saying goodbye.

As soon as we'd finished talking, I rushed into the first cafe I saw, both for heat relief and to watch the news.

And just a few minutes after I'd sat down, I saw a replay of the press conference.

∼

JANICE LOVELACE, Jabaree's mother, walked out onto the podium in front of a group of overexcited journalists, supported by Ruppert Magloire, who was holding her arm. They both sat down in front of a row of microphones, their faces haggard with pain. Inspector Jonas Crimson, impassable but tense, sat down on their left. He was the one who began speaking, in a background noise of cameras taking pictures.

"Ladies and Gentlemen, in the framework of the investigation on the disappearance of young Jabaree Smith, which took place during the night of June 1st to 2nd, followed by an anonymous picture that the media received yesterday, his parents would like to make a public declaration. After that, you can ask them or myself any questions you may have. In the meanwhile, I'll let Miss Janice Lovelace take the floor."

Turning towards the lady, the policeman nodded as a sign of encouragement and gave her a slight smile to support her.

The actress, though used to cameras, mics, and public speaking, was having a hard time holding back her tears. Her husband put a calming hand on her shoulder, and she took a deep breath.

"Life ground to a halt for us during the night of Saturday to Sunday. The world stopped spinning. Jabaree, our little angel, was no longer in front of the cameras. All of you, both here and in front of your TV screens, you all know Jabaree's face. You've seen him, you've loved him, he moved you and made you burst out laughing in the series my husband Ruppert Magloire, who's here next to me, produced. But without any reason or explanation, Jabaree has disappeared. Up till now, we haven't had any news from our baby. I know he's almost ten, but he'll always be my baby, my angel someone stole from me, and I have no idea where he now is. Yet, I still have a thin trickle of hope running through my veins after having seen the photo of him yesterday, accompanied by those words *Never Forget*. We're sure it is a very recent photo because we both recognized the T-shirt that Jabaree was wearing when he went missing, when he vanished into thin air. We think and hope no one has injured him, that he's still alive, and because of this..."

Janice though could not finish her sentence. She turned her head towards Ruppert, who continued the declaration that both had prepared with the assistance of Detective Crimson.

"Because of this, we are begging the person or persons who kidnapped our son not to hurt him. Jabaree is an innocent child and all he wants to do is live. I'm speaking to you, his kidnappers, who undoubtedly are listening to our message and am begging you to bring him back to us safe and sound. In your anonymous message, you didn't express any ransom demands, so we don't understand your motivations. Why did you kidnap our child? What was the reason for this? Whoever you are, please contact us and let Jabaree go. To help you come to your senses, my wife and I have decided to pay for his freedom. Of course, the life of a child doesn't have a price, and no amount of money could replace Jabaree's presence here with his family, with people who love him and who he also loves. But still, as we have to give you a figure, we are ready to give you the sum of a million dollars if you let Jabaree go. Still, greenbacks aren't speaking here, but our bleeding hearts are. If your heart beats just like that of other human beings' worthy of the name, you must understand our pain and agree to release him."

When Ruppert Magloire finished speaking, there was a moment of silence in the pressroom. Inspector Crimson took the mic.

"Ladies and Gentlemen, journalists, if you have any questions please raise your hands."

A few hands went up in unison. Crimson pointed at one of them and nodded.

"Susan Mappleton, for the *Los Angeles Times*. Miss Lovelace, you have no idea who could be hiding behind this kidnapping? Did you, your husband or your son have any quarrels with people working in show business for example? Some animosities or jealousy that could have sparked this act?"

"What's the worst in what happened, is that we have no idea how or why this happened. You know, the Hollywood cinema world is a different world where anything can happen, both in fiction and in reality. Often reality surpasses fiction. But our Jabaree didn't hurt anyone, except maybe for other child actors who aren't as popular as he is. Yes, Jabaree is famous. Everyone loves him. Yes, he's the ideal child. Is that why he was kidnapped? Frustrated parents who couldn't have children? I have no idea what to think anymore, I keep imagining things, our lives have become hell on earth!"

Once again, she broke down in tears. The inspector asked for another question.

"Anthony LaPaglia, for *LA Weekly*. I don't want to question your investigation or your methodology Inspector, but have you thought about a nationwide call for witnesses, or paying for pertinent information that would help you find Jabaree Smith? And speaking of which, any tips on where he might be?"

"Mr. LaPaglia," said Inspector Crimson to him, "as I'm sure you're aware, at this stage I can't share any information on our investigation. The photo didn't allow us to pinpoint any place. It was a simple photo of the child in front of a white wall. On the other hand, our specialists are working on decrypting the IT file and email that was sent to our colleagues. As for any eventual compensation, I'll let Mr. Magloire answer that question."

"We've thought about monetary compensation for

useful information. We will give ten thousand dollars as a reward for any useful tips leading us to find Jabaree."

There were a few murmurs in the room as the journalists were taking notes. Then another arm rose.

" Victoria Johnson, for the *Los Angeles Daily News*. Should Jabaree never be found, will the third part of the *Daddy, Mommy* trilogy, which I believe has just been finished if all the rumors are correct, still be shown in movie theaters?"

This question sparked various reactions in the room, and on the podium, a response by Janice Lovelace, deeply shocked and offended.

"How dare you? That's despicable!"

"Next question," ordered Crimson, pointing at one of the journalists in the back. "And that will be the last one."

" Steeve Palmer, for the *Los Angeles Vanguard*. Inspector Crimson, the date of June 1st, 1988, associated with '*Never Forget*' of the anonymous email seem to refer to another case where someone disappeared, a Hollywood actress named Shondra Wallace, someone I'd personally never heard of. Can you confirm that these two cases that took place on the same day thirty-five years one from the other are linked? If so, what have you concluded?"

Crimson took a few seconds before answering.

"This is one of the leads we are following up, amongst others. This is an unsettling coincidence, and we hope that its resolution will give us some answers that will lead to freeing Jabaree Smith. That'll be all, thank you very much."

∼

Looking away from the TV, I had the feeling that Inspector Crimson would soon be putting pressure on me about the Wallace case... *Karen, it's time to roll up your sleeves and start hopping!*

CHAPTER 14
Just another dud

How could I shed light on an event over thirty-five years old where the majority of protagonists, witnesses or players in it had disappeared, died, or couldn't remember a thing? Whether their memory was defective, or they were voluntarily trying to hide information from me, was something I still had to determine for myself.

That evening, after having spoken once again to Inspector Jonas Crimson, who urged me to do everything I could to try to understand what happened to Shondra Wallace, I decided to choose the formula that I'd already tried and tested in many of my previous investigations, such as the one in the Veronika Lake case[*], meaning I had to go to the premises where it

---

[*] *Sugar Island: Where Veronika Lake vanished into thin air...* (Karen Blackstone Thrillers vol. 1) Nino. S. Theveny, 2023, independently published.

took place. Visualizing, feeling, smelling the atmosphere to better embrace the environment where the events occurred and trying to comprehend the circumstances. Those are the secrets of the Blackstone method! Total immersion!

So I headed off to Lone Pine, a four-hour drive from Los Angeles, if I ever managed to get out of the traffic jams omnipresent in this Californian megapolis, in my rental car. Which didn't make me forget my beloved Ford Ranchero, though I did appreciate my rental's air conditioning.

If it wasn't so very important to establish a link between this case in the 80s and Jabaree Smith's kidnapping, I could have imagined myself on a road trip in the middle of the Californian desert. The scenery on Highway 395 was just breathtaking. You start off in the hills in northern L.A. before penetrating into California's arid plains. Then once you've passed Mojave, you can see the beginnings of the Sierra Nevada Mountain range to the west, as far as the eye can see. Finally, after three stops to stretch my legs and have a pit stop after having downed two huge bottles of water in that infernal heat, I drove along the beautiful shores of Lake Owens for about five miles.

And finally arrived in Lone Pine. It looked like one of those little desert towns that you see in Lucky Luke comic books or when you watch westerns on TV. The town sign said it has a population of two thousand,

and also listed its main activities and attractions. All that was missing were buffalo horns above the sign to complete the picturesque painting.

The tiny town was spread for roughly half a mile on each side of Highway 395, which became Main Street and had a dozen roads branching out from it, with houses on each block. To the west of the town, Mont Whitney, with its 14,500 feet of rock, stood tall like a sentinel guarding Owens Valley.

In that picture-perfect decor over four hundred movies, mostly westerns, had been shot there since 1920.

And also in this idyllic decor, without any explanation nor media coverage, the actress Shondra Wallace, vanished into thin air.

And this was the place where I was hoping to find answers to my host of questions.

∽

As there wasn't much choice for accommodations, I put my suitcase and my fatigue down in Trails Motel, on the southern side of the town. Lone Pine was worlds apart from downtown L.A. Here, you immediately felt you were far from everyone and everything. Time seemed to have ground to a halt, and I was nearly expecting to see tumbleweeds rolling down that dusty Main Street in front of the saloon, though it was now paved.

I quickly understood how a commonplace B-series

actress could disappear in a place like this without people panicking. I had to try to identify myself with Shondra, virtually enter her body, take her identity as if I was putting on her clothing, in the middle of that isolated little town in a decor made for westerns. But walking on her tracks, going back in time and second guessing what took place here in May and June of 1988 wasn't going to be easy.

Where should I begin?

Who should I meet? Were there still any witnesses left? Would anyone remember having crossed paths with Shondra?

I DECIDED to start my investigations at the Museum of Western Film History, which recounted the famous cinematographic activity that had taken place for over a century in this little town, as it was not far from my motel.

"Welcome to our Museum, Ma'am," said a charming young lady with a large smile. "My name is Peggy and I'll be your guide and answer any questions you may have. Is this your first trip to Lone Pine?"

As I was the only visitor in the museum, I presumed that this place wasn't often crowded. As I didn't want to waste time in circumlocutions, I went right to the point and handed her my press card.

"Pleased to meet you, Peggy. To be frank with you, I'm not here as a tourist. My name is Karen Blackstone and I'm an investigative journalist for *True Crime*

Mysteries. Right now I'm investigating a disappearance that happened right here, in Lone Pine."

My speech astonished her.

"Good Lord, someone went missing?"

"Yes. But I don't want you to panic, it happened in 1988. I'm sure you weren't even born then," I said to calm her down and thinking she couldn't be over twenty-five. "To tell you the truth, the person who disappeared was an actress named Shondra Wallace, and she was shooting a movie here. So when I saw your museum, I thought maybe there would be an exhibit about what took place. But seeing your reaction, I'm not so sure there is. Am I wrong?"

"The young lady brunette nodded.

"No, you're right, Karen. Not a word about that event here. I would imagine that the people who founded the museum thought that it would be bad publicity for our little town, as tourism is the most important industry here. Did you know that in the twentieth century, a lot of inhabitants were employed by the studios for menial labor? And some were even hired as extras, or cascade artists, or standbys! Plus I remember a rancher rented out his horses, covered wagons and accessories for cowboy scenes. But is it okay if we do a quick tour... and if that doesn't bother you, could you please give a donation of five dollars to support..."

"No, no, of course that doesn't bother me, excuse me, here. And yes, I'm sure that a few explanations would be useful."

So with Peggy as my private guide, I discovered the cinematographic activity that had taken place here, with a myriad of photos, rolls of film, costumes and posters. I learned that not only westerns had been shot here, but adventure and action movies, as well as horror films like *Tremors*, science-fiction movies, including many in the *Star Trek* series or *Godzilla*, and comic movies like *Iron Man* and *Transformers*. Same thing for Quentin Tarantino's western, *Django Unchained*.

"The scenery in Alabama Hills is so incredible that it not only makes you think you're out West, in the States, but you can also imagine that you're on a different planet or in a different part of the world, like Nepal or Afghanistan, places where producing movies would be more difficult and expensive. Lone Pine is like the suburbs of Hollywood, a natural stage set served on a silver platter," Peggy joked.

"What about B-series movies?"

"That too."

"And if I mentioned *The Coyote-Woman of the Desert*, does that ring a bell?"

My personal guide looked up as if trying to remember.

"Sorry, no. Should it?"

"Probably not, as it was an unfinished movie, and the actress that I talked about before who went missing, starred in it. And according to your explanations, it must have been shot here in Alabama Hills?"

"If they used natural decors and the team went here, it probably was. Would you like to go there?"

"Is it possible?"

"Of course. One of my friends has a four-wheel drive and takes you in the middle of incredible geological formations. He'd be able to tell you where this movie or that one was shot."

"Except the one that interests me…"

"*The Coyote-Woman of the Desert*, I'm afraid so. That's a funny title," Peggy said. "A B or Z-series movie then."

"One that would have been just another dud, had it been finished."

Then I had another idea.

WHATEVER HAPPENED to the reels of film of the scenes that had been shot before she vanished?

CHAPTER 15

Hollywood's canteen

As the afternoon was winding down and my stomach was winding up with hunger, I walked down Main Street, the only street in Lone Pine where there were shops including Jake's Saloon, and it won me over when I looked at their menu.

Peggy, that sweet guide from the Museum, had told me that its owner, George Mavis, was a friend of her father's and that back in 1988, he already had a restaurant here and would probably be able to tell me things.

Peggy also arranged a private tour for me of the places in Alabama Hills where movies had been shot, this time with one of her childhood friends, Jake Pinkerton.

While waiting for the owner to join me, I savored some crispy fried squid with a cardamom sauce on the side, cucumbers with mint, and a portion of chipotle mayonnaise as a starter. Then, as I was still famished and he hadn't come, I decided to continue with grilled salmon and au gratin potatoes with a side of salad with cherry tomato vinaigrette.

"Miss Blackstone?"

I raised my eyes and saw a man who was a good sixty years old, salt and pepper hair pulled back into a man-bun, and a leathery sun-kissed face.

"Mr. Mavis," I said, wiping off my mouth, "thanks for giving me a few minutes."

"Just call me George," he said, pulling up a chair. "What can I do for you, Karen? I heard you're interested in my memories? I would have preferred it to be me," he joked.

"George, with all due respect, my only motivations are professional."

Then I briefly told him why I was here in Lone Pine and what I was trying to find out for the Wallace case. He nodded.

"Yup, I remember! At that time I was the chef in another restaurant and the crew of that movie always ate there. It was as if they were going to the Hollywood canteen but in Lone Pine, probably because the food was good and the portions generous, without wanting to boast. And the name of the restaurant was actually The Lone Pine Canteen. You're going to ask me why I remember those people so well?"

"You took the words right out of my mouth, George. Please, go ahead."

"Well, first of all, because there was that tragedy that shook our whole town up for a couple of days. I'm sure you've noticed how we generally remember what we were doing at some tragic moment? Like the day Kennedy died, or on 9-11, everyone remembers what they were doing when they heard the news."

"That's true," I replied pensively.

"And then, because the camera crew wasn't exactly very discrete," he continued.

"Meaning?"

He smiled nostalgically.

"They were loud and really extroverted. Always laughing noisily, but sometimes yelling at each other just as noisily."

"They actually fought?" I asked, thinking that the theme of anger could have played a role. "A feeling that usually doesn't bode well with peace on earth, good will to men."

"Not the day she went missing. I'd say it was the day before, or two days before. That evening, there were two camera crews in the restaurant. Everyone seemed to know everyone else, but each crew stayed at their own table. Hollywood is a singular universe. Both a large and small family where everyone knows everyone else. After a while, they began to make fun of the others, even insulting them. I wouldn't be able to tell you what they said, I just remember the general atmosphere, at first it was just for fun, then it got pretty heated. Men at each table stood up and they were looking for a fight. My cooks, waiters and I had to butt in to calm things down. We gave them a round of whiskey on the house and then all those film reel crazies calmed down, that time."

I jumped.

"That time? What are you insinuating?"

"Nothing at all. Just saying that with hindsight, it's unsettling that there was a fight that evening and then the next day or day after, one of the actresses mysteriously disappeared and was never seen again. Maybe I'm imagining things... or movies, to match the theme."

I shook my head.

"I also have the annoying tendency to worry about things too, but I think it's just an occupational hazard, though it often helps me shed light on my cases. Did you witness any other incidents between that evening and when Shondra Wallace went missing?"

"Me, no. But I only saw those people when they were having dinner. They lunched together wherever the movie was being shot, probably in their trailers, in Alabama Hills. Or else on the banks of Lake Owens, in the south, because it's got a beautiful panorama."

"Thanks so much for your time, George. And let me compliment you as a chef, everything was delicious."

"Quite welcome. It's not great cuisine like French chefs make, but I try to put my heart and soul into my recipes. Dessert is on me."

The boss and chef got up and winked at me, walking towards the kitchen. Then he turned around.

"Got another idea. Maybe you could meet with old man Bannister, the oldest person still alive here. He's an old fart, a bit bitter and probably no longer has all his wits about him, but... back in the day, he was a horseback rider and stuntman for countless westerns. You know, those where the cowboys and Indians shoot it out and fall off their horses when they're galloping! Well, in the movies that were shot here in Lone Pine, Bannister was often the one who was their stunt artist. And in 1988, he was working, I'm sure of that. He must have run across Shondra Wallace and the others. The only problem is that he must be at least ninety-five. Good luck," he concluded, disappearing into the kitchen.

RIGHT AS OF my first night at the Trails Motel in Lone Pine, I already felt like I was back in the 80s. The decoration of the room, added to what we'd talked about this afternoon with Peggy and George, sparked my nostalgia.

After having conscientiously swallowed, like every day for years now, my meds, I slipped under the sheets and let myself drift into reminiscences and dreams... or nightmares, to be more exact!

Damned

You disappeared, taken away by vile hands who grabbed you from me on a cold winter's night.

What meant the most to me was withdrawn. The flesh of my flesh. The fruit of my womb. The ultimate link, for nine months we spent each second together, a unique, bilateral, irreplaceable connection, one that only mothers know.

When I left that clinic, I was emptied out, empty of you.

They told me I couldn't keep you, that you were born out of sin, that you were damned. A child of shame.

That I wouldn't be a good mother. Because too young, too naive, too much of this, not enough of that.

Yada, yada, yada.

I'd lost my pretensions, but at the same time hadn't lost the shame that stuck to me like a scarlet letter.

They said it was my fault. That I was guilty. Guilty of what?

For having been in the wrong place at the wrong time?

Whereas I was innocent of everything people accused me of without even having tried to understand.

They took the best from me and all I had left was THE WORST.

A few months after you had been taken from me, I learned that you were not the only "present" that I'd kept from that terrible night.

Deep down inside, in my veins, I now had a poisoned gift.

Yes, now true poison was running through my veins.

Twenty-five years later, I still have the stigmas, the daily constraints.

For twenty-five years now, I've had to fight, to struggle against this evil that cannot disappear, this evil that can just be slowed down, controlled, mitigated.

They told me that in my misfortune, I was lucky. That there now was a treatment, and I probably wouldn't die.

I could have.

I would have liked to!

And I tried to, but wasn't strong enough...

Today I want to leave all those painful feelings behind me and progress.

Go to you.

THE LOST SON

Introduce myself.
Talk to you.
Tell you about you, me, us, them.
Why, how, when, where, and if?

Will you want to listen?
   My lost and found son.

CHAPTER 16
Roles learned by heart

LOS ANGELES, June 5, 2024

INSPECTOR JONAS CRIMSON was nearly tearing his hair out, looking at the non-exhaustive list of guests for the gala dinner, the one where Jabaree Smith, Hollywood's little angel, went missing.

Over a hundred people, most of them related to the world of cinema. Meaning that the inspector would have to deal with specialists in lies, sharks used to playing with false pretenses, masks dissimulating their true faces, roles learned by heart that they recited in front of audiences avid for scenarios and diabolic stories.

Crimson had put together a team who would listen to the auditions of the various witnesses who were present that evening. Different types of people, of all ages, in all lines of work, celebrities as well as anonymous, rich as well as... even richer.

They'd already interviewed most of them, but much remained to be done. Now they'd have to separate the wheat from the chaff; they couldn't impose lie detector tests on all those beautiful people, no one was accused of a thing.

Not yet.

After that they'd have to cross-check their statements, cross-reference the sources, note the incoherencies, and compare the inaccuracies and certainties. A colossal amount of work that had to be done in an emergency atmosphere: Jabaree had been missing for three days and no one knew where he was nor even if he was still alive.

A photo is not proof of life.

Nor is it a last warning before execution.

Never Forget, the email said.

A message in guise of a death notice?

MEANING that at the police station, everyone was hopping. Having cross-checked the various testimonials, the investigators were able to draw up a timeline of Jabaree Smith's last hours at the party.

This is what they'd come up with:

6:15 pm on June 1st: Jabaree Smith arrives at DavisProd studios, on Hollywood Boulevard,

where the reception is being held, with Ruppert Magloire, his stepfather.

7:00 pm: Malcolm Davis, the movie producer, Ruppert Magloire, and Jabaree Smith go to the podium.

7:05 pm: Malcolm Davis gives a speech.

7:15 pm: Ruppert Magloire gives a speech.

7:25 pm: Jabaree Smith gives a shy and moving speech, in front of a hundred or so guests, and all thus witnesses of his presence.

7:30 pm: After nourished applause from the audience, the three of them leave the podium and join the crowd in front of the buffet meal.

7:45 pm: One of the assistant producers speaks with Ruppert and Jabaree, while they are all drinking, about a project of spinning off the Daddy, Mommy, etc. triology into a TV series.

8:15 pm: The rushes of the movie are shown in a small movie theater for a handful of VIP guests. Several people affirm that Jabaree is in the front row during the projection and never left the room.

9:50 pm: End of the movie, everyone goes back to the reception room. Ruppert and Jabaree go to the restrooms. Three witnesses confirm they spoke to them in front of the sinks and hand-dryers.

10:00 pm: Jabaree goes back and forth between the guests and the buffet where he comes back with platefuls of petits fours. Everyone wants to spend an instant with the star all Hollywood loves. Several witnesses confirm this up until about 11:30 pm.

11:30 pm: Several witnesses affirm that the little boy is getting tired, something that his young age and all the hustle and bustle in this gala dinner is easily understandable. He's seen curled up on a big sofa across from the buffet.

11:50 pm: Another witness says he saw Ruppert Magloire carrying him, asleep in his arms. They head towards the stairs in the entrance, leading upstairs.

11:55 pm: Another witness says she saw the man and child in the hall upstairs and said she was sorry (it was a woman) to see such a "little kid so worn out" with the life he was living, a ragamuffin life. She sees them go into one of the bedrooms.

12:05 am (June 2nd): Ruppert Magloire goes downstairs into the dining room and he and Malcolm Davis, the producer, raise their glasses to toast the foreseeable success of the movie.

12:25 am: A witness, who was lost upstairs and looking for a restroom, admittedly having had a bit too much to drink, opens the door of the room where the child is sleeping. At least he says he saw a shape under the sheets, and immediately left.

12:45 am: Ruppert Magloire panics publicly. Jabaree is missing. Witnesses say he alerts all those still present at the party, about thirty people, telling them that the child is no longer in the bed where he'd put him a bit earlier. People begin to search for the child in the studio and surrounding areas.

1:00 am: Janice Lovelace receives a call from her husband.

1:15 am: Ruppert Magloire leaves and is seen jumping into his car.

"Good job, guys," said Crimson to his team of investigators. "All these details will allow us to understand what happened. And I'd like to add that once he'd called his wife, there was no sign of Magloire despite the incessant attempts to reach him. A blackout of forty-eight hours during which he said he'd driven to their various homes to try and find Jabaree. Speaking of which, we'll also have to tour them, you never know. Any questions or comments?"

The men and women around the table looked at each other, thinking of what their boss had just said. One of them raised her hand.

"Jonas, I don't think this chronology really matches what Magloire told you. If I remember correctly, he said that Jabaree had disappeared in the middle of the crowd of guests right before he was to give the *People Weekly* journalist an interview, and that was when everyone started looking for him. Is that correct?"

"Affirmative."

"And he never told you that the kid fell asleep on a sofa and that he then took him upstairs and put him to bed. That's unsettling, don't you think? Why would he transform what happened?"

"That's what I'm going to be asking him in a new audition," concluded Inspector Crimson. "You guys wanna know what I think? I hate people who earn a living telling stories... You never know if you should believe them. They *make stuff up* in reality and then pretend to *tell the truth* in their fictive movies... A despicable bunch!"

CHAPTER 17
Movie Road

Lone Pine, June 5, 2024

It was only nine in the morning, but the sun was already beating down on Owens Valley. I went down to the Trails Motel lobby, where a young man who couldn't have been over the age of thirty, candy on the eyes you could say with his unruly blond hair and blue eyes, waved at me. Sitting in a chair, he got up when he saw me and held out his hand at the end of his bulging biceps below his tight white t-shirt.

"Miss Blackstone? Jake Pinkerton, Peggy's friend. I'll be taking you to Alabama Hills."

"Let's go!"

I sat next to him in his dusty Range Rover, and he revved the engine and shot out of the motel's clay parking lot.

"It's not far from here," my guide informed me.

"You'll see, it's totally breathtaking. Where you from, if I'm not being indiscreet?"

"I'm sure that the scenery is going to be different from the forests and lakes in Maine, where I live. I was born in Boston. What about you?"

"From here," he said proudly. "A Californian from the desert!"

We drove to the west of the town and quickly found ourselves in the arid hills that attracted so many Hollywood movie crews. I had the impression of having made a leap into the past, back to the pioneers in the Far West, during the Gold Rush, or when the first railway tracks were constructed, when white settlers stole land from the tribes of Native Americans... It seemed to me that behind each rock, behind each cranny of a hill, we'd find ourselves face to face with a covered wagon, or a horde of Apache's, Comanches, or Sioux, what did I know about Indian tribes, galloping towards us in a cloud of dust.

"Now you understand why so many westerns were shot around here?"

"No doubt at all. I feel like I'm in a movie."

"Crazy, isn't it? This landscape is spread over dozens of square miles, and that's just on the surface, because if you climb up the hills, it enlarges the possibilities. Easy to get lost around here..."

Huh! Words that sparked my curiosity.

"You just saying that to impress me, or were there already cases of lost people?"

Jake looked at me from the corner of his eye while

continuing to keep the other one out on the battered trail we were slowly driving on, with a strange smile on his face.

"Huh. Who knows? A young lady like you, alone in this inhospitable and wild terrain, lost as night begins to fall."

"Stop!" I shouted, nearly scared.

"To tell the truth, yes, it has happened. Human bones were discovered a couple of years ago near here. Remains of a woman, they said. They added that some were half eaten by coyotes, those cute little animals that prowl around at night here."

"Are you trying to scare me, Jake? Did that really happen?"

He winked at me without really answering.

"Hmm. You know, urban legends... Here this is an open sky movie set, you name it, they shoot it here, advertisements, musical clips, lots of things. But my dear little lady, all that's mere fiction. So forget it and just enjoy this incredible scenery. This path is called Picture Rocks Circle, and as you can see by its name, there are geological formations that go way back and are strange or unusual. Here you might see a bear, there an eagle. Or even Hannibal the Cannibal, the feet of a rhinoceros, a toad, a bishop, and who knows what else. Okay, I must admit that sometimes you really have to use your imagination, or tweak the angle, but still, it's impressive."

It was impressive, like he said, and I was duly impressed. I looked at the ocher, yellow or red rocks like an amazed little kid, with a white background of the remaining snow on Mont Whitney. And understood how people could disappear here and end up... as supper for coyotes.

That made me think about Shondra Wallace's unfinished movie.

"Jake, did you ever hear of *The Coysote-Woman of the Desert*?"

"Excuse me? A coyote-woman? What are you talking about? A mutant? As far as I know there were never any nuclear tests in this desert..."

"No, it's the title of a motion picture shot here in 1988 during which an African-American actress, Shondra Wallace, disappeared. Does it ring a bell?"

"Vaguely. But I wasn't even born then! She vanished here?"

"I still don't really know, but right now, in the middle of this landscape, I think it's possible."

"Do you want to see Movie Road?" he proposed, turning to the right without waiting for my answer. "You'll recognize some specific spots if you like westerns."

"Oh. That's not really my cup of tea."

"It wasn't a western, your movie with that coyote lady?"

I thought that over. And it was true that I had wondered the same thing.

"I don't know. I don't think so. Not in the traditional cowboys and Indians sense!"

"You know westerns have really changed since their beginnings! You didn't see that movie?"

"No. It was unfinished because the main actress mysteriously went missing."

"Okay. I see what you mean. Back in the day they still used rolls of film, didn't they? I think it was 35 mm."

"I suppose so."

"So maybe there are rolls of film somewhere! They must be worth a bundle. Can you imagine something like that? The last images of the actress who mysteriously disappeared in the Californian desert. A fortune, let me tell you. If someone finds them, it'll be a jackpot for them."

"She wasn't exactly Marilyn Monroe either!"

"Of course. But Marilyn didn't vanish during a movie shoot never to be seen again! That's pretty mysterious, what you're talking about. And in Hollywood, what's mysterious is worth your weight in gold!"

Driving around with Jake Pinkerton, my mind began to churn.

A fortune! A mystery! Gold! A jackpot!

WHAT I WOULDN'T DO to have those rolls of film...

CHAPTER 18
Fade to black

Los Angeles, June 5, 2024

The shock was as intense as it was unexpected for Inspector Crimson and his team.

While they were wading through the auditions and cross-checking the statements to understand the timeframe for the gala dinner at DavisProd, where each witness could also – and why not ? – become a suspect, a bombshell was dropped on them.

An incredible buzz on all the media, TV, radios, web sites and social media with that video. It was retweeted, shared, commented, taken apart by everyone trying to play private detective, of course giving their opinions, pointing their fingers at the guilty parties.

Journalists and media professionals exploded.

Public opinion panicked.

The cops seethed.

The family trembled with high hopes.

Jabaree was – unless the contrary was proved – still alive!

The video in question only lasted a bit over two minutes, but the intensity of the child's eyes, the words he recited, the tears he couldn't hold back at the end, were all worth more than any other feature movies he'd starred in.

In just a few hours, that tiny rush would have more spectators than the entire *Daddy, Mommy etc.* series.

Millions of pairs of eyes, all over the world but most of all in the United States, were glued to their TVs, smartphones, tablets, or computer screens. Just like on September 11, time seemed to be suspended, whether you were at home, out and about, shopping, at the playground, or at work. Everyone logged on to see the angel face of the most famous child in America.

As was the case in many video clips of hostages, the kid-star was seated on an ordinary wooden stool, in front of a neutral background where nothing could indicate where the message came from.

He was wearing different clothes than when he went missing. Or was kidnapped, as that was now certainly the case.

The positive element that the policemen wanted to remember was that as opposed to the photo they'd previously received, here Jabaree was speaking, here he was *alive*!

∼

TRANSCRIPTION OF THE VIDEO RECEIVED ON JUNE 5, 2024.

`0'00'':` The child appears in the center of the screen, in a three-quarter view. He is sitting, hands on his knees. His head is straight, his eyes looking at the camera.
   A white wall as the background.
   No furniture.
   The room is silent. The child doesn't say anything. Sometimes he slowly nods as if looking at his hands. We only hear shoes on what is probably a tiled floor.

`0'17":` We hear someone clearing their throat. Then a voice, digitally distorted, that could be masculine or feminine, hard to tell without having expertized the file (to be done ASAP).

"Jabaree, you know what you have to do?"

The child nods.

"Do you remember what you have to say? For an actor like you, it can't be too hard, can it?"

The child, lips pursed, nods again silently to the camera.

"Good boy. You're used to cameras, they don't scare you. You know how to memorize texts. You're a pro. A real actor, in spite of your young age. Plus you know how to convey emotions to spectators. Here we go then, we're listening."

0'32'': Slow forward tracking shot on the young actor's face as he licks his lips, a tic he has.

"My name is Jabaree Smith, I'm almost ten and I live in Los Angeles. I want to tell my parents I'm fine. No one has hurt me, and I don't think anyone will. Unless of course, the police aren't trying to find me. Otherwise…"

The camera stops its forward tracking shot, now zooming in on Jabaree's face, slowly but inexorably focusing on his dark eyes. With a close-up face shot, the voice continues.

0'47'': "They give me food and let me drink, they gave me some clean clothes, and I can walk around but I can't leave the place where I'm being held prisoner. I can't tell you where I am. Anyway, I don't even know. I woke up here, but my last souvenir was in the reception room of the studios for that gala dinner for the end of the shoot."

The camera gets closer, and the masked voice embedded in the device begins to speak.

1'13": "What else do you want to say to your parents?"

"Daddy, Mommy, we learned that you decided to pay a million dollars if they free me. I'm all choked up that your love for me is worth a million dollars, but even a cent would have made me jump with joy because I know that you love me and want me back. And I want you to know that I love you too."

Tears begin to well up in the child's eyes. His voice starts to crackle.

"They told me that they'll think about this and will let you know their decision in the next message."

This time the shot only contains Jabaree's eyes that literally invade the screen with his dilated pupils.

1'46": "In the meanwhile, I want everyone to remember June 1st. That's the only thing that counts. *Never forget* June 1st. Every June 1st! That's all I have to say. I love you."

The camera zooms out followed by a slow retreating travelling shot, so Jabaree little by little appears in his globality, from head to foot. Sitting on his wooden stool, his hands on his knees like a good little boy. A poignant image of a ten-year-old kid who seems too serious, so mature.

The distorted voice concludes.

. . .

1'57": "Congratulations, Jabaree! You're going to win the Oscar for the leading masculine role for this splendid interpretation..."

A FEW SECONDS of silence then it fades to black.

2'05": End of the video.

CHAPTER 19
Internet never sleeps

Lone Pine

Even in the most remote part of the Californian desert, in a tiny town that looks like a western studio set, I wouldn't have been able to ignore the new chapter in the Jabaree case.

The info came to me as a notification on my phone, that incredible modern device that knows everything about us, our hobbies, our search engine history, what we talk about. For instance, have you noticed that all you have to do is talk to someone about something so that in a couple of hours or even minutes sometimes, your smartphone will suggest articles to read about it? Scary, isn't it? As if we were being listened to – spied on – via the embedded mic.

But had I not received that notification, I still would not have missed the info that was broadcast on all the televisions in Lone Pine, in bars and in the motel.

And had that not been sufficient, as I'm a VIP, I just got a call from Inspector Crimson.

"Miss Blackstone? I'm sure you didn't miss the video everyone's talking about, even if you're in a hole in the wall like Lone Pine."

I wondered for a second how he knew where I was, but luckily remembered that I'd told him about it before leaving.

"Couldn't miss it, that's true. Influencers would dream of having as many views and likes as Jabaree did on that impromptu clip."

"And I'm sure you didn't miss the reference to June 1st, 1988."

"It couldn't have been clearer."

"So where are you in your investigation, Karen?" asked Crimson impatiently.

"I'm here where she disappeared, Inspector. I'm making progress, slowly but surely."

I could hear him sighing loudly.

"You have to speed things up. I'm counting on you for this. Like I already told you, I can't put my team on this cold case. Can you go any faster?"

That guy made me laugh.

"Cuz you think it's easy to try to chase down something like that? I've got a gap of thirty-five years to fill, me! You, you don't even have a week, and it looks like your missing child is still alive and sending you movies. My missing person shot her last movie back in 1988!

And most of the people who could have seen something – or worse, done something – have also disappeared. Believe me, Inspector Crimson, I'm doing my best."

"Okay, Karen. Don't blame me for being impatient, the life of a ten-year-old kid is at stake and I'm not hiding the fact that all of us here are pretty worried. Do your best. And keep me updated with any little thing that seems to be important to you."

"Roger!"

And just like Myrtille Fairbanks, I hung up on him. Ah! Hanging up on a cop did me a world of good. Especially when he was the one who'd called!

I HAD to admit though that he was right - I had to understand how Shondra Wallace's disappearance could be linked to Jabaree Smith's. We now were sure that the two cases were linked in some way or another for some reason or another and Crimson on his side and I on mine, would have to try to understand how.

But who could I turn to, what could I do?

Continue to investigate in Lone Pine? Rummage around in the huge world of the web? Thirty-five years after, what hope could I have?

Finally, the combination of both types of research could be interesting.

On-site, George Mavis, the restaurant owner, gave me the address where the old Bannister lived, the guy who sometimes was a stuntman or standby in movies shot in Alabama Hills. I'd try to visit him tomorrow morning, it was now too late to bother a ninety-year-old man. Would he be able to give me any useful into? Time would tell.

And in the meanwhile, as internet never sleeps, I continued my investigation online. As soon as Myrtille had assigned me to this investigation, I'd already done a bit of preliminary research on Shondra Wallace but hadn't learned much.

Despite that, I tried again, this time combining several key words such as the names of David, the director, Brad Purcell, the filmmaker that she'd often worked with and Peter Lundgren, the other movie director, the one she was working for when she went missing. Just what I'd been expecting though, meaning movie posters, a few video clips, and a couple of feature movies on streaming sites where they'd been uploaded and that I would have to, but I wasn't looking forward to, watch. I found the titles distasteful, but decided to watch *The Bloody Machete 2*, tough luck for me, work was work!

At least I'd be able to see Shondra Wallace as an actress. If you could really judge her talent by watching a B-series horror movie. But what did I know...

Nonetheless, despite my lack of culture in this domain, I was forced to admit that I was pleasantly surprised by this motion picture that Brad Purcell had produced, and that seemed to have been shot in the tropics, not in Lone Pine. Probably not actually in the tropics, but in a studio. That wasn't important though, but in the last scene were the character she was playing – a girl named Nikki LaToya – was trying to escape a masked psychopath who finally caught up with her holding an unforgiveable machete above her head, her acting was not as caricatural as I had been expecting. Quite the opposite, her expressions seemed realistic, true and not at all exaggerated. You could see the terror in her dark eyes. And in her irises, Death was approaching.

As if she'd really seen the Grim Reaper coming for her…

WHAT CONCLUSIONS DID I have after this hour and a half movie?

Not many, unfortunately. I just got to know Wallace as an actress a bit better, as I still knew nothing about Shondra as a woman.

And speaking about women, what was up with *The Coyote-Woman of the Desert*?

Despite trying everything, all I found was that this was the provisional title of the movie Shondra was playing in when she vanished.

There were neither images of the rushes, nor any video clips, even short ones.

Logical: the movie wasn't finished.

I then tried a few sites and forums about unfinished Hollywood movies. And there were loads of them! Between scenarios that were never shot, crazy products mythical movie producers had – such as

Napoleon by Stanley Kubrick or *Kaleidoscope* by Hitchcock – and feature films that were halted in the middle, it was an encyclopedia of information. Plus passionate internet users often posted comments online.

Nothing though about *The Coyote-Woman of the Desert*. That wasn't surprising though as movies that Purcell or Shondra Wallace had finished weren't big hits. So for an unfinished one...

Still, I decided to toss a bottle into the sea and opened a topic on one of the forums.

CALLING for all B-series fans from the 80s. Anyone ever heard of an unfinished movie whose provisional title was The Coyote-Woman of the Desert, directed by Brad Purcell, produced by David Apfenstein, and starring Shondra Wallace? What's unusual about this movie: Shondra disappeared during the movie's shooting, on June 1st, 1988, in Lone Pine, in the Alabama Hills in California. I'm sure that everyone's noticed that this date is the same as the one where Jabaree Smith went missing too... You think these two cases could be linked? Do you think you could find any reels of film and if so, how?

```
Thank you for your help, even if it's
tiny. Karen Blackstone.
```

I'D HAD ENOUGH for today, my eyes were exploding, and I was getting ready to close my laptop when an image, perhaps subliminal, came to my mind.

An unimportant detail, but one I'd seen.

I put *The Bloody Machete 2* on again in streaming and put the cursor on the final scene, the one where Shondra, alias Nikki, was on the ground, her nightie ripped open, showing one of her shoulders.

And there was a tattoo on that shoulder.

One that seemed to look like a rabbit.

I paused the movie to make sure.

No doubt about it, Shondra – or maybe the person she was playing, how could I know? – had a tattoo on her right shoulder.

I was sure I'd seen that rabbit someplace. Or at least it made me think of something. Would that be possible?

But how could that be linked?

CHAPTER 20
Playboy Bunny

MAYBE I WAS IMAGINING THINGS. The image wasn't clear enough to draw a significant conclusion.

Yet, that tattoo of a rabbit made me think about Hugh Heffner's lucky animal, he who founded *Playboy* magazine back in 1953, and later an empire with the same name. The infamous "Playboy Bunny," the rabbit with its big ears and little tail, spun off into a costume that hostesses in Heffner's orgiastic parties in his various properties wore. The most famous one was the sumptuous Playboy Manor, a neogothic structure built in the Holmby Hills district right here in Los Angeles!

Did Shondra Wallace have any links with *Playboy* or Hugh Heffner himself?

Had she been a Playboy Bunny? Or one of his countless mistresses?

Everyone had heard about Heffner's sulfurous

reputation as a player, his immoderate appetite for sex with two, three, or more partners.

But maybe I was giving myself ideas just because of a commonplace tattoo – and anyway I'd have to do some serious cross-checking before drawing any conclusions – that perhaps were not even related to *Playboy*. I'd have to watch other movies starring Shondra Wallace or find other photos of her.

My eyes were beginning to burn, but I couldn't help but putting in a *bunny tattoo Shondra Wallace* in Google.

I discovered several other pictures of the same tattoo, an incontestable sign that it wasn't reserved for Nikki's character, the one that she had interpreted in *The Bloody Machete 2*. So it was a real tattoo Shondra had.

However, I didn't know what I'd do with that info. Probably not much…

I'd keep it in mind though and closed my laptop before falling asleep.

~

THE NEXT MORNING, all rested up and after having had breakfast at the Trails Motel, I was hoping to have a fruitful discussion with "Old Man Bannister", as George Mavis called him. As he'd given me his address, I went there before it got too hot in Lone Pine.

And the place he lived in belonged to one of his nieces, who preferred to have her doddery great-uncle living with her rather than sending him off to rot in an old people's home. At least that was what she told me when she opened the door.

"I never would have thought that my uncle still would interest anyone," said Felicity Bannister, a plump fifty-something year old with a pleasant chubby face, and graying hair. "But I just want to tell you that he doesn't really have all his marbles anymore up here," she added, tapping her forehead with her index finger. "The poor guy, all the times he fell off horses doing stunt work probably impacted his brain. But as you want to see him, I'm sure he'll appreciate having company."

"Thanks so much. I would have understood if you'd declined my request. I promise to take things slowly."

The niece looked at me and nodded.

"Miss Blackstone, you look like a good person. I trust you, and hope that he can help you with your investigation. You know, I saw the news about that kid in the movies, where my uncle worked a long time ago. But with much less popularity, of course. Maybe that's why he was kidnapped, who knows. Poor kid, I hate hearing stories like that that take place near us. The world is going crazy."

I confirmed.

"Because of my job, I see a lot of awful things."

"I'm sure. Why don't you just follow me, I put my

uncle in the air-conditioned veranda at the back of the house. I always try to keep him out of the sun and the heat. Plus, his vision is now next to nothing, and bright light hurts his eyes. So don't be astonished when you see the blinds are closed and it's pretty dark in there."

When I walked into the veranda, I thus wasn't surprised to see the old man sitting in a wide rattan armchair with cushions on it. A few rays of light filtered between the blades of the mechanical blinds and lit up his crackled and tanned face, one that proved he'd lived for nearly a century in the Californian desert.

"Uncle Paul, it's the lady from the papers, I told you about her earlier. She wants to ask you a couple of questions."

"Mmmm," muttered Paul Bannister between two dried out lips that had sunken into his toothless mouth.

This was going to be fun.

"Hello, Mr. Bannister," I said, getting as close as I could to his closed eyes. "My name is Karen Blackstone and I'm an investigative journalist. I'm working on a cold case that took place here in Lone Pine. I hope you'll be able to tell me something about it."

"Mmmm," he continued, nodding his head and squinting to try to make me out through his dulled irises.

"I heard you were an excellent horseback rider," I continued, trying to flatter him and touch an emotional cord.

And it seemed to work. I saw his eyes light up and

he smiled with his cracked and trembling lips. It took a while though before he answered me with a rocky twang.

"Ah! Horses! Westerns! That's life! I rode horses my whole darn life for movies. You know I worked for lots of famous directors. John Ford, Raoul Walsh, Howard Hawks. And I was a stuntman for John Wayne, Clint Eastwood, Lee Marvin, Robert Mitchum, and lots of others. When you see someone gettin' bucked off or falling off a horse, well that was me! Them actors, they didn't wanna get hurt! Insurance, all that crap. I was young back then."

His eyes looked off to the left, a sign that he was reminiscing. I gave him time to recollect his thoughts before carefully shifting to why I was there.

"Back in the 80s, did you also work for Brad Purcell and Peter Lundgren?"

His forehead wrinkled for a few interminable seconds.

"Don't know them," he answered without any other details.

Next to me his niece looked at me meaning "I told you so," but I wasn't ready to give up.

"Of course, they weren't as well known as the others you told me about. They mostly shot B-series movies. If I mentioned a certain Shondra Wallace, does that ring a bell?"

"Sandra?"

"Shondra. An African-American actress."

"Bof!"

"What do you mean, *bof*?"

"Don't know her neither. Never heard of her."

"She's the person who went missing right here in Lone Pine during a movie shooting, on June 1st, 1988. You were working for that movie Mr. Bannister... You couldn't have forgotten that..."

"Ah! That little Black lady! Don't see too many of them here, that's true. Not like them redskins!"

"Please excuse him," said Felicity. "He doesn't understand today's codes."

I thought to myself that the only fascinating souvenirs he had left were the scenes of cowboys and Indians where he did stunt work.

"Don't worry, I understand. This young lady, who was only twenty-three at that time, went missing, and the film was halted of course. That movie, unfinished, was supposed to be named *The Coyote-Woman of the Desert*."

Suddenly Bannister seemed to have a glimpse of lucidity. His face lit up.

"Ah! Yeah, got it, I remember, Jesus Christ! That's what happens when you lose your memory. Yeah, that black kid that them Indians kidnapped!"

CHAPTER 21
The camera never stops

THE NINETY-FIVE-YEAR-OLD MAN seemed to be losing it. Calling upon his memories only made him think of the movies he'd worked in. Now he was affirming that Shondra Wallace had been kidnapped by the Indians, just like in a typical scene where the redskins kidnap a squaw from the cowboys. White slavery by primitive tribes... Human sacrifices... Cannibalism...

Okay, maybe I was letting my wild imagination get away from me after Paul Bannister's surprising facts. But you had to understand me: now, adding to what he'd just said, he was starting to imitate the Indians just like they did in westerns back in the day, with his hand popping up and down on his mouth and shouting out "*Whowouwouwouwou.*"

"Uncle Paul," his niece said. "Please stop."

But the old man was totally into his insane folly

and now bouncing on his armchair. Now he was shouting out "*Ugh*!" *Ungha-ungha-wha! Ugh*!" and I was becoming uneasy.

General de Gaulle had affirmed that old age is a shipwreck. I think that Frenchie war hero must have been right about that.

Bannister though, didn't agree though his niece kept trying to calm him down, holding his arms and running her hair through the few strands of white hair he had left, like you would do for a baby waking up from a bad nightmare.

"I'm sorry Miss, just let us alone a bit. Could you wait for us in the other room, I'll join you."

Which I did, while apologizing.

While I was waiting in the kitchen, little by little the old man calmed down and a few minutes later Felicity walked in, a contrite smile on her lips.

"I'm so sorry," she said.

"Don't be. I'm the one who's sorry. All that is totally my fault. Going back to the past isn't always beneficial."

"You couldn't know. But I must say, I've never seen him like that, my poor uncle, ever since he came to live with me. He never had any children or never got married. When I saw that he couldn't live alone anymore, I took him under my wing. And that was fifteen years ago."

"That's admirable, Mrs. Bannister. You should be proud of yourself."

"Let's just say that family is important for me. That's life. Do you want to sit down for five minutes? Have an iced tea?"

"Thank you, yes."

She began to serve the beverages.

"That's the first time he's been so agitated. Sometimes he talks to himself or imitates horses when they're neighing. Or other times it's rifles being shot. 'Pow, pow,' is what he says. He worked in westerns for his whole life. They were his life! He did stunt work in over three hundred of the four hundred movies that were shot at Lone Pine. He was their go-to man. He sometimes fell and hit his head and that maybe accelerated the aging of his neurons. You think that's possible?"

"I'm certainly no expert in cognitive functions, but it probably is."

Felicity sighed after taking a long sip of iced tea.

"I think that my uncle mixes his real souvenirs with the fictive ones in the movies he starred in. Often when you work in movies, that mixes up your perception of reality. You end up believing that the camera never stops."

"That's right, sorting what is true from what is false. Not just disassociating truth from lies, but also the reality from fiction. But where the heck did he get this story of kidnapping by Indians?"

Felicity Bannister answer surprised me.

"Right next to here."

"What?"

"You didn't see anything when you drove here from Los Angeles?"

"Like?"

"The Paiutes-Shoshones Reservation."

CHAPTER 22
Portrayed

"You can't miss that Reservation, it's just south of Lone Pine. But if you were expecting a bunch of teepees, you'd be disappointed. It was created in the 30s and now it's mostly a bunch of trailers or prefab houses where the Natives live."

"Now that you mention it. I remember seeing a bunch of prefabs, but there was a campground there and I just thought that was part of it."

"Nope! They're our Indians," Felicity joked.

"What was the name of the tribe again?"

"The Paiutes-Shoshones. I gotta admit that they're not as well-known as those in the westerns, the Apache's, Sioux, Commanche's, Navajo's, Iroquois, Cheyenne's Mojave's, and so on. If you're interested in their history, they're descendants from the Mono and Timbisha tribes."

"How many of them live on the Reservation?

"A little over two hundred. That makes a tenth of Lone Pine's population."

I've always been fascinated by the history of the Native Americans, without even mentioning the genocide that they were victims of by the white settlers, one of America's open and most shameful wounds. Knowing they were parked like that on a reservation made me sick. And I was dumbfounded to learn that one of the tribes lived right here.

"Do both populations mix? Get along well?"

Felicity shook her head, sadly.

"That's one of the sticking points in the daily life of a little town. Everyone goes about their daily lives carefully making sure they don't mix with the others. There are just a few Shoshones who are emancipated from their condition and who have moved off the reservation to 'be civilized,' if you get what I mean. Though we could wonder who is the most civilized in this story."

"A vast subject. Going back to what your uncle said. Do you think any of it could be true?"

"In his delusions?"

"Um hmm. When he was affirming that the Indians kidnapped Shondra Wallace. Was it a fantasy caused by his work in all those westerns or a possible reality? Would it be conceivable that when he was talking about Indians, he wasn't referring to the Apache's that Hollywood actors portrayed but simply to the Shoshones in the Lone Pine Reservation?"

"Frankly, I have no idea. If something happened in our little town, we would have heard of it. Or even retaliated to the Natives. I can't remember any of that happening," the lady said apologetically. "How could I believe a crazy old man like my uncle?"

"Sometimes memory finds unexpected resources. And like the old saying goes, one that seems adequate concerning the Indians, *when there's smoke, there's fire!*"

"Smoke signals," chuckled Felicity ironically. "No, frankly, I don't believe his version. It's true that the Native Americans who live on reservations have a lot of defects like alcohol addictions, violence, unemployment, which are mostly because of their isolation, but I can't imagine them kidnapping a Hollywood actress right in the middle of a movie. Why would they do something like that? With what goal? What interest?"

I thought that over for a bit and summed up my answer to the stuntman's niece.

"In criminology, we call this the *motive*... When you find the motive, you find the person who committed the crime."

"That oh so famous motive in all the cop shows," Felicity agreed. "What all the investigators, from Miss Marple to Sherlock Holmes, from Hercule Poirot to... Karen Blackstone, are looking for. At the end of the day, what's a motive?"

"You're being too nice comparing me to all these bigwigs in fictive police investigations. A motive is what, deep down inside, makes the author commit one crime after another, they commit the crime to satisfy their desires. Jealousy, greed, hatred, revenge, racism. So many possible reasons. Mrs. Bannister, do you think I could go into the reservation to question the Shoshones? People who were alive at that moment, if there are any left?"

My hostess got up and walked up and down in the kitchen. Then she made up her mind.

"I don't advise it at all, Miss Blackstone. Us White people are not welcome in reservations. Especially when they come with accusations of kidnapping and questions."

"I'm not accusing them of anything! I just want to talk to some of them. Get their version of the facts if they have one. As simple witnesses!"

"*Tss, tss*. Once again, I must tell you to be careful. Anyway, you can't just waltz in and waltz out. Even the cops don't do that. The Indians have their own police force, their own local government, their own rules. We wanted to put them away? Perfect, now they're managing very well without us. We wanted to hide them, have nothing to do with them! That's what they want now, nothing to do with us."

I got up too, ready to leave the Bannister's. I thanked Felicity for allowing me to meet her old uncle. I walked through the kitchen, and she began to speak again.

"To go into the reservation, you have to be escorted by a Native American who is assimilated in our society, integrated into the life of our little peaceful town."

"Do you know one?" I asked, hoping she did.

"Actually I do. Go look up Foster Maverick. He works in the Post Office on East Bush Street."

CHAPTER 23
The kid~star

Los Angeles, June 6, 2024

After the nationwide – planetary? – broadcasting of Jabaree Smith's video with his kidnappers, Janice Lovelace, his mother and Ruppert Magloire, his stepfather, both wanted to directly address their public. They wanted to actively look for any witnesses, pool everyone's efforts to try to quickly free Hollywood's kid-star.

They set up a dedicated internet site: www.find-jabaree.com and asked for a dedicated phone number to be manned by volunteers. A huge chain of solidarity was put in place and all of America was impacted.

Well, almost all... Humanly speaking, Inspector Jonas Crimson was the one most impacted by the charity of so many anonymous people. He was touched by the incommensurable heartache of Jabaree's parents, who seemed to want to spend as much as possible – time, energy, and money – to try to find out where their famous child could be.

Yet, beyond his emotions, the policeman couldn't stop thinking about all the incoherencies that he'd noted between Ruppert Magloire's first audition and the testimonials that all seemed to converge taken from dozens of guests during the gala dinner party. When you've got several versions of the same event, one of them is possibly true and the others are probably false, he thought.

Who was telling the truth? Who was lying?

Who had made a mistake? Who had forgotten?

Though he could well imagine the pain the child's parents had, forced to repeatedly dissect the details of the tragic moments they'd gone through, Crimson only wanted one thing now: to summon the successful producer for a second audition, this time a more formal one, in his Hollywood police station.

∼

SECOND AUDITION OF MR. RUPPERT MAGLOIRE BY INSPECTOR JONAS CRIMSON, HOLLYWOOD STATION, LOS ANGELES, JUNE 6, 2024

"MR. Magloire, please sit down. Would you like a coffee? Some water? Anything else?"

The interviewee sat down heavily on the chair across from the policeman. You could feel just by looking at him his hopelessness, perhaps even a type of shame. Shame that he hadn't been able to protect his wife's child.

"Thanks, I'm fine."

"Okay then. I'd like to go over a couple of points that we talked about during your first audition, two days ago. Since then, a lot of things have happened, and I think I know a bit more about the circumstances of Jabaree's disappearance. About this, and before I ask you any other questions, I'd like to know if you spontaneously have any other elements you want to bring to my attention or any things that you had omitted to tell me last time."

Magloire thought that over for a couple of seconds.

"No, I don't see anything. Like what?"

"I don't know... The other day, you were still completely shocked – and of course I'm not insinuating that you aren't today – and in circumstances like that, it's easy to forget little details, that's only human. Today, with a bit of hindsight, perhaps your memory is more serene."

"Inspector, why don't you just ask me what you want?"

The policeman nodded, understanding, opened his notebook and put a sheet of paper on his desk.

"I was able to question most of the guests at your gala dinner and thanks to them, I drew up a reliable timeline of the events concerning Jabaree that evening.

And you. Most of the testimonials converge in the same direction. But that direction doesn't really match what you told me, Mr. Magloire. And I'm wondering why. What do you think?"

Ruppert shrugged.

"How can I think something if you don't tell me about the differences between their versions and mine?"

"That's true. So, there's one point in particulier that's bothering me. Last time, you told me, and I'm quoting you here: '*One second Jabaree was next to me and the next one, I couldn't see where he was in the middle of the crowd. I thought he went to the bathroom or maybe went to get himself another glass of soda or something. Then after about ten minutes, I started to seriously get worried. He was supposed to be giving an interview to* People Weekly *and both the journalist and I went looking for him. Unsuccessfully. I went through all the rooms in the studio, plus outside, but it was dark out. He'd vanished!*' Do you maintain that declaration?"

Biting his lower lip, Ruppert Magloire hesitated an instant.

"Like you said, Inspector, it happened right after, and I was shocked. Perhaps things took place a bit differently, I don't know anymore."

"Right after, but there still were those forty-eight hours where you disappeared. But I'll get back to that. For right now, here's the version that the witnesses all seemed to have seen."

Crimson took the sheet of paper and raised it.

"11:50 pm. Jabaree had fallen asleep on the sofa in the reception hall, you carry him upstairs and you put him to bed in one of the bedrooms. A person confirms that he saw both of you in the hall and then going into the bedroom. Another person says that at about twelve-thirty, he inadvertently opened that bedroom door, and he saw the child beneath the covers. Then at 12:45 am, you go back into that bedroom, you can't find Jabaree and you alert all those still present, then they all actively try to find him, but to no avail. A half an hour later, you decide to go to your car, and you take off."

The policeman finished his story by lowering his voice and leaving an instant of silence to observe Magloire's reaction. He said nothing though.

"Don't you think there's an enormous difference between those two versions? On the one hand, you affirm that you suddenly couldn't find Jabaree, and on the other, people see you putting him to bed upstairs after he'd fallen asleep in the reception room. Mr. Magloire, frankly, even though I'm sure you indulged in a few alcoholic beverages that evening, that you were tired, or the shock made you make a mistake, but still... How can you sincerely have forgotten that you put your son to bed?"

Magloire sighed loudly, his head lowered.

"You're right, Inspector, I lied."

CHAPTER 24
Cut!

"You lied?" echoed Jonas Crimson. "Why?"

He hesitated, still looking down.

"Because I was ashamed, that's why. Ashamed!"

"Ashamed of what, Mr. Magloire?"

"Ashamed of myself. Ashamed of having forced Jabaree to go to a party like that, things that kids of his age shouldn't have to do. Ashamed to have seen him fall over from exhaustion on the couch in front of a bunch of people who were overjoyed to see that little genius kid actor sleeping just like the ten-year-old boy that he was. I even saw lots of them taking pictures of him, probably to be posted on social media and boast that they'd been there. They'd be making comments like *OMG, it was so touching*! Whereas in reality, they were just proud of their gossip. That's why I took him upstairs, far from any prying and mocking eyes. But I was ashamed of that too. Because what I should have done was simply to have left the studio and taken

Jabaree back home, where his mother was in bed with a horrible migraine and let him go to bed in his own room. But instead of that, I was selfish. Because I still had some people to meet, some interviews to give, some hands to be shaken and I wanted to increase my popularity as a successful movie director. And a lot of my success was due to Jabaree, I humbly admit. So that's why I lied to you, Inspector, and why I'm not proud of myself. A useless lie, you're right."

Crimson shook his head in compassion.

"So I can document that your version matches that of the others? Meaning that Jabaree disappeared between the time when a witness saw him in bed and when you went back upstairs to check on him, meaning a gap of only twenty little minutes between 12:25 and 12:45 am?"

"That's seems right to me. He must have been kidnapped then. It's horrible, I couldn't do anything, I didn't see that coming. It must have been someone who was there that night, don't you think?"

"Probably so, but who knows, maybe someone outside could have gotten in without being noticed. In big gala parties like that..."

"But how would that person have known that Jabaree was sleeping upstairs?" wondered Magloire.

"Maybe they saw his picture on social media that one of your guests posted? But that seems to be much too short to have organized an operation that went off without a hitch."

"I agree, Inspector. It must have been arranged in advance, prepared, anticipated."

"Including anticipating that Jabaree would fall asleep?" asked the cop, surprised, jotting some notes down in his book.

"They must have already had a plan and then they just tweaked it."

"You said *they*, talking about the kidnappers, in the plural, this time," said Crimson.

"I can't imagine that only one person could kidnap a child, especially one that a hundred or so people were paying attention to, without being noticed. It's inconceivable!"

"Are you suggesting that we look for an organized gang then? Any hypotheses to advance on the authors of such a rapt? And do you have any enemies, or more mundanely, any animosities? In your job, for example? Or in your family or neighborhood? I'm not asking you to accuse anyone at this stage of the investigation though. Just to try to get some leads here. Do you owe anyone money? Any gambling debts, for instance?"

"I don't have that vice, Inspector. Others, certainly, but not gambling. And I only went to Caesars Palace in Las Vegas once, if you can believe that! And that was with a tour."

"Were you ever threatened? Any threats concerning you, your wife, or Jabaree?"

"Never."

"Are people jealous of you? Your success in the

Daddy, Mommy, etc. series, could generate jealousy for your colleagues or your business rivals."

To Crimson's surprise, Ruppert Magloire began to chuckle.

"I can see that you only have a very superficial understanding of Hollywood, Inspector. People seemingly say, or let's say when they're being filmed 'oh what a wonderful world it is.' Everyone loves everyone else, congratulates them on their successes. Or congratulates themselves! They all want to attend the Oscars or Golden Globes ceremonies! The Palme d'Or in hypocrisy, that's it! But once there's no one on the sets, when the cameras are no longer running and the director has shouted out 'Cut,' that's when their masks are lowered. Grudges and bitterness appear. Low blows and cheap shots are legion. So, yes, maybe you're right and we should be investigating those who are jealous of my success. Or especially of Jabaree's success."

"Got any names for me?"

The movie director sighed and closed his eyes. He seemed to mentally be listing people in showbiz that could have been capable of committing a crime, of kidnapping and sequestration of a child, and demanding a ransom.

"I sincerely don't know. In the people surrounding me, I can't believe anyone would be capable of such infamy. But I do agree with your hypothesis of premeditation, and because of that I think that the author or authors of the rapt must have been someone amongst my guests at the gala dinner."

"So one of the hundred or so people that my teams and I had questioned as witnesses then..."

"Even if they didn't take part themselves in the kidnapping, they could have been accomplices or have ordered it."

"I'll look into that hypothesis. With your help, Mr. Magloire."

"I'll be happy to help," said the movie director, getting up from his chair.

But Crimson raised a hand.

"Sit back down, Mr. Magloire, there's still one crucial element we have to go over," he told him in an authoritarian voice.

CHAPTER 25
Radio silence

SUDDENLY CUT off in his gesture, Ruppert Magloire raised his eyebrows, worried. He thought his second audition had finished, but the Inspector didn't agree. The movie director sat back down, docile.

"What else then?"

"Oh. Don't worry, I just wanted to go over precisely what you did after you left the party that evening," the policeman said, trying to reassure him. "So, as of 1:15 am, according to the witnesses who saw you rush away from the party in your car, up until the time when you spontaneously came to see me, there's a gap of a bit over fifty hours. Mr. Magloire, what did you do during those fifty hours of radio silence? Fifty hours, that's a heck of a long time, which left you a lot of time to do a lot of things."

The movie director felt his anger building with that insinuation.

"But I already told you! I desperately tried to find

Jabaree. I drove to our different homes just in case he had run away and had decided to hide in one of them. You know in a situation like that you're not always really logical, you must understand that better than anyone."

"Better than anyone, I don't know, but yes, you're right, this is something I've often noted. Whether you're a criminal, a victim, a partner-in-crime, or witness, you can panic, make mistakes, do unfortunate or stupid things. Even us investigators, we can panic and make mistakes too. I'm not blaming you for that, it's only human. I'm just asking you to clearly tell me what you did during those fifty hours. In detail."

"Okay. Sorry, I was a little emotional there. Let me try to remember because I must admit that my stress led me to act as if I was running on autopilot. Even now, I sort of feel like I can't remember even half of the things I did that night. Like there are little black holes in my brain. But I'll do what I can. So when I left the party, about 1:15 a.m. like you said, I headed first to Pasadena, north of L.A. which is our closest country house. At that time of the night there weren't any traffic jams, and I got there at about 1:45, so half an hour later or so. I looked all over the property, inside and out, and as Jabaree wasn't there obviously, I continued to Malibu, where we've got another house."

"Looks like business is good," Crimson said ironically. "How many houses do you have? Sorry, you can continue."

"We have three country houses in the States. And

one apartment in Paris. Of course, I didn't go to France…"

"In fifty hours? You could have," Crimson said, cutting him off. "So, Malibu and…?'

"Yes, the same thing in Malibu. I looked all over the property, inside and out, and then I rushed to our last villa, which isn't in California, but in neighboring Nevada, in Las Vegas. And that's where I holed up before coming back to Los Angeles."

"Laying prostrate? Explain that to me."

"Like I said earlier, I was ashamed of myself for all the reasons I gave you before. And there was another one: I wasn't able to find Jabaree despite all my efforts. But also ashamed to go back home, to look my wife in the eyes, with what happened to her son. The only son she'd had with her late husband. I felt so terribly guilty!"

The man seemed sincerely afflicted by his incompetence as Jabaree's substitute father. Not worthy of it. His words stuck in his throat and his eyes filled with tears. Crimson knew he was at the point of an emotional breakdown. Yet, the cop continued.

"You gave up and you refused to look reality in the face. To assume your mistakes. Wouldn't it have been more logical to go home to your wife, who was in bed with a migraine and support her when you told her that her son had disappeared? To act responsibly! That's not very glorious, is it, Magloire!"

Those last words completely overthrew the tiny bit

of self-confidence Ruppert had, and he burst into tears, holding his head in his hands.

"I was pathetic," he managed to articulate between two sobs.

"That you were," confirmed the police officer. "You screwed up, Magloire. Now you have to repair things, if you still have time... If Jabaree is still alive."

"Don't say that!" protested the movie director. "You saw the video like everyone did. He's alive, he'll come back. My wife and I are doing all we can."

"So are we," added the inspector. "Never forget that. In the meanwhile though, please give me the addresses of your country homes in Pasadena, Malibu and Las Vegas."

"What good will that do?"

"It's for our investigation, Mr. Magloire. Plus, I'd like you to accompany us there. A private tour, if you like."

"I don't understand. What do you think you'll find there? Not Jabaree, as I just told you that he wasn't there. Plus, how would he have gotten there? With all due respect, Inspector, don't you think you're going in the wrong direction? Wasting time with me rather than having all your men look for our child's kidnappers?"

"As I'm not a soothsayer nor a fortune-teller, all I believe is what I see, Mr. Magloire. Ah! One more question before we go. In the video, Jabaree insists that we should not forget June 1st, *every June 1st*. Does the disappearance of an actress named Shondra Wallace that took place on June 1st, 1988 ring a bell for you?"

"I never heard of her."

CHAPTER 26
Glitter and glamor

LONE PINE, June 6, 2024

I WAS SITTING on a bench across from the post office in that snoozing town. A few minutes before, I had gone in and asked to see Foster Maverick, the Native American who moved from the Paiutes-Shoshones Reservation to become an active citizen in what was referred to as "New Americans." I quickly told him why I was there and could feel that he was open to discussion. And had to say that in this investigation, contrary to those I'd carried out before, I hadn't run up against a brick wall of suspicion or silence in those people I'd met. But I still had no leads in this case that would allow me to understand why and how Shondra Wallace had gone missing.

The young man told me that he finished at 4:00, and that I could wait for him outside. He was someone who was easy to recognize walking out of the side door. With tanned and copper-colored skin, typical of those with a Native American ascendance, and his long black hair tied back in a ponytail. He reminded me of books I'd read when I was a kid, that villain, *Injun Joe,* who scared me so much in *The Adventures of Tom Sawyer*! And when the heroes went to the cemetery, at night... Just thinking about it gave me the willies and I was instantly transformed into that little girl who hid under her sheets at night with a flashlight and trembled while reading my comic strips, scared of the images in Mark Twain's novel.

But Foster Maverick wasn't scary. Quite the opposite really with a friendly face and a huge smile. He crossed the street, and I immediately felt like I could trust him. He was a tall man with large shoulders, like a heavyweight, but with delicate features. He must only have been thirty max.

"Here I am, Miss!" he said, holding out his hand. "But just for half an hour, because I've got an appointment at five. As it's scorching hot in this darn desert, why don't we get something to drink at the saloon?"

When we walked in, the owner greeted Maverick saying "*Ugh,* Foster Born Under the Red Moon at Winter Solstice." The Native American visibly didn't consider this as a racist remark and immediately replied, "*Ugh,* Pale Face like your Butt," while laughing. I guessed that was how they usually greeted each other.

We both sat down at one of the tables made from wood weathered by years of elbows and glasses put down then raised on them, and appreciated a sip of Californian beer, Lagunitas IPA that Foster had recommended. I never drink much beer but had to admit that its coolness in that hot weather did me good.

"Thanks so much for granting me a few moments of your precious time, Mr. Maverick."

"How can I help you?" he said, nodding, as if my request had not bothered him. "You interested in the postman or the Indian?"

"I have to humbly admit that I'd like to ask the man from the reservation a couple of questions. Felicity Bannister suggested that I meet you."

"You're interested in the Reservation, aren't you? Like all the White people who've never met a real Native American... You wanna do a paper on us? You're a journalist? I have to tell you that our reservations aren't zoos where you observe Indians in cages. Still... even if there aren't any bars, we're still..."

I stopped him right there, feeling that this conversation was starting with a false pretense, and immediately wanted to put things right.

"Just a second, Mr. Maverick, let me put things straight. I'm a journalist, that's right, but in a very special domain, in criminal and cold cases. So I don't have any intentions of voyeurism regarding your Native American countrymen. I'm not here for any social feature articles. I'm just investigating a disappearance that took place in Lone Pine on June 1st, 1988 and that might be linked to Jabaree Smith's disappearance, you know that young actor, that wonder child that you've certainly seen on the news."

"Of course. But how does that tie in with the Lone Pine Reservation?"

"To be frank with you, at this stage in my investigation, I have no idea. Maybe it doesn't. But the reason why I'm here stems from the elucubrations of Mrs. Bannister's old uncle, who, in his fantasies, told us that Shondra Wallace, the actress who went missing, had been kidnapped by the Indians."

Foster Maverick laughed ironically.

"Pure fantasy, I confirm. That crazy old man is making things up. He's still living in his world of westerns that fried his brain. Old Gramps fell off one too many horses! I know him well. Everyone knows everyone else in this little town in the middle of nowhere. Lone Pine, Hollywood's annex, but without its glitter or glamour. A population of two thousand at the most, stuck between natural landscapes that Hollywood studios love, splendid mountains, a lake, a peaceful little river, the desert, and the Paiutes-Shoshones Reservation. Talk about a set! Wannabe cowboys – look at them all, around us, with their boots and hats – and real Indians don't mix, or if they have to, the strict minimum. They just tolerate each other. Anyway, it's easy when something happens in this little town that's usually calm, to blame the Indians on the

Reservation for it. Too easy. And that's what you believe?"

"No," I replied, raising my hand. "Far from it. Like I said, those were just elucubrations of a half-senile old man. I don't want to incriminate anyone. On the contrary, I consider the people on the Reservation as inhabitants of Lone Pine in their own right, and that's why I believe that they've got their own opinion on the disappearance of Shondra Wallace. I'm sure that they have their own version of what happened and that's what I'd like to hear, to help me make some progress, who knows."

"Okay. I believe you have good intensions. But what do you expect me to do?"

The Native American finished his sentence and beer at the same time.

"From what I understand, you can't just enter the Reservation like that, especially when you're White like me. That you needed a recommendation, some sort of authorization. That's why Felicity told me to contact you, hoping that maybe you could open the doors for me."

A long silence followed. Maverick seemed to be thinking things over.

"You know, I left my fellow Indian citizens many years ago. I didn't want to end up like them, like most of my childhood friends or family members. Unemployed, nothing to do, pariahs, alcoholics, violent, you name it. I burned my bridges and freed myself. Since then, I'm not someone they really appreciate, though

I've not become a *persona non grata*. So I will try to defend your cause for the elected delegates of our tribe and especially its president, Mary Hansen."

"You've got a president?"

"Yup, and a vice-president, a treasurer, a secretary, a curator, and all those functions are held by women. The Paiutes-Shoshones have a long matriarchal tradition, as do most Native American tribes. They organize themselves inside their reservations. But you must be aware that I'm not guaranteeing a thing here. I doubt that they'll be overjoyed to stir the muck in a case that probably doesn't even concern them."

"You think you'll be able to give me an answer soon?"

"Don't be in such a hurry! The Natives have their own rhythms, one that's not as hectic as that of Americans today. Your Shondra Wallace lady went missing thirty-five years ago, is that right?"

"Totally."

"So, you're not in a big rush."

"But the life of a ten-year-old kid is at stake…"

CHAPTER 27
Stuntman

NIGHT HAD FALLEN upon Lone Pine when I left Forest Maverick.

The emancipated and assimilated Native American hadn't given me much hope for an eventual meeting with members of his tribe. I hoped he'd be able to get me a pass of safe conduct quickly, but until he did, I couldn't hang around there much longer.

I had to delve more deeply into my investigation, find the answers to my – way too many – questions. And sooner rather than later, to support Inspector Jonas Crimson in his search for the truth and hopefully save Jabaree Smith, who still was being held captive in an unknown place by his anonymous kidnappers.

Find the kid before it was too late.

It was a race against time – against death? – that was picking up speed. A clock with several needles. One of them, the big one, had slowly been turning since 1988. The other one, the little one, had panicked since June 1st, 2024.

Two contrary but inseparable rates of speed.

In my room at Trails Motel, I wasn't sure of what to do next. Wait till I could get into the Paiutes-Shoshones Reservation, or rush back to Los Angeles where I still had some people to see or see again?

Know where I stood. Link the leads I'd already explored.

I had to think. Who had I met up until now who had been in close or distant contact with Shondra?

Opening a Word file, I jotted down some quick notes.

Brad Purcell. Shondra Wallace's preferred movie director. In a couple with the actress? Lives in L.A. Now unsuccessful, decided to retire. But never had much success…

David Apfenstein. Purcell and Lundgren's producer. Lives in L.A. in a fortified villa. His HQ is the Bel-Air Country Club golf course. Disappointed by Lundgren when he quit shooting *The Coyote-Woman of the Desert*.

George Mavis. Owns a restaurant in Lone Pine. Knew Purcell and Lundgren's shooting crews. Confrontation between those two groups the day before Shondra went missing.

Paul Bannister. 95 years old. Was the professional stuntman in over three hundred movies shot in Alabama Hills, including *The Coyote-Woman of the Desert*. Lives in his niece's home in Lone Pine. Repeats that Shondra was kidnapped by the Indians. Fantasy or reality?

"Pretty slim pickings," I muttered.

Whether it was in Hollywood or in Lone Pine, I still couldn't fathom how the actress disappeared back in 1988. But as for elements to be explored, I had a ton of them.

Try to meet *Peter Lundgren*.

Ask him if he knew what happened to those *reels of film* that had been shot for *The Coyote-Woman*.

Ask *Apfenstein* the same questions, as he was the movie's producer, making him the *owner* of those aforementioned reels.

Watch *other feature films* that Shondra starred in. You never know. That tattoo...

Maybe I should head off to *Watts*, try to understand where the young lady was born and raised? Find someone who knew her as a *child*, or her *family*. Once again, go back to the past.

Tomorrow morning, after a good night's sleep, I'd head back to Los Angeles. And if Foster Maverick was able to get me into the Paiutes-Shoshones Reservation, I'd return to the desert.

While getting ready to go to bed after having decided that, my heart tightened up again with the idea of going back to L.A.

Because I'd never forgotten that I'd come to California not just for the investigation into the disappearance of Jabaree and Shondra, but also, to answer some personal questions, ones that would be the completion of an entire life of questions without answers. At the age of over forty, I finally was going to make that happen, finally going to be able to touch my own ghosts of the past.

A few days ago, I was getting ready to see that ghost.

To introduce myself to him.

To talk to him. About me, about himself, about this *us* that had never existed. Or just a little. Not enough.

I wouldn't leave California without having affronted my own past.

A FEROCIOUS NOSTALGIA came over me stemming from the mixture of all those investigations taking place at the same time.

I felt I was selfish not devoting a hundred percent of my time and energy to solving the Wallace case, and who knew, maybe that little something that seemed to be linking it to the freeing of the kid-star.

That nostalgia caused tears to well up in the corners of my eyes and my underlying anxiety kicked in once again. My life was painful. What had I done in it? Did I screw everything up?

I was over forty years old, and I didn't have – or almost didn't have – any children. No husband, not really anyone in my life.

I grabbed the phone and called Paul.

Paul Nollington, who I met in one of my previous investigations, had jumped into my life, one winter's day on a beach on Long Island.

Paul, with whom I had an episodic relationship, often a long-distance one. We hadn't promised each other anything. And I never forgot that I was over fifteen years older than him. We were simply happy to talk to each other on the phone from time to time, to meet up, when our respective jobs allowed it, as mine took me all over the United States.

Not quite a couple, more than just friends. Something between the two. Lovers?

We hadn't talked for a couple of days. I needed to hear his voice that evening.

He picked up at the third ringtone.

"Hey! My beautiful Karen. Happy to hear from you."

"Paul, you've got my number too..." I said between my teeth. And immediately regretted it. "Excuse me, I didn't mean to say that. It's just that I'm really scared, Paul. I'm freaking out."

And then I explained to him everything I that was

weighing me down in my head, in my body, in my heart. As I often did with him, I opened my soul to him and knew that I'd be able to count on him to comfort me.

When we hung up, an hour later, I swallowed my indispensable treatment and hit the sack.

Tomorrow is another day.

Distance

Once again I'm on the lookout.

I'm watching you. Following you.

You have no idea. Either you're too carefree to notice it or I'm too used to tailing people discreetly. Anyway, I'm the shadow of your shadow on the Los Angeles sidewalks, between Westwood and Bel-Air.

When you left your apartment, without realizing it, you led me right to your school. UCLA, what a fantastic university! I'm proud of you, but you don't know it.

What did you decide to major in? Medicine, physiques, chemistry, literature, math, law, astronomy, management? There are so many prestigious sectors in this huge world-renowned university that has over forty thousand students. Over a dozen Nobel Prizes and three Pulitzer Prizes were UCLA alumni! What do you want to do with your life? What projects do you have?

Will I ever find out?

To do that, the only options I have are to introduce

myself, rather than allow you to slip through my fingers one more time.

Good Lord, you're so big now! The first time you were taken from me you weren't even twenty inches long. Today, you're a strapping young man of over six-foot-three, walking ten steps ahead of me.

A handsome young man with a mixed complexion, with black hair like me. Girls must love you! Do you have a girlfriend? I'd like to know that too. A mother has the right, doesn't she?

With that thought, I had a mirthless chuckle. A mother? Am I one? Was I ever one?

Does giving birth make you a mother?

Is maternal love innate, or does it occur as years together go by?

In that case...

I walk faster, and the distance between us becomes smaller.

The distance in feet and yards. The emotional distance...

I dream of shattering both of them.

I have to try.

We both go through one of the doors of the UCLA campus. I don't look like a student. More like a professor?

Whatever, no one prevents me from entering the mythical belly of Californian higher education. The building seems immense. I'd read someplace that there are nearly three hundred research projects and thou-

sands of scientific projects going on in the hundred and sixty-three buildings here on the campus. I turn my head from right to left, subjugated.

When suddenly.

I run into you.

You stopped suddenly to get something out of your backpack, and I didn't notice it.

"Oh! Excuse me," I say with a choked-up voice. "I wasn't paying attention, I..."

"No problem, Ma'am. You didn't hurt yourself?"

I hear his voice for the first time. Or should I say since he was first born...

"No, I'm fine," I stutter.

"Can I help you?"

"No... I mean... I... You... I'm fine, thanks. And once again, sorry."

"Okay. Great. Have a good one then. I gotta go, I've got my comparative anatomy course in five minutes."

Haggard, paralyzed, I let him go again.

What an idiot I am! I'd slap myself in the face.

So close finally and ... still so far...

CHAPTER 28
Moguls, nabobs, fat cats

Los Angeles, June 7, 2024

Had Ruppert Magloire thought he'd be going on a road trip on that sunny Californian morning, he would have been mistaken. And not just a little. The movie director, sitting in the back seat of Inspector Crimson's unmarked vehicle that his deputy was driving with Crimson in the passenger seat, was silent.

The investigators wanted to do the exact same itinerary that Magloire had taken a few days earlier when he left the gala dinner to look for Jabaree. They consequently began their trip at the studios where the party had taken place. Crimson looked at his watch when they left and Agent Payton put the car in drive, heading to Pasadena.

"Mr. Magloire, can you give my colleague the exact roads you took? I'd like to take the same ones."

"How could this help you, Detective? I'm going to end up thinking that you suspect me of doing something," the movie director said.

"I just like things to be clear and precise. That's it."

"Okay. Head east and turn left then after the TCL Chinese Theater. You go around Park Griffith and the Hollywood sign up to Universal Studios. Then after, east through Glendale. And after that straight to Pasadena."

An hour later, the car stopped in front of the address Magloire had given them. It had of course taken them quite a bit longer during the day than at one in the morning. Yet Crimson questioned him on this.

"You told me it only took you half an hour to drive here."

"Traffic was really light," Ruppert confirmed.

"Let's get out then. Can you show us around?"

The villa, hidden behind a tall wooden fence, looked like one of the white colonial manors like you see down south and in some Latin American countries. As it was in the middle of a grove of maritime pines, you only noticed it when you got there. Crimson made an admirative face when the gate opened. Nearly whistling between his teeth.

The policeman and his officer, once the instant of fascination past, let the owner show them around, starting off in the yard surrounding the villa, and then inside.

For over half an hour, all three went upstairs and

down, room after room, nook and cranny after nook and cranny, while Crimson asked Magloire a few questions, jotting the answers down in his notebook.

"So then Mr. Magloire, you went to Malibu after, is that right?"

"Just like I told you time after time during our interviews, Inspector," said the movie director ironically.

"Let's go then!"

Following the same procedure as before, Ruppert Magloire told Agent Payton and Crimson the road he'd taken, and Crimson consulted his watch. This time they went back to Glendale, then headed west taking Road 101 along the Pacific, until they turned south after Calabasas and went through the Santa Monica Mountains.

There, overlooking Santa Monica Bay, Ruppert Magloire and Janice Lovelace's property was just as breathtaking as the previous one in Pasadena. That large white wooden villa, almost directly on the beach, symbolized another aspect of the wealth that some of the movers and shakers in the Hollywood cinema world enjoyed. The opulent producers – those recently called *moguls**, nabobs, fat cats –, those who produced blockbusters and were known throughout the world, all those who loved to flaunt their dough, thought Crimson.

---

* Moguls are magnates of the Hollywood cinematographic industry, and producers in the most powerful studios.

He hated their "*better than you*" mentality. You could tell that by his hint of a smile, no words were needed to describe what he thought of the country houses that the couple had. As for their kid, that Jabaree, born with a silver spoon in his mouth and already a star at not even ten years old, what would come of him when he grew up, wondered Crimson when he walked into the villa with Magloire.

If of course, the kidnappers hadn't already killed him...

They looked up and down like in Pasadena for three-quarters of an hour. After the first residence in a cluster of trees, this one was like a seaside resort. Whether they chose to stay in one rather than the other must have depended on the weather. How lucky they were to have so many choices!

They went back into the unmarked car.

"Mr. Magloire, there's something that's bothering me here. When you left Hollywood that evening, first you went to Pasadena, then to Malibu, and you ended up in Las Vegas. You took the same road several times, back and forth, in particular through Glendale. Wouldn't it have been more logical, simple, and less tiring to take Malibu-Pasadena-Vegas? It would have been quicker too."

"Inspector, do I have to repeat that I was shocked? Do you think I'd planned my route before trying to find Jabaree? I knew I only had a slim chance of finding him, but I drove instinctively, starting off with the house that seemed to be closest to the studios. And continued farther and farther even if I knew I probably wouldn't find him in Las Vegas. Then finally, I told you why I holed up there. Shame..."

"I understand. We'll go there anyway. I'd like to see what kind of place you have in Nevada. As it'll take us over four hours, we'll stop for something to eat along the way. I always get hungry when I'm driving."

ONCE THEY'D GONE through the mountains in the north of Los Angeles, the trio began to cross the Mojave Desert and Mojave National Preserve, with its constantly changing landscape on Highway 15. Crimson thought of Karen Blackstone, who was also in the Californian desert, a bit farther north, in Lone Pine. Had she made any progress? Had she linked the two Jabaree-Shondra cases together? The two cases that took place on June 1st? Of course not, the inspector thought, otherwise she would have reached out to me.

After having stopped for a quick lunch in a diner, Jonas took the wheel so Agent Diane Payton could rest. The trip was mostly a silent one as Agent Payton and the movie director were half-asleep listening to the noise of the tires on the road and the air-conditioned breeze, as outside the temperature was climbing in that month of June between California and Nevada. They quickly crossed the border between the two states and Vegas wasn't far.

In the middle of the afternoon, Crimson stopped

THE LOST SON

the car in front of the third – and last – home they owned, this one on the outskirts of the city that never sleeps, discovering a hacienda-like building in the middle of a huge yard planted with palm trees, banana trees and other tropical plantations that seemed bizarre in that arid landscape. He could see Vegas's skyline in the distance, with its internationally recognized hotel-casinos. The policeman had recently read that out of the thirty largest hotels in the world, twenty of them were located there! The Venetian, with over seven thousand rooms, The MGM Grand Las Vegas, Mandala Bay, Caesars Palace and so many other venues with their debaucheries of money, celebrities... and poor taste, in his opinion anyway.

"Glad I'm here," he said, opening the door and stepping out in the dry desert torpidity. "It's like an oven here!"

"You'll feel better inside," Magloire said, escorting the duo.

When they walked in, it was like walking into a palace. The rooms were enormous, decorated with state-of-the-art furniture, white ceilings nearly ten feet high, picture windows as large as those in an airport, looking out over the immensity of Nevada's arid plains. Sumptuous!

Just like in the two previous villas, the policeman didn't find a single trace of Jabaree. But that wasn't really what he was looking for, during this road trip with Ruppert Magloire...

The residence had at least five suites, including one

with a jacuzzi-spa, a spacious open kitchen, a living room, a library and a video library.

Upstairs, Crimson saw another door at the end of the hall. That one was different from the others, which were made from wood and glass. It was upholstered with a type of quilted bright black leather making him think of a sofa that was vertical. He immediately thought of an armored door or soundproof one, like you imagine in psychiatric hospitals.

"What's in there?"

"My private little sanctuary," replied Magloire mysteriously.

"Can I go in?"

A moment of silence, then Magloire put his hand in his pocket, taking out a key.

He unlocked the door, and when he opened it to allow Crimson in, his mouth literally fell wide open.

He was dumbfounded by what he discovered inside.

CHAPTER 29
The creator's den

It wasn't the first time that Inspector Crimson discovered an original and unusual room like that one.

He had seen several of them during his numerous investigations, especially in Los Angeles and in particular in Hollywood.

But like that one, never.

The room was simply frightening... with beauty. When Magloire turned the lights on, a myriad of spotlights lit up the ceiling, immersing the room in a powerful aura.

A white canvas was hung on the huge wall at the back, immaculate and just as tight as a drum.

On the floor, a dozen rows of individual luxuriously comfortable armchairs. All identical, in black leather, with wide arm rests and cavities to hold bottles or glasses.

The ceiling, two side walls as well as most of the

back wall where they had entered the room, were all covered with a wasp-like nest's special coating.

"That gives you perfect acoustics," explained Magloire proudly, noting the officers' subjugated eyes.

To top it all off, opposite the huge screen, there was a narrow opening in the wall with an old school movie projector.

"My secret pleasure," continued their host. "The least a well-known movie director should have, don't you think?"

"I don't exactly have a shooting range at home," replied Crimson, stung by Magloire's haughtiness.

The pride that those *nouveaux riches* had, with fortunes built on air, fiction, fantasy... But as that was what the public wanted, that was what they got, noted the cop bitterly to himself.

"This is where I often find my inspiration for my next movies," the owner explained. "I watch old feature movies with reels of film that I buy at a specialized market or that my colleagues or producers sometimes give me."

"Sort of like people who collect vinyl records, you mean?"

"Exactly. What's retro and vintage is popular nowadays. Whether we're talking about clothing, culture, or entertainment. Have you noticed how old arcade games are now popular too? Machines that we played with when we were kids in cafes or gaming centers, like Street Fighter, PacMan, Space Invaders,

Tetris, simple games like that, but addictive ones. They're back!"

"That's true," agreed Crimson. "But we're not here to talk about video games, Mr. Magloire. Can we go into the projection room? I'd like to see what one really looks like."

"Umm... it's sort of a mess right now, I'm working on a tough project and there's not even enough room to turn around in there, especially if all three of us go up."

"No problem, my colleague will stay down here. Okay with you, Diane?"

"Will do, Boss."

"I really want to see it."

"I understand. You wanna see what goes on behind the stage, don't you?"

Crimson nodded, happy like a kid on Christmas, and followed Magloire who led them to a door hidden in one of the sides of the room. A small stairwell led up to the projection room.

Then another door, this one with a digital code, opened, with an electronic noise.

"Welcome to the creator's den!" shouted out the film director, emphasizing the words.

"The word *den* seems to be the correct one," said Crimson when he saw the room.

"I told you so."

The tiny or even confined room for two people at the same time, was filled with incredible devices for movie fans. Fitted out like a projection room in a movie theater back in the day, it had several projectors, one of which was aimed at the tiny hole. On the wall there were reels of 35 mm film hanging, others were already installed on the projector. There was a console on the table next to the projector, which looked like a mixing table or an old record player for vinyl records that a disc jockey could have in a nightclub. Buttons here, there, and everywhere, that you turned, pushed, pulled or pressed. Cranks and other accessories that Crimson had no idea what they were for. But the most surprising thing was at the feet of the policeman, who was afraid to move.

On the shiny flooring there were several pieces of 35 mm film, of all different sizes – some only as long as your thumb, others at least three feet long, all rolled up like transparent streamers.

"I think this is the first time in my life that I've actually seen a roll of 35 mm film," said the policeman. "For me this is awesome! That's Hollywood! And just to think that engraved on these thin pieces of plastic, you've got my best souvenirs of a movie fan. Things I've never forgotten. It's magical! I'm afraid to step on them and wreck something precious."

"Don't worry, those are things I won't be using," said Magloire. "I was doing some editing on an old project that's important for me."

"A new movie with Jabaree?"

"Not at all," replied Ruppert with a smile. "The movies I've directed with Jabaree all use digital technology, not film. What you see here are old reels that I bought from a producer who declared bankruptcy a couple of years ago and I play with them, mixing and editing them. A movie director's little whim. A hobby. Like a musician who rearranges songs other artists have written."

"I get it. Can I touch one?"

"Sure."

Crimson bent down to pick up a few inches of film with his fingertips. He raised it to his eyes, hoping to make out some images. For a fleeting moment he felt like a Peeping Tom, as if he was discovering some fabulous or forbidden relic.

"Quite moving."

"That's the magic of cinema. What an invention! The Edisons, Lumière, Gaumont, Marconi and all the others subjugated the whole world with their twenty-four images per second! Or how to recreate the illusion of movement with twenty-four pictures one after the other. Sort of like those books when we were kids that had a drawing on each corner of the page, and you had to flip the pages with a finger at a certain speed to animate the character. Remember those?"

"I do. I loved them."

"It's nearly the same here. On these reels of film, movement is generated by how they're driven using the little holes on each side. And on this thin little roll of film, you also have the soundtrack! Except for silent films, obviously. Isn't that fantastic? It sure beats today's digital technology."

"It looks like you regret it," the policeman asked,

quite astonished, before slowly putting the bits of film back down on the mixing table and putting his hands in his pockets, so he wouldn't wreck anything.

"No, no regrets, you have to adapt to your era. But nostalgia, of course. That's why I'm interested in these old reels of film."

Crimson, still fascinated by the projectors and afraid to move in the middle of all the snippets of film on the floor, had another question.

"Can you show me a few minutes of your work?"

Magloire raised his eyebrows and hesitated before answering.

"I'd prefer not to. Just like all serious artists, I'm afraid that if I show someone an ongoing project, I'll ruin it... But I promise you that when, or should I say if, you'll be one of the first ones to see it, with a sneak preview!"

"It's a deal then! I can't wait."

"You won't be disappointed, Inspector..."

CHAPTER 30
Front row seats

Los Angeles, June 7, 2024

I still hadn't had any news from Foster Maverick about going to the Paiutes-Shoshones Reservation. I wasn't going to harass him the day after my request, but internally I couldn't wait to discover the universe of the Natives of Lone Pine and their version of what happened in 1988.

In the meanwhile, I still had some leads to follow up on and wanted to meet Peter Lundgren, who'd produced *The Coyote-Woman of the Desert*, that unfinished movie. As he had front row seats when Shondra Wallace vanished, I was sure that he'd have interesting things to tell me.

Just like I'd done before for Apfenstein and Purcell, I logged into the IMDb website, looking for the film director's file. I learned that Lundgren, a

Swede, had begun by directing several "artistic" movies in his homeland. After that, he moved to the States and begun a more lucrative career, churning out B-series feature films with strange and sometimes disturbing titles like *The Long-Toothed Crocodile*, *Zombie Wonderland*, *Revenge of the Killer Zucchinis*, *The Nerds Counterattack*, and *Caligula's Wild Nights*... Crazy stuff, I thought. But after all, if that allowed him to put bread and butter on his table, and satisfy the appetite that fans of that kind of movies had... Anyway, Shondra Wallace had starred in several of them.

The Coyote-Woman of the Desert was certainly like the scenarios of the previous movies, written on the kitchen table during two nights of insomnia, produced as quickly as possible by pragmatic David Apfenstein, with his flair.

I found Lundgren's contact details in his file and called his agent. I introduced myself and explained why I was calling.

"Miss Blackstone, my client won't give you an interview like that. Plus, right now he's on vacation in Sweden. You want advice from a friend: forget him!"

Then he hung up on me.

I hate that! Myrtille could do that to me, but some unknown person, *niet*! Advice from a friend? I'd give him some of mine!

I called back.

"You don't give up, do you? I told you that..."

"Listen up, Mr. Voygt, you must have heard of the case that's now on the front pages of papers and has impacted the Hollywood universe, Jabaree Smith's kidnapping."

"Of course, I don't live like a hermit in a cave. What does my client have to do with it?"

"I'll give you the short version. On June 1st, 1988, Shondra Wallace disappeared and was never seen again. At that time she was starring in *The Coyote-Woman of the Desert*, an unfinished movie that your client, Peter Lundgren, produced. On June 1st, 2024, Jabaree Smith disappeared, kidnapped by a mysterious person or persons who, in a video clip, had the child say that we must never forget June 1st... You don't see any link between the two cases in your pitiful little brain? So quit trying to stonewall me and let me contact your client, wherever he is! Here's some advice from a friend... It's a question of life or death for Jabaree!"

"Hey! Hey! Hey! No one talks to me like that! I'm not your dog. I don't owe you anything."

"If you had just an ounce of humanity, you wouldn't be totally insensitive."

"Okay. I'll give you Lundgren's number, even though I don't see anything linking these two cases. But I'm not going to guarantee you a warm welcome. Peter is a mixture of a polar bear and a cold-blooded Viking. Freezing inside and wild outside. Good luck."

And he gave me his number. I immediately dialed it.

"This is Peter Lundgren's voicemail. If I'm not answering, two hypotheses. Either I'm busy or I don't trust your number and that explains why I didn't pick

up. *If you still want to leave me a message, go ahead. I'll see if I want to call you back."*

I confirmed, not a warm welcome from that Swedish bear!

But as I wasn't afraid of bears, I left him a message and underscored the importance of calling me back. What he could tell me could potentially lead me to understand the whys and wherefores of the Shondra case, and from that one, Jabaree's case.

Hoping he'd agree to meet me, I went to check my emails, something I hadn't done for the past couple of days.

Nothing that exasperates me more than stalling in an investigation when I'm waiting for someone to phone me back, decide something, or grant me an interview. Right now I had no news from the Lone Pine Indian Reservation, I was still waiting for that old Swedish bear to phone me back and had no serious leads. I was fuming.

Ever since I'd arrived in California, to be frank, I thus hadn't checked my emails. For me that wasn't a reflex. I usually let myself be guided by notifications of messages that arrived on my phone rather than systematically consulting my computer. That meant that when an email concerned "promotions," "social networking," or most often and unfortunately "spam", those mails were something I missed.

Looking through the "social networking" category, I stumbled upon the following subject line:

`Karen, you have an answer to the`

thread you opened on MovieGeeks.com. Click here to identify yourself and consult it.

Right below, there were the first words of the message as a teaser.

"Hi Karen! Here's a lead that might be interesting for The Coyote-Woman..."

End of the preview.

I clicked.

And was excited by what I read.

CHAPTER 31
Lights, camera, action

I FRENETICALLY OPENED the message in response to my thread I began without much hope on the forum, throwing a bottle into the sea.

And it looked like that bottle had crossed the Atlantic as I was reading the response of a person with the pseudonym meganoc1970, and according to the forum's IP location, I thought he or she must be in the United Kingdom.

HI KAREN! You might want to check this out for *The Coyote-Woman of the Desert*. I don't know what it's worth, but it deserves to be looked into. You're talking about Peter Lundgren's unfinished movie? It's a title that is a part of the myths or urban legends of American filmmaking. The select few, unconditional fans of B-series, have all heard it one day. Mythical because unfinished. Mythical too because of the disappearance linked to it. An unsolved disappearance if I understood your message right. So your work must consist in shedding light on cold cases like this. Good luck! As for me, my job, or should I say my passion and favorite hobby, is finding forgotten little gems, forbidden movies, duds that you cringe at when watching them, movies that were censured, unfinished, lost, not released, salacious or said to have been destroyed. There are parallel distribution circuits for these types of movies that the general public can't find. But we know how and where to look, where to get the right information, the right supplier of cinematographic goods. Don't bother going on platforms like YouTube or Dailymotion, you won't find anything. How come? 'Cuz a movie like that, if there's anything left of it, was never edited! All that's left, at the best, are two or three reels of film depending on what they actually shot, rushes, alpha takes, nothing polished. As opposed to a movie whose takes had never been viewed, arranged, sorted to choose the best ones, then edited, mixed with the soundtrack and additional music, produced and distributed, and that one day you'll fatally unearth on a platform, even if — and especially — if they're the worst duds ever! As for your *Coyote-Woman*, none of this had been done. A low-cost B-series movie that was shot in ten days. Generally, the director and producer don't even bother to view the rushes each day. They shoot everything, sometimes the same scene several times, and keep the best one. Plus, in this type of production, reels of film are expensive, and they don't want to waste money, so they often do just one or two takes, and tough luck if they're crappy. And that's what we like about duds! LOL! Like when we see part of the sound boom up in one of the corners, or when an actor mumbles his text, or when a technician walks through the background, all that. So, in your case, all we would be able to find would be unedited snippets with front slates or tail slates and the assistant directing shouting out *"Lights, camera, aaaaaannnnd action!"* Then, at the end, *"Cut!" "That's a wrap!"* or *"That's shit, let's redo it!"* or even *"That's shit, but we don't give a damn, we're keeping it!"* Like I said, LOL! So Karen, listen up. If you're hoping to unearth some images of a cult-movie-that-never-existed, you gotta go right to the sources. To the producer or the film director. Good luck and keep us in the loop. Us MovieGeeks, we're loving it!

So the production back in the day... Apfenstein or Lundgren... Lundgren or Purcell? Interesting. So if that Swedish bear deigned call me back, I'd have a crucial question for him!

I was getting ready to log off the MovieGeeks forum, when I saw that *meganoc1970* had added an answer to her own answer, and I'd nearly missed it. She added:

By the way, you said that Peter Lundgren produced the *Coyote-Woman* motion picture. I doubt it. Every B-series specialist would agree with me here… In my opinion, it's more of a movie that Brad Purcell directed, as he usually had Shondra Wallace as his star actress. So for me, it's Purcell. Maybe Purcell began to shoot it and for some unknown reason the producer fired him and continued with Lundgren? Or another supposition: the movie was directed by Lundgren, but the main actress wasn't Shondra Wallace… But maybe I'm the crazy one here! So think about it, Karen. LOL! :-) Good luck! And don't thank me for this headache!

SHE WAS RIGHT, I didn't know if I should thank her – or him – that *meganoc1970* who was helping me out here while bringing in more unknowns and questions. Amongst everything that person suggested, the sentence *the main actress wasn't Shondra Wallace*, was the one that bothered me the most. What if everyone had been looking in the wrong direction since the beginning?

What if Shondra Wallace had never even starred in *The Coyote-Woman of the Desert*?

And what if, by extension, Shondra Wallace had never disappeared?

CHAPTER 32
Backstage

I WENT BACK to my room in L.A. and my phone started to vibrate on my bedside table in my hotel room downtown.

An international number with a prefix I didn't know.

"Good Lord," said a deep Nordic and heavily accented voice, "you know what time it is here in Stockholm?"

"Thanks so much for getting back to me so quickly, Mr. Lundgren," I replied.

"I seem to think I didn't have much of a choice, Miss Blackstone. Like you put a knife to my throat with your story about that kid, the one everyone in Hollywood's in love with... I can understand the urgency of this but have no idea how it concerns me. So consequently, I don't know how I can help you."

"Let me be the judge of that, Mr. Lundgren. Without realizing it, perhaps you have an element that would help me make progress in my investigation on the disappearance of Shondra Wallace."

"Pff! What for? All that happened ages ago. No one cares about that anymore! And I don't either."

"I can see that. But Jabaree's kidnapping would tend to prove the opposite. Did you see his video clip?"

"Yup. So what?"

Hmm, that polar bear had thick skin.

"He insisted on the fact that we should never forget June 1st, *each June 1st*. That seems clear to me. You're one of the last witnesses and you took part in what happened in Lone Pine on June 1st, 1988. Do you understand why they made Jabaree say that the date should never be forgotten? You see any link between the two cases?"

"None! There's a thirty-five-year difference between them. I don't see anything in common except for the date and the fact that it concerns movies produced in Hollywood. That's it."

"At first, I thought it might be a copycat. Maybe one of Shondra's secret and unconditional admirers. Someone close to her at that time and who wanted the whole world to pay attention to her tragic fate that no one seems to care about. What do you think?"

There was a moment of silence between Scandinavia and California.

"I think you're right on one point: no one gave a damn about what happened to Shondra. She was a second-rate actress, one who only starred in flops that idiot Apfenstein produced, and Purcell and I directed.

She didn't leave any souvenirs about her talent as an actress. Her body, maybe a few. She was worth taking a look at, and a lot of people certainly did."

"Who, for example?"

"Well, her fans, already. If they watched our two-bits movies, it was above all to see scenes where Shondra would be half-naked, or even more than half. And then her acting partners too. And of course, Purcell himself."

"Really?"

"You sound astonished. Believe me, those two rubbed shoulders together for a long time. Why do you think they worked together so often?"

"Okay, I get it... but you also shot several feature-length films with her..."

"Except I never slept with her! Apfenstein, on the other hand..."

"The producer? Him too?"

I could hear Peter Lundgren's guffaw on the other end of the line.

"Ah! Miss Blackstone. I see you have no idea what takes place in Hollywood. Hollywood is a city of whores and pimps! Fucking is a local sport in hopes of becoming a leading actor, not playing in minor roles all your life, like Shondra Wallace who vegetated in that category. You want to be on top of the bill? Sleep with an influential producer! Apfenstein, though he looked like a too serious accountant, wasn't the last one to drop his pants and have ambitious starlets kneeling in front of him... while promising them a key role! It's only when they're successful that actresses forget they were whores and become capricious bitches with short memories!"

"That's quite the picture you're painting there, Mr. Lundgren."

"I assure you, it's realistic. As I come from a European culture, Scandinavian to be exact, I don't agree with their Hollywoodian practices. But that's how the world of movie making turns. What goes on behind the cameras! It's just as fascinating as on the screens. A totally hypocritical world. And one that crushes and destroys innocence. Hey, you know how you say 'Go fuck yourself' in Hollywood?

"No."

"You say, 'Trust me.'"

And once again his rocky guffaw rang out. I interrupted him to try to get back to the point.

"So you think that Shondra gave in to Apfenstein's advances?"

"Rumor has it. Backstage rumors. When the cameras weren't filming."

"Even when she was in a couple with Purcell?"

"For sure. In Hollywood or in Lone Pine, it was like you were on vacation, everyone slept with everyone else. That's one of the reasons, in my opinion, why *Coyote-Woman* failed."

"Meaning?"

While Peter Lundgren was telling me what went on backstage when *The Coyote-Woman of the Desert* was being shot, my pen was racing in my notebook.

"At the beginning, Brad Purcell, Apfenstein's little pet, was directing the movie. Then rumors began that the producer had been very up close and personal with Shondra for months – not just getting regular head from her, but probably much more – and in exchange, he'd been promising her the moon and the stars, leading roles, Oscars, and who knows what else. So like many rumors, it grew, and Purcell got wind of it and one night, in a restaurant, he let it all out and started badmouthing Apfenstein. But Apfenstein had him by the balls, he was the one financing his movies! If Purcell kept on making movies, eating and paying his rent, it was thanks to Apfenstein, as no other producers wanted to sink their dough into his films. So in a nutshell, Apfenstein fired him! 'There you go! You're out, you loser. Scram!' And that's where I came in. Up until Shondra went missing, without any reasons or explanations... At least, according to the official version. Because that explanation, I don't think it's hard to understand..."

Now things were getting interesting.

"Give me your version then."

CHAPTER 33
Hollywood's working class

ON THE OTHER end of the line, the Scandinavian producer told me about when Shondra Wallace had disappeared in Lone Pine.

"Rumors saying that Apfenstein was one of Shondra's friends with loads of benefits went even farther. Backstage everyone knew he'd been fucking her for months, but we also heard that there was a bun in her oven... And people noticed that the wannabe starlet's silhouette was getting larger and larger. But who knows, maybe it was something else! Alcoholic beverages? An excess of sugar? She was letting herself go? So, as you must know, when rumors begin to spread, they never stop. Just like a snowball that gets bigger as it rolls down a hill, rumors also grow from word of mouth. Anyway, the most imaginative people insinuated that Shondra was ashamed of that situation and that she wanted to disappear to get an abortion or have the baby in secret. Or that Purcell, feeling she'd betrayed him, had kicked her out."

While writing a summary of what Peter Lundgren was telling me in my notebook, I thought about his version of what happened, thinking it could be logical. Yet I wasn't quite convinced.

"If we admit your hypothesis, we legitimately can think that Shondra Wallace isn't dead. Or at least, that she didn't die thirty-five years ago. Since then, a lot of water has flowed under the bridge and who knows what happened in someone's life for over three decades. But why would she have wanted to disappear and never be seen again?"

"To change her life!" Lundgren said, sure of himself. "She wouldn't be the first or the last person to turn her back on the past and want to start over again from nothing, someplace else. A new life. You told me in your message that you're specialized in solving cold cases. Sometimes they're easy to solve meaning people disappear intentionally. I'm sure that a lot of your cases were solved with that explanation!"

"That's true. It's estimated that there are about ten thousand voluntary disappearances in the United States each year. Sometimes they're simulated deaths. You delete everything and start over. Erase the blackboard. Or white. A choice you have to respect. No one is obligated to love and undergo their present life."

"Totally. Were you able to talk to that outdated Purcell or that robotic-voiced Apfenstein?"

"Yes, but I'll have the pleasure of asking them new questions with what you just told me. Ah! One more thing, Mr. Lundgren. As you worked shooting a part of *The Coyote-Woman*, would you be able to tell me if the reels of film of that unfinished movie are someplace? Any idea where they could be? Or maybe you have them?"

"Not at all, my little lady. Producers rarely keep reels of films. They legally belong to the production studio. I'm sure you have no idea how many reels of film are rotting in their reserves. Gold mines! Treasures for cinephiles, including B-series fans, Hollywood's working class!"

"So then David Apfenstein is the one who would have the rushes of *The Coyote-Woman of the Desert*, if they exist?"

"Logically, yes. Unless he decided to eliminate them too."

"What do you mean, '*too*?' I jumped in. "Are you insinuating that Apfenstein would benefit from 'eliminating' Shondra Wallace?"

"After what I just told you, don't you agree with me?"

"It's true, that could be a motive. Burying the secret of a nonconsensual pregnancy, I said with a lump in my throat, operating despite myself a personal parallel.

"There you go... Eliminate Shondra Wallace, literally or figuratively, by deleting the rushes of her last movie... One or the other... or both! Good luck, Miss Blackstone," concluded the old Swedish bear, leaving me with even more leads to pursue this time.

CHAPTER 34
Planetary star

Night had already fallen when the police car, driven by Inspector Crimson, with Agent Diane Payton next to him and Ruppert Magloire in the backseat, arrived at the movie director's villa.

Just looking at that beautiful home with its huge bay windows all lit up was breathtaking. Crimson saw Janice's silhouette, walking up and down in their vast living-room, her head hanging and dragging her feet, her arms wrapped around her shoulders as if she were freezing and trying to warm up, though the night was still warm. She heard the vehicle turn into the driveway leading to the front porch, supported by Doric style marble pillars, and briefly glanced at it before continuing her phantasmagorical steps.

"Here we are back at home, Mr. Magloire. I mean, back at your main home," said Crimson ironically after a very long a tiring all-day drive going between the successful director's various abodes.

Los Angeles, Pasadena, Malibu, Las Vegas, and then back to L.A.

"So now you know what I did during those fifty hours between the time that Jabaree disappeared and when I came back home," clarified Magloire.

"At least we know what you told us and what you wanted to show us. I see your wife is still up. Do you think I could ask her a few questions at this time of the night?"

"Be my guest," he said, inviting them in.

Agent Payton turned the car off and both police officers followed Ruppert Magloire inside.

"Jani," he shouted out. "Inspector Crimson wants to talk to you. Are you visible?"

"Tell him to come up," replied his wife in a whiny little voice.

The husband showed the police officers up. Crimson saw the actress wearing a pink, silk bathrobe, her hair in a mess, and her eyes reddened by tears.

"Miss Lovelace, I'm sorry to be speaking to you so late, but I'd just like to take advantage of our presence here to talk to you briefly. Ask you a couple of questions. Alone," added the inspector, glancing at Magloire.

With a movement of her chin, Jabaree's mother invited Crimson to follow her into the next room, one that had a huge carom billiard, also known as a French pool table, the version with only three balls and no holes, smack in the middle of it.

"Do you play?"

"When my migraines allow me to, yes, I do, it relaxes me. But tonight, my head is killing me again. Like every night since my little angel left. Tell me you'll bring him back quickly, Inspector. I'm begging you. I can't sleep, I can't eat, I can't live anymore. Without my son, I think I could let myself die from sadness."

The lady dropped down into an armchair at the corner of the billiard and burst into tears. Her hands putting pressure on her temple, she could feel the migraine growing and knew she'd be bedridden soon.

"We're doing everything we can. I'll soon get the results from the analysis of the video your son did, and maybe that will give us some idea of where he is. We're still interviewing everyone who was at the party that night and are cross-checking their versions. Plus my teams are going through the footage of the CCTV cameras in the roads that were adjacent to the studio. And finally, thanks to the phone number that we created for your call for witnesses, we now have other leads, though so far not very convincing ones. People tell us they saw Jabaree in Vegas, San Francisco, or in the Venice or Watts districts in L.A. Please believe us, Miss Lovelace, we're doing our best. Just a couple questions then I'll let you rest."

"Okay. What do you want to know?"

"This is a bit delicate, but how much do you trust your husband?"

The actress's eyes popped wide open with surprise.

"What do you mean by that? Are you asking me if

my husband is cheating on me, if he has mistresses? You know, in this line of work..."

"No, that wasn't what I meant. Do you think that your husband, who's not Jabaree's father, could be hiding something from you? Lie to you? For example, even though I understood it when he told me he was ashamed to not have been able to prevent your son from being kidnapped, and that was why he didn't want to come home before fifty hours had gone by... But during all that time he didn't give you any news except for the phone call an hour after the kidnapping. Do you believe his explanation here?"

Janice Lovelace closed her eyes, both to concentrate and to ease her ophthalmic pains.

"Why wouldn't I? He's my husband. We tell each other everything."

"Miss, that's something I hear every day... And when all is said and done, you often learn that you didn't know a thing or at least not everything, about your spouse, with whom you share their life, for the best and for the worst, with whom you sleep and make love. Because one day, out of the blue, you discover a terrible secret about the person you thought you knew so intimately. I'm not saying that's the case for your husband, I'm just asking if you trust him."

"Blindly. Ruppert has always been there for me, even at the worst of times. There when Dwayne, my first husband and Jabaree's father, died. May he rest in peace, my poor Dwayne who passed away so quickly. He didn't see his son grow up, didn't know he'd become a planetary star. He would have been so proud of him."

"When did he pass?"

"It'll be six years ago in a couple of weeks. Jabaree was only four then, still a baby for me. And he still is. My baby..." she whispered, despondent.

"And you met Ruppert shortly after that?"

"No, actually Ruppert and I had known each other for ages. You could say we were colleagues. He was already a movie director, I was a young actress. Dwayne's death brought us closer. I could count on him, he was always there to help me through that difficult period of mourning. Plus he was always there for Jabaree too. A substitute father, you could say. Inspector, Ruppert is a good man. That's why I don't have any reasons not to trust him. Any reason at all. I know that he feels terrible, that he's punishing himself, for Jabaree's kidnapping. His adoptive child! His cinematographic son. He's the one who made him."

"Would you happen to have a photo of Dwayne?"

Dwayne Smith's widow slowly got up, walked into the next room and came back a few seconds later, a picture in her hand.

"Dwayne, Jabaree and me, for his fourth birthday. This is that last photo where all three of us are together."

"Could I hold on to it?" asked Inspector Jonas Crimson.

CHAPTER 35
Ultimatum

Los Angeles, June 8, 2024

I discovered the video at the same time as everyone in the United States.

At the same time, undoubtedly, as Inspector Crimson and his team. I'd know in just a few seconds.

Two tiny minutes that would curdle the spectators' blood.

An abject threat.

A key turning point in the Jabaree case.

A terrifying ultimatum.

On the video, you saw a closeup of a masked person, only seeing their pupils through the two holes in the hood that was as black as clotted blood.

Their voice was artificially distorted through some

electronic means and so you couldn't be sure if it was a man or a woman speaking.

Here is what they said:

"Today, Jabaree's not the one talking to you. Parents, friends, colleagues, everyone, don't worry: Jabaree is fine.

For now!

This message is addressed more particularly to all the investigators who are trying, in vain, to understand our motivations.

Who are making no progress in their investigations.

Who have no idea where we are.

Who can't solve our riddles.

In this case, we'll make things clearer for them.

Know that time is now of the essence.

This is what we want to tell you: *Those who died on June 1st didn't die in vain!*

Let me repeat myself: *Those who died on June 1st didn't die in vain!*... Now is that clearer?

And now that we're hoping you'll have finally established a vague link between Jabaree Smith and a certain Shondra Wallace, here is our ultimatum:

If, in forty-eight hours as of now — meaning June 8th, 2024 at 12:00 sharp — you haven't shed any light on Shondra Wallace's disappearance, Jabaree will be paying the price...

So if on June 10th at noon, the truth is not known, we will cut one of Jabaree Smith's fingers off and send this tender bit of pink flesh, blood and pale bones to whom it may concern.

Then another one, then again another one... every forty-eight hours, until the truth is known. Or there are no more fingers to cut off...

INVESTIGATORS, listen well: Tick tock, tick tock, the countdown has begun!"

∼

I WASN'T ASTONISHED when my phone rang, and I saw Inspector Crimson's name on the screen.

CHAPTER 36
Cowboys and Indians

Countdown - 48 hours

"THIS IS TURNING INTO AN UNSPEAKABLE CLUSTERFUCK," swore the inspector in my ear on the phone. "Their fucking countdown is forcing us to cut corners in our investigation. And yours too, Miss Blackstone."

"Hey, Inspector, calm down! I can't replace your police force, okay!"

I raised my voice, trying to contain the anger I had receiving pressure from him like that. I wasn't responsible for Jabaree Smith's kidnapping nor for the abject images that his kidnappers were showing the world. Their ultimatum was causing us, and especially me, to urgently find a conclusion to the Shondra Wallace case, and the life of the Hollywood kid-star now depended on it. Crimson was insisting on that point.

"Karen, you've got two days max to solve that 1988 cold case."

"Listen, Inspector, are you trying to make me assume the entire responsibility for the incompetence of your services in not being able to find Jabaree Smith? Don't you think it's your job to find that kid who was kidnapped, whatever the reasons might have been for that? I understand that there's a link between his kidnapping and Shondra Wallace's disappearance thirty-five years ago, but still, this is your job, not mine!"

"Miss Blackstone, you aren't here to give me any lessons. Let me remind you that you're the one who contacted me about your copycat hypothesis."

"Well, I was right, wasn't I? I'm sure you agree that right now, my theory seems to have been true. The kidnappers explained the link very clearly. The problem, Inspector, is that when you investigate a cold case that's over thirty-five years old, you can't do anything quickly. How can you expect me to solve a mystery that old without hardly any witnesses left or just a handful of old doddery men who are drooling down out of their toothless mouths? It's nearly impossible, and I feel just as bad as you do. It's killing me to know that the kid is threatened like that while I'm moving between a robot-voiced producer (Apfenstein), a has-been and creepy movie director (Purcell), another producer who's on vacation in Sweden (Lundgren), a senile stuntman and standby who plays cowboys and Indians in his head (Bannister) and a starlet who went missing but was missed by no one (Shondra Wallace). Without even counting the reservation where real Indians who are pretty untalkative live (the Paiutes-Shoshones from Lone Pine). A nice painting, isn't it? So how can I draw a clear and definitive conclusion in forty-eight hours?"

I could hear the police officer mumbling during my tirade. I finally finished though.

"Are you in Los Angeles now? Get your butt over to my police station. Debriefing with my team in an hour. With you and two surprise guests..." added Crimson bitterly.

I knew I had no other solution than to obey him.

∽

FORTY-FIVE MINUTES LATER, I was sitting in the conference room of the Hollywood police station with Inspector Jonas Crimson who introduced me to his team members. I met Officer Diane Payton, his deputy, as well as half a dozen members of his main team. Two men wearing civilian clothing, spotlessly clean suits and ties, completed his squad.

"These two are Agents Lawrence McCormick and Maleeva Perez, from the FBI," said the inspector in a scratchy voice, casting a furtive glance at the two agents.

The mood in the room was glum. Their faces were

all wearing masks of helplessness. Events were following each other at a pace making it impossible for them to progress in their investigation, which was what Crimson said after having introduced me.

"Miss Karen Blackstone here is an investigative journalist specialized in solving cold cases. She was the first person to have understood the link between Shondra Wallace's disappearance and Jabaree's. At first I didn't believe her, nonetheless the latest video tends to prove that she was right. Karen will brief us on the current status of her investigation, and after that I'll tell her what we've learned to date. The reason I asked her to come is a simple one. We have to pool our strengths and resources – local, federal and private" –, he said, looking at the two FBI agents –, "work together, and brainstorm so we'll be able to solve this case quickly and no one will be hurt. Karen, we're listening."

In the following minutes, I repeated what I'd already told Crimson on the phone an hour ago about the various protagonists I'd interviewed ever since I'd arrived in L.A. Then I told them about the recent emails I'd exchanged with the person called *meganoc1970* on MovieGeeks, about the reels of film on possible unknown rushes of *The Coyote-Woman of the Desert* movie. I concluded with the sex scandal theory between the Brad Purcell, Shondra Wallace and David Apfenstein trio and the possible pregnancy of the actress which could have been one of the reasons she suddenly and voluntarily went missing.

"A simple fuck story?" said one of the Feds ironically.

"Unfortunately, that's what has driven the world for ages," replied the inspector. "But what links Shondra to Jabaree, that's the unknown skewing the equation. Now, let's go over what we know on our side. Which is not much. Moses, how are you doing on the analysis of the email and videos?"

A young policeman with red buzz cut hair looked in his notes only to end up saying that the teams specialized in electronic decryption still hadn't managed to find out where the documents came from.

"The person who did this is a pro in encryption and interference with sources, Inspector. All we know is that it came from the American continent."

"That's reassuring. At least we don't have to worry about Interpol sticking their noses in our business too," said Crimson – a poorly disguised insult to the Feds that he didn't appreciate much. Then, he turned to another of his team members. "So what about the CCTV cameras in the studio where the gala dinner was held?"

"We went through all the footage available from the cameras in the adjacent streets and compared it to the license plates of the cars that those invited to the event said they had driven. All the vehicles leaving the studio's underground parking lot and surrounding streets were scanned, between the time that Magloire took Jabaree upstairs, which was 11:50 pm and the time when he alerted everyone that he was missing,

12:45 am. We recognized most of the witnesses – all potentially suspects –, but never saw the child."

"Did you also check any eventual vehicles that drove around in that time slot?" McCormick asked.

"There were quite a few of them in the vicinity of the studios. It was Saturday night and there are apartments around there. People come and go, guests come to see friends or family, people go to parties or bars, but we never saw any ten-year-old kids."

"What about Magloire?" asked Agent Perez.

"Like he said, his vehicle left the underground parking lot at 1:15. You could see his Corvette leaving from level -2, but as the cameras were placed at the ends of the rows, we don't know his exact spot. All we saw was a long flash and then his warning lights followed by a more rapid double flash a few seconds before the vehicle appeared. What's surprising though, is that we saw the same flash from roughly the same place about half an hour earlier, but no cars left the parking lot then. Or at least not Magloire's Corvette. As if someone had unlocked the car to pick up or put something in it, and then had walked back to the studio after having locked it again a few seconds later, when we saw the flash once again. But we can't affirm that it came from his Corvette. It could have been a car that was parked in the same row. I don't know if this could be useful, Boss."

"We'll see," replied Crimson, pensively rubbing his chin. "Maybe there's a way we can see if it's a Corvette... You'll have to contact a dealership to see if the flashes to open and close the car are all identical or if they're vehicle specific. Also if they make noise."

"The CCTV cameras don't record sounds," said one of the policemen.

"Okay. That's too bad. For example, what does your car do when you unlock it?"

"Two short flashes."

"Mine has two short ones, then a long one."

"Mine three short ones," said another policeman.

"Mine two long ones," continued McCormick.

"And mine, nothing at all," I added, thinking of my old Ford Ranchero that only opens when you put the key in the car door.

Crimson closed the question by asking his subordinate to note the brands and models of cars that left the parking lot in the concerned time slot and to contact automobile makers to find out the types of flashes when locking or unlocking vehicles. Just by looking at his face, you could tell the policeman wasn't thrilled by that mission. But sometimes when you're an investigator, you have to do boring jobs like that one. Been there, done that.

"So, whatever, we have to act fast," said Agent McCormick, the most experienced of the two Feds. "Otherwise, if the kidnappers cut a finger off the boy in two days, things will escalate, and that's something I don't want to see happening, got it, guys? So back to work, you too Karen. Do you need the Bureau's help to make progress?"

"Give me twenty-four hours, Agent McCormick."

"And why should I, Miss Blackstone?"

I hated the FBI agent's condescending tone but didn't want to show it. I knew that with people like him, you have to keep your head down and produce good arguments, without patronizing them.

"I've always solved the investigations I've been given. Whether the events took place a few weeks ago or several years ago. And I've already worked with the Bureau, and no one complained about my services. I don't see why it should be different for you. Of course, I'll keep you in the loop, both Inspector Crimson and you, whenever I make any progress. And as the inspector said, we have to pool our resources to multiply our chances to solve this case. So, will you trust me, Agent McCormick?"

He smiled lopsidedly at her after having looked her right in the eyes, his eyelids down, as if trying to read what was going down deep inside of her soul.

"Tomorrow at noon, I want results here on this table. Otherwise, we'll take over the entire case. Is that clear?"

"Clear as spring water," concluded Crimson before adjourning the meeting.

CHAPTER 37
Silver bromide

WHEN THE POLICE all left the debriefing room and once the Feds had disappeared, Inspector Crimson held me back.

"Karen, I hope you understand why I'm putting so much pressure on you."

"The images of Jabaree and his kidnappers are there to remind us of the urgency. I must admit though that I've rarely had to stir up and rekindle the past so quickly though. I'll get going right now."

∽

Countdown - 46 hours

THE FIRST PERSON I wanted to talk to was David Apfenstein. I'd learned too much about him not to want to listen to his version of the facts and had the idea that he'd hidden a couple of things from me during our first interview at the Bel-Air Country Club.

This time, the ninety-five-year-old didn't feel up to having me come either to the Golf Club or to his air-conditioned house, where he'd now holed down with the terrible heat that was increasing day by day in Los Angeles. Like a lead blanket tossed over the heads of the Angelinos.

The former producer nonetheless was convinced of the urgency of the situation and said he'd speak to me on the phone. His metallic voice in my EarPods was even more unsettling than when I'd spoken to him in person.

"If that can help find the kid..." his synthetic vocal cords coughed out. "What do you want to know that I didn't already tell you, Miss Blackstone?"

I went straight to the point.

"How about telling me the truth this time."

"What are you insinuating?" Apfenstein asked.

"That you lied to me, either by omission or intentionally. Why didn't you tell me that you had a nonconsensual or forced relationship by blackmail in *exchange for screen time* with Shondra Wallace? Or that the actress was pregnant? And that you had a confrontation about this in Lone Pine with Brad Purcell, the person she was unofficially in a couple with..."

The laughter his synthetic voice generated was even worse than when he spoke.

"Because all that is a load of crap! And I can guess who the son of a bitch was who must have been ranting and raving about me. Dumb ass Lundgren, right? That bland Eskimo who I supported for years with my production company. Let me tell you, he wasn't biting the hand that fed him back then when he was looking for money to finance his inept scenarios! Forty years later it's easy to blame an old man!"

"Are you denying that you didn't force Shondra Wallace to have sex with you?"

"That's a bit personal as a question."

"Please answer, Mr. Apfenstein. I sort of feel this happened a long time ago."

"Let's say there were no crimes or misdemeanors. Let's be frank, Hollywood is a huge fuckodrome where sex is how things are paid for. *You wanna be in a movie? Deserve it!* That's what happens on movie sets. Of course, Shondra gave me her favors every once in a while. Stuff like that happens all the time in our line of work. But I can guarantee you that I never fathered a child. Too many problems, believe me. And if she had a bun in the oven, it certainly wasn't mine. Hey, and why wouldn't it have been Lundgren himself? Accusing others of what he himself did, that's a great tactic!"

"Are you accusing Lundgren?"

"I'm too old now to be accusing anyone. I'm simply reiterating my innocence: I didn't impregnate Shondra Wallace. Consequently, I still have no idea what caused her sudden disappearance."

Feeling that I wouldn't get any further on that soapy hill, I changed subjects.

"Let's talk about *The Coyote-Woman's* rushes. Though the movie was never finished, you still had takes of a slew of scenes, either directed by Brad Purcell or by Peter Lundgren. Is that correct?"

"Affirmative, Miss. So?"

"So those rushes must be someplace. Lundgren told me that the reels of film belong to the production studios. Meaning to you, Mr. Apfenstein."

"Correct."

His laconic answers were beginning to seriously piss me off. Either he was out of breath because of the heat, or he was hiding info from me on purpose.

"Do you think then that I could access those video rushes of the scenes shot in 1988?"

A guttural sound emanated from Apfenstein's electronic throat, making me think he was strangling.

"Miss Blackstone, I quit working fifteen years ago. I sold my business to a larger studio, a major one, more financially robust than me. So, for those reels of film, I remember that after our movie in Lone Pine was interrupted, they must have directly gone to the studio's archives."

"They must be accessible then in the large studio that acquired your business. I'd imagine that when you buy out a studio, you also purchase its archives?"

"You imagine correctly."

"What major studio is it then? You can tell me, it's no big deal now. Please."

This was beginning to get very tiring.

"I can tell you, it was Warner Bros. But don't bother asking them."

"How come?"

He sighed metallically before answering.

"Do you know what a 35 mm silver print film used in the movies is made of?"

"You're the specialist, tell me."

"It's a plastic band topped with a thin layer of gelatine, another of silver bromide plus a couple of other chemical components that are light reagents. All of that is... very, very flammable. See where I'm going here?"

"You destroyed the rushes?"

"Not me."

"Who?"

"A couple of weeks after the precipitated ending of *The Coyote-Woman of the Desert* shooting, a fire broke out in the facility where all the reels of film rushes that had never been edited were sleeping calmly. Just imagine my despair when I saw it, the day after the fire. Heaps of melted, twisted, carbonized plastic. Tens of thousands of miles of film and hours of work that all went up in smoke. Cultural treasures destroyed in just a few minutes. Millions of dollars of losses. Luckily covered though by my insurance that I paid a fortune for."

"Was it an accident caused by the heat?"

"Not at all. Insurance experts came around and they concluded that it was arson. They found boxes of matches in the heaps of carbonized plastic. But the person who caused the fire, who committed that criminal act deliberately, was never found."

"Someone who had an interest then in seeing those reels of film disappear..."

CHAPTER 38
Avatar

Countdown - 44 hours

How can you understand someone if you don't understand their past or their origins?

That was what I was focusing on now, while treading water in the quagmire of open questions I had in my investigation. Open and unanswered questions, leads I was following without seeing any proverbial light at the end of the tunnel.

I was furious when I learned that the rushes of *The Coyote-Woman* all went up in smoke and melted plastic. I had hoped to discover a few clues or indications from the scenes shot in Lone Pine, Shondra Wallace's last minutes before she went missing, just like her cinematographic avatar, the fictional character she was playing. I knew that sometimes actors, movie directors or screenwriters had fun putting subliminal messages into their works, things that explained explicitly their problems *in real life*. But was afraid, in the case that took up all my time, that I'd have to simply forget about that possibility.

I began another private message to *meganoc1970* on the MovieGeeks forum.

Hi Meganoc1970. I'm sorry to have to tell you that the rushes of *The Coyote-Woman of the Desert*, that mythical unfinished and unedited movie, have all totally disappeared. David Apfenstein, who was the producer at that time, told me that the reels of film that had been stored in the archives of his studio all burned in a fire caused by arson, just a few weeks after they'd been stored there. In the summer of 1988. Shondra Wallace's last role only survived for a few days after she disappeared. A double disappearance, if I can put it like that, the actress and then her avatar. As if she'd died twice! It's sad and really too bad. The myth of the forbidden film has fallen apart. Hope all is well with you and thanks again for having tried to help me with this case. Karen.

So now I had to try to find another explanation for Shondra's disappearance.

If the past in 1988 hadn't helped me, if the present of 2024 wouldn't allow me to investigate either, I had to find another approach.

But where? Maybe in her childhood and youth, that of someone dreaming of becoming a star. Psychoanalysts make their bread and butter by affirming that the adults we now have become are merely the sum of all the dreams, hopes, fears, anxieties, desires, aspirations, experiences, relationships or disillusions of our childhood. So why not try to understand Shondra Wallace's youth?

What did I know already? Not much, that was for sure. I had no idea who her parents were, if she had any brothers or sisters, if she was raised with them, in what conditions... Nothing.

I could ask Purcell. Insofar as he'd shared a part of her life, slept with her, maybe that was something they'd talked about. No sooner said than done, I phoned the retired movie director but got his voicemail.

. . .

"Brad, Karen Blackstone here. Can you call me back ASAP? I'd like you to tell me about Shondra's childhood, if of course you know something, and I'm sure that you do, as opposed to what you told me in our first interview, you didn't just consider her as 'a little sister,' but... a bit more than that. It would be appreciated if you could tell me the truth, this time. Please call me back, Jabaree Smith's life depends on this, I'm sure you can't ignore this fact."

While waiting, I thought back and remembered having read a short article on the web on Shondra's very succinct biography, and that she was born in Watts, L.A. As if that was useful to mention. Either the author of her biography hadn't found anything more interesting to write, or they'd put in this tidbit of information for a specific reason. In which case, what was it?

After I'd hopped into my rental car, I programmed its GPS to lead me to downtown Watts, leaving the device the choice of the road, as I didn't know where to go more precisely. Persuading myself that for a change, fate would lead me where it wanted, and it wouldn't be any worse than elsewhere.

Traffic jams were holding me up in downtown L.A., and my phone rang. I used the hands-free kit in my car and picked up, hearing a man's voice booming inside, covering the A/C running at full speed.

"Miss Blackstone? Brad Purcell here. I got your message. Please know that I'd like to apologize for not having been completely honest with you the other day at the Griddle."

"There's still time to come clean," I encouraged him.

"Well, it's true that Shondra and I did have a romantic idyll. Nothing regular nor permanent. In Hollywood, love is quite versatile. But working together for years only strengthened our episodic relationship. We were important to each other, that's true. And I was devastated to see her disappear so brutally, without any apparent reason."

The honking horns were playing a cacophonic symphony at the loggerheaded intersections, and I had to raise my voice to cut him off.

"Without any apparent reason, you're sure? Could Shondra have wanted to disappear to hide her non-consensual pregnancy? Get an abortion or raise her child alone, like a wolf... or a coyote? A coyote-woman..."

"Jesus Christ Karen, who puts ideas like those in your head? That's mind-boggling."

"My source isn't important, Mr. Purcell. For me it's a valid hypothesis. Maybe she didn't tell you everything!"

He sighed noisily.

"Shondra was naturally a bit secretive. A discrete woman. I can't imagine that she'd hide something like that from me, it would have been too incredible. A child... maybe mine... that would have been so..."

The last words of the former movie director got

caught in his throat. I could tell he was not faking his emotions.

My stop-and-start driving started up again. My car's radiator was working full-time and suffering under the blazing heat that softened the tar on the crowded streets.

"Brad, would you say you knew Shondra well?"

"I'm not sure of anything anymore," he admitted after a few seconds of silence. "Who can be sure they know their partner? Without the tiniest zones of shadows? Or having glimpsed their hidden sides? Everything's possible in real life, in the life of real people."

"Real people?"

"Yeah. You, your neighbor, your parents, normal people. Those are real individuals. But actors, screenwriters, authors, movie directors? All those despicable people live in spurious worlds, ones full of false pretenses, roles, masks! They're used to acting, interpreting, pretending, and that's a habit that penetrates right into the deepest parts of your soul and your heart. And then you can no longer separate things that are true from things that aren't. You start lying because you're used to it, first to yourself, then to others. As if your life was a movie. As if the camera, like the Earth, never stopped... And you become a living lie!"

"Was Shondra like that?"

"Possibly. Maybe Shondra's life was only a huge lie..."

CHAPTER 39
Crossfading

WHILE I WAS DRIVING, at a snail's pace, towards the south of Los Angeles, Purcell's words resonated in the car, as if they'd been bouncing around inside.

"*Maybe Shondra's life was only a huge lie...*"

And if he was right?

"Brad, what do you know about her past? What did she tell you? About her parents, her childhood, when she was a teen. I know she was born in Watts, in an African-American community. That's where I'm going right now."

"At least that's what she said."

"You guys never went there together? To have dinner with her family or something? How old was she when you first met her?"

"The first time she starred in one of my productions, she must have just turned twenty. That was back in 1980. Yeah, that's it, in *Black Panther in Brazil*, it was a total flop, but at least that brought us together.

She always told me that her parents died in a fire in their home in Watts when she was sixteen, and then after that she either lived with her aunt and uncle or friends. Up until she dared try her hand at the great Hollywood adventure, leaving Watts, where she often said she 'would have ended up dead.' Ended up, like loads of young women in that underprivileged neighborhood, by turning tricks, becoming an alcoholic, a drug addict, or by being raped and then beaten to death in some dark alley. You know Watts is a very different part of Los Angeles, you'll see it soon. Watch out, with your snow-white skin, you'll stick out like a sore thumb."

"It's that dangerous?" I asked, worried, while turning onto Central Avenue.

"Well, let's just say that it's not the most touristic district in L.A. Generally speaking, non-residents carefully avoid South Central. But those who live there only have one wish: to leave, and that as quickly as possible, like Shondra insightfully did. Before it was too late for her."

"Have you got any names of streets? Where she lived when she was little?"

"I can't give you any precise ones, but I remember she told me she could see those infamous Watts Towers from her bedroom window. That's the only highlight in Watts, Karen. So they must not have lived too far from there. Can I ask you a question now?"

"Go ahead."

"Why do you want to go there, especially all alone?"

"Because I'm not making any progress in my investigation, and I think I have to plunge into the places where the person I'm looking for grew up. That helps me understand, by empathy, the impressions, feelings, motivations, lots of things about that person. As if I'm her, actually. I try to comprehend the environment through her eyes, listen with her ears. And for a couple of hours, I'll live her life by procuration. Understanding what's implied. So today, I want to become the child Shondra was, the one who grew up in Watts."

"Be careful, Karen," Purcell concluded grimly. "Make sure you're out of there before it's dark."

TRAFFIC HAD FINALLY LET up as I got farther from downtown. At the same time, the environment had substantially changed, and I began to understand, now apprehensively, what I was getting myself into. I remembered that huge riots had taken place here in 1965, as well as urban guerilla fighting back in 1975. Entire blocks of buildings seemed to be abandoned, having been looted or burned in a new wave of riots in 1992. You're not always reborn from your ashes, like a Phoenix... Going past filthy gas stations, pitiful fast-food joints and empty warehouses or shops with bars on their windows as if they were expecting new troubles any day now, was beginning to make me uneasy. It was terrifying. Groups of young unemployed people were roaming around on broken sidewalks, dragging their feet in the Angelina sun. Everything around me stunk of poverty, unequal opportunities, of how hard it was to escape from a ghetto where you had been born.

This was the gateway to Hollywood, light years away from its gloss and glitter, its stars on the Walk of Fame, its gigantic studios, Sunset Boulevard, and the Bel-Air Country Club. I had the impression of listening to Elvis's stabbing and poignant lyrics in his timeless song, *In the Ghetto*:

"*People, don't you understand?*
The child needs a helping hand
Or he'll grow to be an angry young man someday.
Take a look at you and me.
Are we too blind to see?
Do we simply turn our heads
And look the other way?"[*]

AT THE END of the street, I could now see the Watts Towers, standing like huge lighthouses in the turmoil of the neighborhood, with their porcelain or glass inlays reflecting the blinding light of the sun. *Are we too blind to see?* wondered the King.

So little Shondra must have lived close to those

---

[*] Elvis Presley. *In the Ghetto*. A 1969 hit that spoke of one of his friends who lived on the wrong side of the tracks.

improbable sculptural towers. Was she living or merely surviving?

Those strange structures, something I'd never heard of and would learn about their origins later, stood out in the semi-abandoned urban decor. Despite their eclectic aspect, there was something poetic and surrealistic in the towers. A small park covered with yellow and dried grass surrounded them, like an island between the pot-holed streets next to it. Gangs of young men were roaming aimlessly on the sidewalks, looking for something to do. High-voltage cables, antennas and dishes were entangled in this environment of raw poverty.

I was afraid to stop my car and get out. Young men were staring at me while I was slowly driving, some of them giving me ambiguous gestures making me uncomfortable.

I kept on going, I didn't want to stop there. Yet I wanted to understand.

I turned on a street leading east, and suddenly saw a little girl who must not have been older than seven or eight, a pretty African-American with beautiful kinky black hair, playing on the sidewalk. It looked like she was playing hopscotch or something similar. A few steps with her left foot, then two or three jumps with her feet together, before returning to her right foot. That was the first impression of joy I'd seen around here, all the rest was merely boredom and morosity.

I turned slowly in her direction, to retain that positive image as long as I could. As my car was slowly driving past the child, she turned her head towards me.

Right then, at that precise moment where we looked each other in the eyes, her little, black and brilliant eyes seemed to pierce my soul.

I had a flash.

I looked into her eyes, and then like in Hollywood movies, a scene little by little replaced the preceding one by a process that cinephiles perfectly recognize: crossfading.

I was no longer gazing at that little girl, I was looking at Shondra Wallace!

CHAPTER 40
Top of the bill

WATTS, Los Angeles, 1976.

SHONDRA WALLACE WAS NO LONGER the carefree little girl playing hopscotch on the cracked sidewalks of the roads near Watts Towers.

TIME HAD GONE by for her. As it had for all those who lived in that district. She was now fifteen, nearly sixteen, and had just undergone one of the worst atrocities of her young existence. Her parents had both perished in a fire that had ravaged their home, a sad little house made from cheap wood, just like their neighbors' houses, while she was at school. While walking home, like every afternoon, she first smelled the odor of burnt wood hundreds of steps from the house. Then she saw spirals of black smoke in the perfectly blue Californian sky.

She ran as fast as she could because she'd just understood. Understood that a part of her life was now over and that now, now she could only count on herself to survive in a world that was too hostile for her. Too hostile for all the people living in her African-American community, who, like in many other places in the States, were victims of police brutality and overzealousness. Things that had caused riots in the previous years, the last one dating back only a few months. Even the army had been called in to help and soldiers walked up and down the streets in Watts with their tanks and machine guns on their shoulders. Except when they were aiming at someone, and pulled the trigger...

Was that what war was? A war between Americans? Because some citizens were more American than others? On what basis? Birth? Skin color? Where you were born? Because you're more American in Hollywood, Bel-Air, Beverly Hills than in Watts, Compton, or South L.A.?

Isn't the blood flowing in your veins the same color as the blood dripping from the bodies of those lying in the gutters?

SHONDRA THOUGHT of all of that while walking down the sidewalks in Watts. Of that and of her future. Since her parents had passed, she'd been living right and left, sometimes with uncles and aunts, sometimes with family friends. Mutual assistance was an essential lifestyle in poverty-ridden districts.

Either you stand together, or you die.

But Shondra didn't want to die. Not now, not that young. She thought she had all her life ahead of her, but for that, she had to flee the morosity in Watts. She had to go north to the nice districts, on the hills, on Sunset Boulevard, the Walk of Fame, where the studios were. Where those movers and shakers and decision makers lived, those working in the movie industry. As Hollywood was the center of the world, that was where she wanted to go. And stay.

Sometimes she took the subway and got off at Hollywood/Highland, not too far from the Walk of Stars. She would gaze at the stars on the sidewalk, being careful never to walk on them, a sacrilege! Often she would stop and contemplate one of them, such as Barbara Streisand's star, one that had recently been inaugurated. She dreamed of the day when she'd put her hands on fresh concrete to leave her own trace. The indelible trace of her success. But she knew that her dream was inaccessible. Was there even one African-American actress who had a star? One black woman? It was impossible in those puritan studios directed with an iron fist by WASP and Jewish moguls.

Yet, in the past few years, things had started to change for roles given to African-American actors. The fight for civil rights had begun and that was something newsworthy. The 30s, 40s, and 50s, were finished, years when Hollywood only employed black people in roles of waiters, cabaret dancers, bandits, or slaves... They now could hope to have less caricatural roles, nearly like those held by white actors. Of course, they still wouldn't be at the top of the bill, but there was a glint of hope. Sidney Poitier had been a huge hit in *Guess Who's Coming to Dinner* and had nearly won an Oscar for *Lilies of the Field* in 1964.

Not yet a global star, it was still too early! No, gender cinema was what would open the door for him.

What was called exploitation films, those shot quickly and cheaply, exploiting current trends or niche genders, in hopes of a quick profit. Movies that Shondra could have seen in drive-ins or grindhouses with friends a bit older than she was.

Those theaters where B-series movies were shown, those where spectators could watch two feature-length films for the price of one ticket. Those that Shondra preferred were a sub-gender called *blaxploitation*, starring an actress that she dreamed of resembling, a certain Pam Grier, a hit.

Resemble her or succeed her?

How does one become the new Pam Grier? wondered Shondra while ambling down Sunset Boulevard.

I have to be noticed by a successful screenwriter, an ambitious director, an influential movie producer.

I'm ready for anything, I can do it...

CHAPTER 41
The art of make-believe

THAT's what that little girl I'd run across while driving through Watts inspired me. A little girl who I imagined as a young lady now. A teen who, mortified by those singularly cruel events, had to grow up, and grow up fast.

I now thought that I could begin to understand what drove Shondra Wallace to flee this desolate part of Los Angeles and try the great cinematic adventure, that art of make-believe that put stars on sidewalks and above all, in the eyes of spectators throughout the entire world. Amongst them, how many souls had dreamed of glory only to harvest disillusions?

Shondra saw herself right at the top of the bill, filling theaters, attending festivals all over the world wearing brilliant *haute couture* dresses, blinking because of the flashes of cameras. In her dreams, she undoubtedly was sure that one day she'd be walking down the red carpet in Cannes, going on stage on

Oscar night to lift that golden statue whose name came from a librarian who had an uncle named Oscar and whose face looked like the trophy...

Instead of that though, in 1988, she was only and still a second zone actress, shooting B-series movies, unknown to the public.

How could you explain that chasm between her dreams as a young lady and the pitiful reality?

Now that I thought I'd understood the origins of her ambitions, why wouldn't I be able to understand the reasons behind her disappearance? Was there a link between the two or did the solution reside in that twelve-year interval?

I kept driving at a snail's pace in the streets of Watts and the silhouette of that little girl faded in my rear-view mirror. My suppositions weren't going to be enough. I wanted to have them confirmed by witnesses. In the streets adjacent to Watts Towers, I looked at the passersby, at inhabitants sitting on their front steps or in front of a bar-grocery store with bars on its windows.

There wasn't any place to park, so I kept going until I found one and parked my car, making sure to lock it. You might say that it was a bit of a cliché, but I wanted to make sure my rental car would still be there when I went back.

A few white-haired African-Americans were killing the time they still had left by playing dominoes and drinking coffee. *Nothing ventured, nothing gained*, I thought to myself. After having quickly guessed the age of those calm old men, I thought that with a bit of luck, they could have known the Wallace family back in the 70s. I was sure no one had forgotten the drama of that house that had burned down.

When I arrived at the patio, which was merely the sidewalk with three rusty iron tables and six chairs in the same state, people were looking at me curiously. I ordered an iced coffee. The sweltering heat, though the afternoon was drawing to an end, made me want a thirst-quenching drink that a lady whose breasts were so huge that she seemed to have two watermelons in her bra brought me.

"You lost?" she asked me suspiciously.

"What do you mean?"

"Bah! You know, 'chalk faces' like you – beautiful though, let me compliment you – we don't see too many of them sitting here outside in front of our store. Except for the cops that tour around here now and then, this ain't no playground for Whites."

The old men all chortled after the lady's verbal admonition, showing their mostly toothless mouths, with the few teeth they had left quite a disgusting yellowish color.

"Last time I saw one," continued one of the men, "it was one of them deputies of the L.A. mayor, who gain merit by promising a golden future for this district. Gimme a break! Just words, no actions. They smile when they're being filmed for the news, but once their backs are turned, they rush off in their limos with tinted windows, and it's *adios, amigos*!"

"I'm not here to show off or promise you anything. Quite the opposite, I'm humbly here because I need your help."

"What kinda help, beautiful lady?"

I rummaged around in my purse and took out my press card.

"Karen Blackstone. I'm a journalist specialized in trying to solve cold cases. I'm sure you couldn't have missed that event that shook all of Hollywood up," I said, as I saw a TV inside the shop with the kidnapping of Jabaree Smith on it."

"For sure. Poor kid. But what can we do about that?"

"It happens that his kidnapping is linked to the disappearance, thirty-five years ago, of a certain Shondra Wallace. A forgotten and poorly known actress, but someone people around here would know."

"Why would we know her?"

"Because the Wallace family lived around here up until 1976. Then there was a tragedy: Shondra's parents died when their house burned down. Only the little girl escaped because she was at school when it happened. After that she lived right and left, with friends or family members, in Watts, up until she decided to stand on her own two feet and try the great Hollywoodian adventure. Did any of you know the Wallace family?"

There was a moment of silence on the patio, one of

the players was holding a domino suspended in the air while seemingly thinking.

"There were Wallaces around her, almost as many as Jacksons or Browns. But yeah, I was here in 76 and remember that. It was the year after the second wave of riots... I personally didn't know the Wallace family, but I can find you someone who must remember little Shondra."

"That would really be useful for me."

"Wait a sec."

The old man, who must have been north of eighty, put his wrinkled and trembling hand into his pocket and took out a brand-new phone on which he looked for a number, then stuck it against his ear with its oversized lobe and stiff hairs sticking out of it like parsley. He waited for a few seconds, then began shouting into the phone.

"Hey Russell, if you're able to get up from your sagging couch, get your old flabby butt over to Lilah's place, there's a pale face who wants to talk to you. Yeah, you. I know it's a surprise. She says you could be useful. So turn off that crap you're watching on TV and put some pants on, hoping they're clean and hurry up, she says it's urgent."

I thanked the old man for his both spontaneous and vividly descriptive solicitude and waited a couple of minutes before a man who must have been at least sixty-five or seventy walked up to us. He fist-bumped his friends' hands and sat down right across from me. No need to say that the pale face was mine.

"Hey, Missy! What can I do for you?"

I repeated what I'd told the other clients and finished with a question.

"So, you knew Shondra Wallace quite well then?"

"That I did. Before she split from Watts, never to set foot here again, I was her boyfriend."

"Tell me about her."

CHAPTER 42
Those damned big white screens

"Shondra, when she was sixteen, she was quite the looker, I swear to you. Attracted men like flies. As for me, maybe you can't see it now, but I wasn't bad myself neither. Right, Malcolm?"

The aforementioned Malcolm nodded, not quite as convinced as his friend. Without an acquiescence from his mates, Russell Eubanks, as that was his whole name, continued.

"We fell in love with each other, it was just evident for us. A couple that had hype in our district. When they saw us walking, people called us the Romeo and Juliette of Watts."

"But like in Shakespeare's play, it didn't end well?" I asked.

"That's right. And I'll tell you why."

I was all ears.

"Because of those movie theaters! Those damned big white screens! Shondra was obsessed with movies.

You gotta understand how ironic that was. Here, we're just a couple of miles from Hollywood, but for us people who live in Watts, it's inaccessible. But Shondra dreamed of that so much that I knew that one day she'd give in to the call of them projectors, just like a moth who's attracted to streetlights. But just like a moth, she got so close that she burned her wings... Forever. If you'd only known how passionate she was! That was all she talked about. Cinema, its stars, the glitter and glory, money, everything we don't got here! Except for the movies that came to us at that time. As soon as I got my driver's license, I took all the gals around here to the drive-in, on Friday or Saturday night, they all loved it. In the car, when we were watching the movies, often two back-to-back B-series that made us laugh more than shiver, having a beer or a Coke and some popcorn, my Shondra never stopped staring at the screen. She had stars in her eyes. She was one of Pam Grier's fans, the blaxploitation star, in movies where Black people like us had roles. She wanted to become like her, an icon for Black American actresses."

I had been right then, when I mentally had delved into Shondra's mine a bit earlier.

"How did she leave Watts?"

"Suddenly! She told me that, one night when we were kissing while watching a movie we'd already seen at least three times. 'Russ, I love you, but I gotta go. If I stay here, I'll die.' Jesus, it was the opposite that happened. She left to die in Hollywood."

"In Lone Pine," I corrected him.

"Same thing. You understood me."

"Yes, I did. Go ahead."

The old man, whose souvenirs went back over forty years, was still as moved as he was when he was a teen.

"I don't know how she managed to live in Hollywood. She didn't have a dime on her, a place to sleep, nothing. She left with nothing. Okay, at that time it wasn't that unusual either, the peace and love mindset, a backpack, you put out your thumb to hitch, you met good or not so good people, and that was life. She did phone me from two or three hostels where she was able to sleep a couple of days, between petty jobs to make enough dough to get something to eat before landing THE role that would 'put her in the limelight,' as she always said. She told me that she'd met famous actors, screenwriters and producers who had promised to hire her. Like I said, she was beautiful, and I imagine that a lot of those guys noticed her. But she had to wait for a long time, even for years, before landing a role in a movie. You wanna know what I think? I think she earned a living doing something else…"

"Meaning?"

"You know what happens in Hollywood's artificial world? There's thousands of wannabe actresses, trying to get a role, even a tiny one, who'd do anything to star in a movie. Anything! And very few who actually make a living from it."

I thought about Apfenstein's admitted affair with her.

"Like giving men their bodies?"

"I wouldn't say 'giving,' it's more like an 'exchange currency.' They start by giving them head in exchange for a role as an extra. Then a little more for a secondary role, and who knows what for a leading one! Something they get caught up in. Months go by, the career they'd been hoping for doesn't take off, then the budding starlets become depressed, or alcoholic, or start taking drugs to keep going and forget their lost illusions... But for that, you need money! So you end up accepting even worse, you sell your body to anyone as long as he pays enough to buy a package, a pill, a dose, or a bottle of scotch."

"You think that was what happened to her? She did have a career. Even though it didn't fulfill her dreams as a young lady."

"You call that a career? Dozens of flops shot quickly by untalented movie directors and shady producers? I saw a couple of her movies at the beginning of the 80s. After that, too disgusted by what I'd seen, I quit watching. It made me sick to see her as ridiculous as that in public. Even if there wasn't much of a public..."

What Russell Eubanks was describing to me was an intimate aspect of what went on behind closed curtains. Behind the scenes.

"I understand what you must have felt. I watched some of her feature-length movies too and I have to admit that they inspired more pity than admiration. But still, I thought I found a spark in her eyes that led me to believe that she did have undeniable potential."

"But one that was never used. Maybe she didn't meet the right people at the right time. Or she only met the wrong ones."

Those words were like a sudden electric spart in my thoughts.

"Concerning her disappearance, do you think it could have stemmed from when she was trying to break into this line of work... maybe she met the wrong person at the wrong time?"

"That's something we see here in Watts. When you rub shoulders with people selling drugs or their bodies, one day or another you always end up meeting the wrong person at the wrong time..."

CHAPTER 43
Admiration or derision?

Countdown - 40 hours

"WE'VE ALREADY SEEN mules ending up at the bottom of the lake weighed down so they wouldn't come back up or eaten by coyotes in the middle of the desert," continued Eubanks with a muted voice. "Or with a bullet in their forehead in the middle of an abandoned construction site."

"Do you think Shondra could have been one of those drug runners who ended up, like so many others, by being eliminated because she'd become a problem or was useless?"

Eubanks shook his head.

"I wouldn't be able to tell you. It was just a hypothesis. I tried to understand why she vanished into thin air like that and have never been able to find a logical explanation. Maybe you'll have more luck!"

The sun was disappearing behind the horizon, and I glanced at the clock on the wall of the grocery store and bar. Time had rushed by so quickly since Jabaree's kidnappers had given the world their ultimatum, whereas time had stretched itself too slowly since Shondra Wallace's disappearance. I shivered.

"I hope so too," I said, getting up, "because the clock is ticking. Thanks so much for your time, Mr. Eubanks."

"And thank you too for trying to rehabilitate Shondra's memory."

I collectively thanked all the customers in the bar, who'd already begun playing dominoes again, paid and walked back to my car.

The sun had already set in the ghetto in Watts. I picked up my pace, less reassured than when I'd come earlier on in the afternoon. The little girl skipping on the sidewalk had gone home, replaced by groups of young unemployed gang members, their caps on backwards and a fag hanging out of their mouths.

I spotted my car, my heels tapping on the still hot sidewalk. I was sure the night wouldn't refresh the atmosphere. I couldn't wait to get back to my comfortable air-conditioned room, I was smothering here. The heat? The urgency? Fear? Or a mixture of all above?

Turning my head each time I heard murmurs behind me, I saw those young men, with nothing to do and all day to do it, whose slow steps wearing sneakers mixed with the click clack of my heels. I had the feeling I was being followed.

I accelerated and finally reached my car, opening it with the remote control. I was afraid to lose time if I manually opened the lock.

Only when I was opening the door did I hear some snickers behind my back – admiration or derision? – followed by words that pierced my soul.

"Hey, little Lifesaver! Sweetheart, don't leave like that!"

"Wait for us, Whipped Cream!"

"We wanna have a good time!"

My knees buckled. I hit my hip on the corner of the door, a sharp pain ripped through my ribs. I swore, getting into the car as quickly as possible. Locked the doors. My hands were shaking so much I could hardly put the key in.

The gang rushed up to me.

I turned the key, pressing on the brake. The engine coughed and stalled. I turned the key one more time. This time it coughed but started.

In the meanwhile, four young men had encircled my car. One of them was in front, his hands on the hood, another one behind and the two others on each side.

I could see a kid, who must not have been older than eighteen, through my window, though I refused to look at him. He was wincing at me lasciviously, moving his tongue obscenely, a hand on his zipper and mimicking sickening caresses.

Terrorized, my mind went back in time. Tears began to fall, I closed my eyes and found myself plunged into atrocious memories of one spring night in Boston.

I was seventeen…

Stalemate

Being in the wrong place at the wrong time. That perhaps was the case for Shondra Wallace, but that certainly was true for me.

I was young and carefree, still a child, my parents said.

I was seventeen, I had my driver's license, drove a clunker.

It was night, I had gone out. There were raindrops forming puddles in the road.

It was in Boston, in Roxbury.

What was I doing there alone at night, in those filthy roads flanked by buildings that had seen better days?

I didn't hear them come.

They jumped on me out of nowhere.

There were three of them, I remember that perfectly, because I had the time to count them, one by one.

I couldn't make out their features. Only their

reddened eyes were visible in the middle of their black skins and shadows of the night.

They grabbed my arms, picking me up.

One of them put his hand over my mouth to prevent me from screaming, from calling for help.

They dragged me to a cul de sac, where the lights of the adjacent street only generated long, black, and frightening shadows.

A pestilential stench was coming from the rusty garbage cans or bags that stray cats or dogs had ripped open. Maybe rats too, as I saw yellow eyes in the corners when they forced me down on the ground, my back in slimy puddles with the reflection of the cold moon in it, impassable to the drama taking place under its eyes.

The hand over my mouth came off, and in that second I wanted to scream.

But very quickly I knew it would be a terrible mistake when I saw a switchblade shining right next to my left eye.

"You open your mouth, you're dead," whispered a terrible voice smelling of alcohol and rot. "Don't move, it won't take long, you'll see".

They pulled up my dress, ripped my panties off.

Someone jumped on me, and I closed my eyes tight when I felt myself being ripped apart between my legs.

Then a warm and sticky liquid ran down my thighs.

It stopped, and then a couple of seconds later, started again.

Still as strong, still as painful.

But I remained silent. I bit my lip until it bled, I swallowed my shame. I waited till it was over.

Then it was. Three times.

Those unknown teens drunk with alcohol, drugs, hatred, and perversity assaulted me three times.

Then they sauntered on, leaving me alone on the cold and wet concrete in that alley in Boston.

I cried silently for long minutes before finding the strength to get back up.

I got back up.

Physically. Mentally.

I didn't tell anyone. Especially not my parents. I was too ashamed.

I was in a stalemate.

Nine months later, they took you from me forever.

Twenty-five years later, I'm coming back for you, my lost son...

CHAPTER 44
Cacophony

Countdown - 40 hours

"Hey! You guys! Get the hell outta there you, you assholes, before I call the cops!"

I recognized that voice from inside my car. Opening my eyes. I saw the four idiots who were having fun scaring me skedaddle.

How far would they have gone had Russell Eubanks not chased them away.

I'd relived, in a memorial flash, the drama of my youth, that instant that changed my life forever and that partially explained my presence today in Los Angeles.

I lowered my car window.

"Thank you, thank you so much, Mr. Eubanks. I have no idea how I can thank you for that."

"Come on, everything's alright now. Don't stay here, this isn't a place for people like you. Get going and find my Shondra, that'll be how you can thank me."

I stepped on the gas, fleeing Watts, just like that young lady who had dreamed of becoming an actress did, forty years ago.

A FEW HOURS LATER, back at my motel and nearly asleep, I heard people shouting outside. I looked at the alarm clock and it was exactly midnight. Bells were ringing in the nearest churches.

It was getting louder. I got out of bed, walked up to the window that I could only open in oscillation mode for safety measures. I thought I heard several different tones. Both men and women were shouting. Shouts of joy... rather than fear?

From my observation post, I could see that several windows were open in the neighboring buildings. And I thought I saw young people in them. They were the ones shouting, one after another and then all together in a strange cacophony. They made me think of a pack of wolves who had gotten together with this battle cry. Little by little, the clamor diminished in intensity and ceased just as mysteriously as it had begun.

It had only lasted a minute.

I went back to bed, but only fell asleep at about three in the morning, my head still buzzing with my enigmas and fears. Fear of my past. Fear of what I was going to do with those memories. Fear of not being quick enough for Shondra. Fear that Jabaree would be hurt because I wouldn't have been able to overcome those fears.

∼

Countdown - 28 hours

THE NEXT DAY, at the hotel lobby, I questioned the concierge, a sixty-something man wearing a red jacket with gold buttons on it making him look like someone to be respected.

"Did you hear all that shouting last night?"

I strangely felt that he was holding his laughter in. He was having trouble controlling the movement of his lips and his nostrils, before asking me a strange question.

"Is this the first time you've been to Los Angeles in June?"

"The first time ever. What does that have to do with it?"

"Because that confirms that you were never a UCLA student."

I had a flashback of Luke Virgil. I pushed that gut-wrenching thought out of my mind.

"Can you please stop talking to me like the Sphinx, in riddles?"

"Sorry. So what you heard last night, at midnight, was the *midnight yell*, which is when all the UCLA students shout each night during their exam week. It's a tradition said to help them evacuate stress caused by their finals. I have no idea if it works, but you have to admit it's quite quirky and unique."

I thanked him for his explanations while thinking that amongst those thousands of anonymous voices that night in Los Angeles, my son could have been one of them.

A voice lost in the night.

My phone rang as I was walking into the dining room downstairs.

It was an unknown caller, but I still picked up and was glad to hear a voice that was not unknown to me.

"Miss Blackstone? Foster Maverick. Can you jump into your car and drive to Lone Pine?"

"Of course, why?"

"The Paiutes-Shoshones Reservation President has accepted to speak to you."

I grabbed a couple of croissants in a basket in the dining room and a coffee to go and rushed off to the parking lot.

CHAPTER 45
Strip of film

Countdown - 26 hours

"INSPECTOR? I got those analyses that you asked for."

The police officer who'd stuck his head through Inspector Jonas Crimson's half-opened door was proudly holding some sheets of paper.

"Come on in, Melvin. Let's have a look."

The day before, when he'd returned from his Pasadena-Malibu-Las Vegas journey with Ruppert Magloire, Crimson had given LAPD's scientific laboratory the strip of 35 mm film he'd taken from the movie director, having put the inch or so of strip of film in his pocket.

JUST LIKE A FLY FISHERMAN DOES, the cop had thrown a line out, to see if he'd get a bite. "Nothing ventured, nothing gained," he'd thought in the private projection room of the hacienda in the middle of the desert.

Crimson ran through the three very technical paragraphs that experts had written about the tiny strip of film. The main conclusions of their report affirmed that without much risk of errors, the film dated back at least thirty years but not more than forty. The brand and model of the film were visible on the sides of the film, which hadn't been produced since the beginning of the 90s, said the specialist, a retired photographer. That was also the beginning of the decline of movies made with silver-halide film, and the increase of digital technology.

The death of cinema, some people had said.

Moreover, the experts had analyzed the cuts at both ends of the strip and had concluded that though the strip itself was old, the cuts made by scissors or shears were very recent. A week or two at the most.

The double scissors' cuts were very precise, clean, and determined. Only six images were present, what the specialists described as "a quarter of a second of a movie," as cinematographic standards, since "motion pictures" had been invented, were composed of twenty-four images for one minuscule second of a film. Not including slomo and accelerations, of course!

The editor had thus wanted to cut six "instants" meaning a quarter of a second from a reel that when empty, could have up to three hundred and five yards of length for a twenty-seven-minute shoot. The experts then gave the inspector the following equivalences:

Twenty-seven minutes equals one thousand six hundred and twenty seconds.

One thousand six hundred and twenty seconds multiplied by twenty-four images per second represents thirty-eight thousand eight hundred and eighty instants printed on the reel.

And for feature-length films, should it be the case, the amount would be six or seven times this length. Miles of film to be edited to end up with an hour and a half movie.

To make a long story short, the analysis only included six of those thirty-eight thousand eight hundred and eighty pictures! Two hundred seventy-two thousand one hundred and sixty images if the filmmaker used seven reels of film... meaning a needle in a haystack.

And that was what Crimson had to draw his conclusions from.

But conclusions on what?

What could that tiny strip of film he'd pinched from Ruppert Magloire tell him?

Magloire had told him two days ago that he was working on an old project. The inspector looked at his notes.

"What you see here are old reels that I bought from a producer who declared bankruptcy a couple of years ago and I play with them, mixing and editing them. A movie director's little whim. A hobby. Like a musician who rearranges songs other artists have written."

A producer who went bankrupt? Other artists? Maybe Apfenstein, Purcell, or Lundgren, people who Karen Blackstone had mentioned last night when they met?

Could those snippets of film from the 1980s that he'd picked up from the floor of Magloire's editing room, correspond to a quarter of a second from *The Coyote-Woman of the Desert*, that unfinished movie that had supposedly gone up in smoke in 1988, Crimson wondered.

The expert's report only focused on the physical analysis of the bits of film. Not on the content of those six images. The policeman wanted to get to the bottom of that.

He picked up the bit of orangish-brown plastic, straightened it between his two hands and put it above his eyes, aiming at the light of the neon lights in his office.

What he found on those six images baffled him.

CHAPTER 46
The Far West

Countdown - 24 hours

WHEN I HEARD that the news was to begin on my car radio while driving to Lone Pine, right after the ads, my heart jumped.

It had already been twenty-four hours since Jabaree's kidnappers had given us their terrible ultimatum.

Twenty-four hours until their atrocious threat would come live: cutting off one of the child's fingers and sending it as proof they were serious.

Tomorrow, at noon, if Crimson's and the FBI's teams, not forgetting myself, had not solved the double mystery about Shondra Wallace's disappearance and Jabaree Smith's kidnapping, it would be too late.

And it seemed to me, much to my despair, that I was still ages from finding some explanations about the hodgepodge of contradictory leads I was trying to make sense of.

Would I find an answer with the Paiutes-Shoshones? I was certainly hoping to. Anyway, it was a great honor to be allowed into their reservation.

I sped down the deserted desert highway in the blazing hot sun that gave the road the illusion of burning steam, as if it was being distorted by the star we saw during the day.

Miles went by, I must have had about another hour before reaching Lone Pine.

∽

Countdown - 22 hours

TWO HOURS LATER, I met up with Foster Maverick. The little town's mailman, that Native American now assimilated to the local life in Lone Pine, would facilitate my introduction to Mary Hansen, the president of the Paiutes-Shoshones tribe. I was astonished by that very western name that the Indian who was in charge of the reservation's autonomous administration. She welcomed us at the closed gate. I hadn't imagined of course an Indian wearing traditional clothing, with black braids on each side of a face with war paint on it, a feather in her hair, however. Yet I still hadn't been expecting to see a lady with short hair, wearing jeans and a shirt.

In front of the fence-gate that two men manually pushed open, I thought of the cages for animals... A zoo in which we'd parked human beings.

"Come in, Miss Blackstone," said Mary Hansen, without a smile and turning her back on me to being quickly walking down the reservation's main path.

I glanced at Foster, questioning him with my eyes, but he just shrugged, as if asking me what I'd been expecting.

Following in the footsteps of the president, we went past homes made from corrugated iron sheeting, wooden pallets and a few concrete blocks. Others had mobile homes, trailers, or prefabricated ones in which the temperature must have been scorching, without any air conditioning. I imagined an old fan at the best moving the hot air around, without cooling it. Hell on earth!

We continued for roughly five hundred feet and then Mary Hansen stopped in front of one of those buildings, probably the least miserable of all I'd seen, and showed me in.

The fears I'd had about the temperature inside were founded. Inside the walls made from sheeting, it was unbearably hot. Used to conditions like that, she invited me to sit on one of the plastic chairs in front of a desk covered with sheets of paper. On the walls there were portraits of Indians wearing their traditional costumes, this time with feathers, bows and arrows, posing in front of real brightly colored teepees.

"This is our administrative center," said the chief of the tribe. "This is the place where we make all the decisions about how to manage our reservation. What you white people call 'town halls.'"

I tried to look interested.

"From what I understand, you are completely autonomous?"

"Of course we are. We don't have a choice. The Western world is so ashamed of us, the original inhabitants of this country before they came. I'm talking about the land, of course. Even though settlers had their way with our squaws, back in the day... But let's not talk about the half-open scars of the past and get down to business. You wanted to talk to us, the Paiutes-Shoshones, about a case concerning you settlers."

"Please Ma'am, I don't want to talk about controversial subjects that eat away at good relationships between our two nations. I'm personally for the recognition of Native American rights. And to be frank, the living conditions of your nation, out of sight here in the reservation, are terrible. I want to believe in the possibility of a complete assimilation."

"Utopia!" Mary Hansen said loudly. "Whatever. Let's continue. Foster begged me to help you understand what could have happened here in Lone Pine, in 1988, a long time ago. I was only eight at that time. From what I was told, you think the Natives played a part in that disappearance, simply because an old half-senile stuntman had told you that Shondra Wallace had been kidnapped by one of them..."

Paul's head popped into my mind when she said that, that toothless old ninety-year-old who shouted out "*Whouwouwouwouwouwou*" and "*Ugh*! "*Ungha-*

ungha-wha! Ugh!" by tapping his dry lips with his calloused and knotty hand.

"I must admit that, from your point of view, it does seem completely incongruous and unfounded. Yet there was an unexplained disappearance that took place on June 1st, 1988. A kidnapping? She ran away? An accidental death? Or maybe a murder? Whatever happened, as your reservation is right next to where the crime took place, if it was a crime, I think that maybe somebody could have something useful to tell me."

President Hansen sighed and shook her head.

"I frankly don't see how my people could have been involved in that. As no one wants us, as we leave you all alone, though we didn't smoke that famous peace pipe, I'd say that what happens in Lone Pine and in Alabama Hills is of no interest to us. We're far removed from all that craziness behind our fences and barbed wires."

When she said that, she glanced at Foster Maverick, who was squirming in his chair, uncomfortable and silent.

"And like I said, I was way too young to remember anything. And Miss Blackstone, I'm not so sure either that there's a huge number of witnesses between our fences who are still alive."

"Well, it doesn't go back that far," I corrected her ironically. "Only thirty-five years."

The president burst out laughing.

"My poor lady," she finally said, "don't get things wrong, laughing for me was a type of playing down the importance of what you said. What do you know about our living conditions? You must ignore that life expectancy in Indian reservations is only forty-seven years for men and fifty-two for women! That's why I said that there wouldn't be a huge number of witnesses to what happened in 1988..."

My eyes popped wide open, flabbergasted.

"Just think of the problems I have to deal with every day here. The population of this reservation, like all the others in the States, has serious health problems. First of all, diabetes, due to malnutrition: too much sugar, not enough fresh food. Problems of depression and alcohol addiction. Even though selling alcohol is forbidden, consumption is enormous: 85% of the families here. All you have to do is leave the reservation and go to a grocery store in Lone Pine and you'll see rows and rows of hard liquor. And when they've drunk all their stock, you know what my fellow countrymen drink?"

"I have no idea."

"Just have a look in the stores around here, the 90° rubbing alcohol, hand gel, methylated spirits, all those aisles are empty! And as if that wasn't enough, we also have to fight against drug addiction, especially because of all the meth that's sold. Even though we're in reservations, drugs are omnipresent wherever there's poverty and misery. You put all that together, without forgetting that the infant mortality rate is 300% higher than the national average in the United States, the rate of suicide in teens is 150% higher, and the mortality rate of adults is also high. Unemployment here in the reservation is 90% and 97% of our population live below the poverty line. A third of our families doesn't have electricity, phones, running water, or drainage. So you see, all your little problems that you pale-faced people have on the other side of the fence, Miss Blackstone, I really couldn't care less."

"I'm really sorry to have learned all that. Sincerely. I had no idea..."

The president raised an authoritarian hand to cut me off.

"Don't apologize, it's not your fault. No, I'm not totally insensitive to what is taking place between this double case that's targeting African-Americans. I consider them to be equal to us souls of the First Nations. They're descendants of slaves, their ancestors were violently dominated by the White settlers. Black slaves, Native Americans, same war. Even today, ghettos in big cities are the spitting images of our reservations, from a human point of view."

When she said this, the image of Watts came back to me. I let the president finish her speech.

"I'll help you out, at least I'll do what I can," Mary Hansen assured me. "Here in Lone Pine Reservation, there's an ancestor who was able to resist all those scourges. That venerable man is the living memory of our reservation. Some people say he's over a hundred years old, but you know, birth certificates aren't our specialization here. But when you see him, you'll understand that Methuselah was just a kid next to him!

He was here in 1988, so maybe he was a witness – or a participant – in the events you're concerned about."

The president got up from her chair, inviting Foster and I to do the same. She wasn't quite finished though.

"You'll be meeting "Prancing Horse under Winter's Red Moon."

My eyes must have opened wide, thinking about Indians in movies of the Far West.

"That's really his name?"

Mary burst out laughing.

"No, I was pulling your leg. It's Joshua Cutler! But I have to warn you, he's hard of hearing and nearly blind."

CHAPTER 47
Smoke and mirrors

Countdown - 21 hours

WHILE WALKING down the roads (if you could call roads those simple, dusty clay paths between the rows of sheet iron houses), with Mary Hansen and Foster Maverick, I looked right and left towards the sad dwellings where people must have been sweltering under the scorching desert sun. After what Mary Hansen had told me, I was wondering what kind of life those living here actually had. As we walked towards the center of the Indian reservation, I could make out little groans, people crying or shouting in a language I didn't know.

"Almost there," said Mary.

Then I saw an enormous teepee covered with colored canvas. I thought that the ancestor must live there, in a traditional home like his ancestors had.

"Is this it?" I asked, pointing to the teepee.

"Ah! No, not at all, that's just for the folklore. Once per year, we have what you white people call an 'open house,' for tourists. People who think they're going back into the good old days, during the Goldrush and conquest of the West. On that day, we all put on our costumes, with feathers, a peace pipe, totem poles, all that. We organize fake ancestral ceremonies, with traditional dances and songs. The tourists are happy, they take selfies with feathers in their hair in front of the teepee and two Indians next to them with a war hatchet. Then they leave with some stuff we made, we earn a couple of bucks... which will quickly be spent in the grocery stores around here. Only smoke and mirrors. No, Joshua lives in the trailer right behind. This one."

The president knocked on the trailer door. We heard a muffled groan. She opened the door.

"Josh? This is the lady I was talking to you about yesterday, remember?"

She added a couple of words in some unintelligible tribal dialect and a dark shadow came from the back on the trailer.

A low shadow, almost on the ground, accompanied by the sound of wheels. I was astonished to see a little stunted man emerge, just like a wrinkled apple, sitting on a wooden wagon with wheels that he used his hands to advance. Mary had told me that the old Indian was half deaf and blind but had forgotten to mention that he didn't have any legs either. There was a yellowish blanket covering his legs, which ended with two stumps above his knees.

"Come here little lady," he said with a throaty and tremulous voice. "So I can have a look at you."

I obeyed and stepped forward in the scorching heat of the trailer. A foul odor tickled my nostrils, a mixture of dust, sweat, mold, tobacco and other undefinable substances. I gagged, but resisted fleeing, while trying to breathe in and out slowly to get used to it.

Leaning down over the old man with his wrinkled face, his nearly bald head with a few rare white hairs sticking straight up, his tanned skin betraying his belonging to the people from the First Nations, called the Red Skins, by the white settlers, I tried to look into his glassy and strangely blue dead eyes, covered with an unsettling opaque veil.

"Thank you for having me, Mr. Cutler."

"Louder!" he shouted, putting a hand to his ear.

"Thanks for allowing me to come," I repeated a bit louder. "I'm here to use your memory."

"Ah! My memory. You're lucky, that's about all I've got left. You wanna talk about the last century, right?"

"Yes, about 1988. Someone disappeared here in Lone Pine."

In a few sentences, I summarized, quite loudly, what I knew, what I thought, and what I hoped to find with him. To finish, I told him about Paul Bannister's hypothesis, that senile man who had affirmed that Shondra Wallace had been kidnapped by the Indians.

"That crazy Bannister who played Indians in the

movies? But still, maybe that old codger wasn't completely wrong..."

"Meaning?" I asked, interested.

"If I'm not getting everything mixed up, I think that was the year that we took in a woman who wasn't one of us. And I said, 'took in,' not kidnapped. We're not wild Indians! Even though that's what you like to think..."

"Do you remember that lady?"

"Vaguely."

"Was it Shondra Wallace, the actress?"

"You know what? I never went to the movies in my life, Ma'am. So I had no idea who she was. And I couldn't have cared less!"

"She didn't tell you her name?"

The hundred-year-old Paiute-Shoshone Indian shook his head.

"What is a name? A name doesn't make you the human being you are or were born. She didn't tell us, we didn't ask."

"Why not?"

"Because she was desperate. Like her life was at stake. She was black, like I told you, and because of that, we considered her as our equal. An oppressed person, an exploited one, one banned from the society that Whites imposed on her. So when she came, in the middle of the night, begging for hospitality – at that time I was the chief of the reservation –, that was all we wanted to know. We took her in, like one of us. We hid her behind our barbed wires."

I was subjugated by what the old Indian had told me. He seemed to have put his finger on the key to Shondra Wallace's disappearance. I wanted to know more but Joshua seemed tired of having spoken so much, of having solicited his memory. His lifeless eyes were occulted intermittently behind his wrinkled eyelids. The scorching heat in his trailer must also have contributed to his exhaustion. I was afraid I'd lose him, so I quickly continued my questions.

"Then what happened? How long did she stay? What happened to her? Where is she now?"

My plethora of questions slowly drew him out of his lethargy, though Mary Hansen and Foster Maverick, at my sides, both looked at me severely.

"Sorry, Ma'am, that's a lot to remember. It was so long ago and I'm so old. But I still can tell you one thing that's sure and that I can't forget."

"What?"

WHAT THE OLD Joshua Cutler told me was completely unbelievable. It both terrified me and gave me hope...

CHAPTER 48
A miniscule snippet

Los Angeles, June 9, 2024

Countdown - 18

Lawrence McCormick, the FBI agent, hands in his pockets and visibly impressed with his self-importance, was sitting across from Inspector Jonas Crimson, who was holding the inch or so of 35mm film that he'd just examined.

"Inspector, you can't just produce this film as incriminating evidence against Ruppert Magloire for a motive. You took it without him knowing it. Any court would close the case in five seconds on grounds of procedural errors. Can you run through again what you're hoping to prove?"

"Listen, Agent McCormick, I'm convinced that this little six-image piece of film could be a miniscule snippet of an unfinished motion picture that was shot in Lone Pine in 1988 when Shondra Wallace went missing!"

"How can you confirm that? What did you see on those six images?"

Crimson shook his head, not liking where that conversation was headed.

"Agent McCormick, I want to point out that this little piece of film only represents a quarter of a second of a movie. I know it's not much, I understand, but the experts are formal for the date and have said that it could have been shot back in 1988."

"Just like a load of other movies that were shot that year or even that decade. Back to earth Crimson, you can't prove a thing with so few tangible elements. Anyway, what are you trying to prove?"

The Hollywood cop glared at the Fed, chafing with the FBI agent's warnings.

"Well," he finally said, "let's just imagine that this bit of film is a miniscule snippet of a movie starring Shondra Wallace, and even better, part of her last unfinished motion picture, the one where she vanished... That would be the missing link between the Jabaree case and the Wallace case. We'd have come full circle!"

The federal agent shook his head, trying to follow the cop's line of thought.

"That doesn't prove a thing," he concluded. "All that would mean is that Ruppert Magloire is interested in films in the 1980s. Big deal! And that he's also, as everyone knows, keen on movies starring Shondra Wallace. So what? Is that going to help us find his stepson who was kidnapped? No Crimson, quit dreaming and get back to work!"

"McCormick, quit talking to me like that! I'm not one of your underlings, don't forget."

McCormick raised both of his hands, to calm things down.

"Hey, don't get on your high horses. What I'm telling you is to avoid you being ridiculous if you go to the prosecutor with your allegations stemming from the discovery – whoops, I should have said illegal misappropriation – of a so-called piece of incriminating evidence. What are you convinced of? Of nothing. You got allegations, that's it. Show me the snippet of film so I can check it myself."

Crimson hesitated for a moment, still holding the film in his fingertips.

"Here. Now you're interested in it?" he asked ironically.

"Quit trying to be cute."

The FBI Agent took the tiny piece of film that Crimson handed to him, raised it to eye level and turned towards the neon light shining down in the room with his bright and crude light. He looked like a radiologist examining the cliches of a patient.

For a few long seconds, the Fed examined the six images while squinting. Hard to make things out.

"Jesus, you could go blind trying to look at this," he muttered. "You should be looking at it with a projector, or I don't know, scan it to study it on a computer screen or project it onto a white screen."

"Congratulations, you've just reinvented the principle of cinema," Crimson said mockingly.

"Plus, all the images look the same..."

"Quite logical, McCormick, as, like I already told you, it's a part of a movie that was shot with twenty-four images per second. So what you're looking at is a quarter of a second. What do you want to happen in so little time?"

"Just another reason for me to think that this thing is useless. What do we see? A horse's ass that's galloping away... Really interesting!"

"With someone riding it. Someone who could be Shondra Wallace. Black hair, black skin, the same silhouette."

"But we only see her back. What can you conclude from so little material Crimson? That it was a western they shot in Lone Pine? Talk about a scoop! Like hundreds of others. A horse and its rider in a western..."

"Exactly! You hardly ever see ladies riding horses in westerns. That seems to be a good tip, don't you think?"

"Frankly, it's pitiful. You're exhausting yourself dealing with insignificant details. Forget it and focus on trying to find Jabaree. Time is of the essence. And I'm repeating, you don't have the right to use that film."

"We could ask for a perquisition of Magloire's projection room in Vegas," Crimson tried.

"You'd never get a search warrant, and you know that. So get down to work," concluded McCormick, leaving Inspector Jonas Crimson's office.

Who did just that, picking up his phone and dialing a number he knew all too well now.

CHAPTER 49
The common thread

Lone Pine, June 9, 2024

Countdown - 18

I FELT my phone vibrating in my purse on my lap, but I didn't pick up, as I was sure that the old Joshua Cutler, calling on his memories of the past, was going to reveal something important.

Mary Hansen and Foster Maverick were also hanging on to the old man's cracked lips, looking at his red toothless gums, listening to his scratchy voice.

"Like I said, there are some things you can't forget, even after forty years. Because they're things that impact your life, simply. Life and death, the two extremities of your existence, that's all that's important, right? Everything that goes on in between them is just smoke and mirrors," the old Paiute-Shoshone Indian said philosophically.

"Come on Joshua, we're getting impatient here," said Mary Hansen.

"Hold your horses! My brain ain't twenty years old anymore! If I lose the thread, it's shot. But for sure, I'm not going to lose the common thread of what happened that year that I can't remember which one it was, but that you told me it was in 1988. Calendars don't mean a thing to me. So, that year, it was the beginning of summer, or pretty close to it, because it was already really hot, like today in the trailer."

I mentally confirmed what the old Indian said, because we were boiling here. He continued.

"Anyway, like I said, it was hot, but all that happened at night. So that night, when everyone on the reservation was sleeping except for a couple of drunkards who were watching TV or beating up their squaws, all of a sudden there was some agitation at the entrance. You gotta know that we always have someone making the rounds here at night. Ya never know! With all them pale faces prowling around not too far away," joked Cutler with a guffaw sending me bitter scents to my nose and drops of saliva onto his chest.

"Cutler..." Mary Hansen protested.

"Sorry, I like to laugh now and then, it's like the only thing I got left here in this lowly world before I join my illustrious ancestors. So, as you don't like my sense of humor, we'll start where I stopped then. So, someone was trying to get in and they came to wake me up 'cuz like I said, I was the Chief at that time."

He slowly turned his head towards Mary, as if saying to her that only his venerable age was preventing him from still assuming that function.

"The guardian ran inside my hut and started yelling: 'Chief, there's a lady outside! She's crying, panicking, and begging me to let her in. She says she's in danger and needs our protection!' So I rushed out and I saw a grieving woman, on the ground, all curled up, looking behind her fearfully, then looking towards the city, to the north. I bent down to ask her what she was afraid of, what she was trying to get away from. And then she answered me..."

∽

Lone Pine, the night of June 1st to June 2nd, 1988

As was the case in most nights in the Californian desert at that time of the year, the clear sky unveiled a myriad of stars twinkling over the sleeping town of Lone Pine.

A distraught and frantic lady was pounding at the locked gate in front of the Paiutes-Shoshones reservation.

"Please, let me hide behind your walls. I'm begging you. I have to disappear. I'm imploring your sense of hospitality..."

"You're not one of us, lady," retorted Joshua Cutler, the Chief of the Indian reservation. "This is only for Paiutes. You're a Paiute? You sure don't look like one, at least from what I can see here in the moonlight."

Sobs and gulps were making it hard for the woman to reply.

"I'm not a Pale Face either, just look at me! Just like you, I'm a minority. From a cast of pariahs. A woman, to boot. Please, I'm begging you, I need you. You're my only hope of escape. And asylum. If you don't let me into your reservation, you'll have my death on your conscience. Even worse than that, you'll be reproaching yourself not to have saved two lives..."

CHAPTER 50
Counterbalance

"Two lives?"

I couldn't help but shouting that question out.

"That's right, Miss Blackstone. Two lives. 'Cuz that little lady all alone in the middle of the desert was carrying a child."

"Shondra Wallace was pregnant then, so it wasn't just a rumor," I said to myself out loud, remembering the interviews I'd had with Lundgren, Purcell, and Apfenstein, where each gave me a different version.

The old Paiute nodded silently.

"Yes, that woman, the one who we never asked what her name was, was expecting. And that's why she was seeking asylum with us. To flee a universe that was rejecting her – who knows why? – and give birth to an innocent child."

"The child was born here?"

"That's right. A couple of months after his mother arrived, in the fall, I think. Our whole community welcomed that lady whose belly quickly expanded, with open arms. Behind our barbed wires, she had nothing to fear, especially as the White People openly ignored us. She'd found asylum with us Paiutes!"

"Why didn't you ask her what her name was?"

I was enraged deep down inside that the old Chief couldn't give me the information I needed to confirm one of my hypotheses.

"What's in a name? Nothing. Letters, sounds, no other meaning than a phonetic one, a way of cataloguing a human being, closing them up in an administrative stranglehold. For us Natives, we don't care about names and ID cards! Dates of birth and death aren't important! The only true identity of a human being resides in their hearts, in their souls. That night, in the milky pale light the moon was giving off, I could read her despair as well as how pure of a soul she was, just by looking in her eyes. That's why we opened our doors – and our hearts – to her, without any further explanations. We didn't need nothing else."

In the sweltering shadows of the trailer, I couldn't take any notes, but the info that the Indian had given me was engraved in my brain. I wanted to know what happened after that.

"So she had her baby then?"

"That's right. All our squaws surrounded her. You probably know that for us Natives, women are sacred. This was the best place for her. So like I said, the baby was born in the fall. A beautiful baby boy who weighed about ten pounds. A chocolate-skinned kid, just like his mother. Maybe not dark chocolate, but with a bit of milk in it, just like the tea English people drink."

"What about the father? Did he ever try to find his wife and his son?"

Joshua Cutler sighed.

"Got me. All I know is that he never stopped in to ask about the kid. Nor to ask about her. Maybe he didn't even know he was gonna be a father, stuff like that happens!"

I counted back in my head and realized that the little boy born in Lone Pine would be thirty-five now. Thirty-five years, like the number of years separating the two "June firsts." Could that have been the missing link between the two disappearances?

"What happened to the mother and child?"

"I remember, like I told you, that the mother stayed here for a couple of months till the baby was born."

"What was his name?"

"Missy Blackstone, you didn't hear a word I said? Names ain't important for us. He was a moon child, that's all. Anyway, I would have forgotten his name after all those years. So, lemme answer your question, 'cuz all this talking is wearing me out. The little baby was born in the fall and the two of them stayed here for several moons in the reservation. We fed them, housed them, took care of them, as did all our squaws. Maybe long enough for them to be totally forgotten."

"That was certainly the case."

"And probably because she felt at home with us,"

the old man said philosophically. "She'd become one of us. Everyone accepted her. Just like her son, who was growing up in our teepees, alongside other little Paiutes-Shoshones born around that time. There's lots of births in the reservation. That counterbalances our high mortality..."

"Infant mortality?"

Mary Hansen answered that question.

"That's right, we deplore a high rate of complicated births, because of a lack of hygiene, and a lack of medical assistance and care before and after birth. Of course, since the dawn of time, women have given birth alone, sometimes without any assistance at all. And Humanity has survived. If there's one domain in which the White People have evolved, it's in safe delivery of babies. Here, conditions are often difficult, and giving birth often causes complications. Sometimes there are stillbirths, sometimes infants only survive a couple of hours. Other times, it's the mother..."

"You mean..."

"A couple of months," Joshua Cutler continued. "The mother and child stayed at the reservation for a couple of months. I think it was until the following spring. Up until it happened... We were all so sad!"

CHAPTER 51
Slides

LOS ANGELES

Countdown - 16 hours

"Why the heck isn't she picking up?"

Inspector Crimson's loud voice resonated in his empty office. Since FBI agent McCormick had left, the policeman had been trying to reach Karen Blackstone. He wanted to tell her about his discovery. Or at least the intuition he had to have discovered something crucial on the snippet of film he'd pinched at Magloire's place.

The cop was sure of himself. He had a hunch, a gut feeling, something that had served him well during other complicated investigations, that he had something there that required attention. He picked up his phone again, looking at the time. It was just a few minutes after eight at night. The colleague he wanted to talk to had finished work of course, but as every minute counted, he needed to progress.

"Patterson? Crimson, Hollywood Station, here. Sorry, but I need your expertise right now. I'm sure you're with your family and please accept my apologies in advance, but I have to go to your lab. Can we meet there in an hour?"

At first his colleague from the LAPD IT expertise department wasn't too happy about that, but he finally consented to join Crimson as soon as possible.

"I owe you one," Jonas thanked him, before hanging up.

AN HOUR LATER, the two policemen dressed in their civilian clothing were in Patterson's lab, a windowless room with a slew of computers, various electronic devices, as well as other equipment that seemed to date back a few decades. Amongst them, in a small adjacent room lit up with ultraviolet light, there was material used to develop photos: a developing bath, a stop bath, fixative, a washing bath, lines to hang the pictures on, etc.

But the technician didn't need to use all those old school devices, having tools that modern science gave its investigators.

"So here's those infamous images," declared Patterson admiratively when Crimson handed him the snippet of film. "Let's see what they can tell us."

He placed the snippet below the hood of a state-of-the-art scanner and pressed the digitalization button, thus transforming the 35 mm bit of film into an IT file that he would be able to be read with a computer and giving them the possibility to virtually manipulate the six images. Little by little, on one of the screens in the room, the slides appeared, much clearer, much larger, and individualized into six distinct files.

"Is this maximum resolution?" Crimson asked.

"Of course. Seeing how old this is, I used optimal digitalization, to correct the lack of light, density, and colors linked to the wear and tear caused by the years gone by. So, there we are, let's have a look."

The two men sat down in front of the screen and Patterson began dancing his fingers around on the keyboard, soliciting the photo touchup software and its various improvement filters, on contrast and light on the six nearly forty-year-old images. After a few minutes, he was satisfied with the result and sat back on his chair to admire it.

"Great job," Jonas confirmed, looking at the images of the bareback African-American horseback rider on the galloping horse. "Too bad we only see her back."

"Except for the sixth image," Patterson nuanced, "where she's slightly three-quarters from the back. You can see the bottom of her chin, a chin pointing forward as if accompanying the horse's movement. And she sure does look like a black Amazon, with her hair streaming out behind her, hunched down on the horse! Someone who must have been riding for ages. And that costume she's wearing, her bare shoulders, her muscles, her skin perspiring with the effort..."

"Hey! Come on! I'm not asking you to go crazy for a woman who died thirty-five years ago!"

"Okay. What else do you want me to do here?"

"To tell me if it really is Shondra Wallace here on these images and if they're a part of *The Coyote-Woman of the Desert*, the last movie she starred in."

"Jonas, I'm busting my gut laughing. You think I'm David Copperfield? That I can pull that info out of a hat, like a white rabbit?"

"Not from your hat. But from your machines with a thousand artificial brains, yes. So get hopping, I've got a sword of Damocles hanging over my head now."

Patterson nodded, sat back in his armchair and once again began using the keyboards of his various devices.

"Let's start at the beginning then. Like an ordinary person now that we have the imagines in digital files. I'm gonna upload them into Lens and we'll see if His Majesty Google recognizes them."

The technician did what he said he'd do, hoping that the images had, one day, someplace or by someone, been uploaded onto the vast web, that same web where so many answers were, to the delight of AI, lazy students or authors staring at their blank pages... They just had to wait a few seconds before the system spit out millions of results... but none of them of them meaningful, much to the dismay of the policemen. All the great G could do was to supply similar images, of ladies galloping on horses, images of westerns, but none of them were strictly identical, none of them pointed their fingers towards the name of Shondra Wallace, nor or an image that had come from *The Coyote-Woman*.

"Nothing ventured, nothing gained," muttered Crimson.

"Don't give up hope yet," Patterson reassured him. "All this failure taught us, but you already knew that, is that no images of the movie you're looking for had been uploaded to the net. It was an unfinished movie, am I right? Or maybe it never even existed."

Hmm, Crimson thought, a ludicrous hypothesis that sure would screw up Karen Blackstone's investigation. He looked down at his phone and saw that the journalist still hadn't tried to call him back.

"Wait a second, I've got an idea," said the technician, surfing the internet. "Is that how Shondra Wallace is written?"

"Yup."

"Okay. Let's see what we find on her, and we'll compare it with our six images."

Though much less well known than Whoopi Goldberg or Halle Berry, there were several pages of pictures of that obscure starlet of the 80s. And it was easy to see that the horseback rider of the rush Crimson had pinched looked quite a bit like Shondra Wallace.

"Pretty darn close," Crimson admitted, suddenly

excited. "But if I could be a hundred percent sure that it was her, that would give me some grounds to continue with Ruppert Magloire. If it's true that he was working with strips of film starring Shondra Wallace, maybe there could be some link with the kidnapping of his stepson!"

"How though?"

"By supposing, for example, that someone panicked at the idea that Magloire had discovered something essential about Shondra Wallace's death and was going to reveal it using that movie. And he or she was thinking of dropping a virtual bomb on the whole world and to make sure that didn't happen, they kidnapped Jabaree? The kidnappers kept on saying that there was a link between those two kidnappings. If we proved that Shondra Wallace was the one on the horse here, that would give me extra ammo."

"Wouldn't it be easier just to ask him?"

"But I'd be admitting that I stole this from him and that wouldn't make a very good impression on the judges. Shit! Patterson, you gotta find me a solution with your stuff here."

"Okay. Let's do things differently then," continued Patterson, while his colleague was busy thinking. "I got some smart software in my little bag of tricks, including one called MorphoNet, a type of digital physiognomist that uses a morphing process that's state-of-the-art, and can cross several images and calculate, using algorithms, the percentage of concordance versus discordance based on hundreds of pixels. In a nutshell, lots of jargon, but let's try to see what it'll find."

The six images, all zoomed in on the horseback rider's silhouette, were uploaded into the software, mixed in with a bunch of others of Shondra they'd found on internet. There was a green cursor that progressed slowly, added to an advancement percentage, then the verdict fell.

"95% of positive occurrence."

"Bingo! With a score like that," exclaimed Patterson, "if that's not Shondra Wallace, it must be her twin sister!"

CHAPTER 52
Twin

On the road in the desert

Countdown - 14 hours

My interview with old Joshua Cutler, unofficially a hundred and fifteen years old, opened my eyes with all his revelations, maybe not all of them completely true because of his age and his memory that perhaps had embellished things. On the too straight road back to Los Angeles through the desert, his last words ran through my head.

"That's it," Cutler continued with his broken voice, "in the spring of 1989 our ancestors called one of them back."

"The child died prematurely?" I asked, saddened at the thought an infant had passed.

Cutler shook his head.

"No. The child survived. It was his mother. On the night she passed away, we all could hear the coyotes howling in the desert."

"Coyotes!" I nearly jumped, thinking of Shondra's last movie.

"That's right, in our ancestral beliefs, we associate their howling with the imminence of death. And I can tell you, that time there was a huge pack of them around the reservation, and they barked, howled and growled for hours on end. It was the end. Right from the very beginning, the delivery took place in difficult conditions, and anyway, the woman was already sick when she came here. She had problems nursing her baby, not enough milk, not enough nutrients in the little bit she had. Other women in our tribe shared their milk with her and her baby. That's how solidarity works with us Natives, Missy Blackstone. The little kid didn't grow up with Indian blood in his veins, but with milk from Indian women in his stomach. That's why we considered him as one of us, despite the color of his skin."

At that moment in the discussion I was sad because I soon would have the confirmation of what I'd thought, – like everyone else, spectators, former colleagues, friends or investigators – since my investigation had begun, meaning that Shondra was dead. Up until that moment, it was just a strong hypothesis, but now with what the former Chief of the Paiutes-Shoshones tribe had told us, it was true.

"What did you do with her body?" I wanted to know, thinking that if there was a grave someplace, at least I'd have some physical evidence.

The old Paiute called on his memory once again.

"As she'd become an unofficial member of our tribe, we buried her body and spirit in accordance with our funeral rites. We took her body outside our reservation towards the north, on horseback. The men dug her a grave, killed the horse so it could bring her spirit back to her ancestors, and then let the tomb open to facilitate her departure. On the reservation we fasted for three days. I hope her spirit is in peace and harmony with nature now."

His tale touched me. Touched me with fear and sadness.

But then I had another feeling.

An ounce of hope!

Hope that the child born to that forgotten woman was still alive. If so, I had to find him. A man who was now thirty-five. I asked another question, spurred on by hope.

"The child grew up here? The man he's become is still here? If so, I have to meet him."

Cutler raised a rheumatic hand.

"Don't get your hopes up Missy."

I suddenly feared the worst.

"Don't tell me he's dead too!"

"I can't answer that question," the old man hesitated.

"Why not?"

"Because I can't confirm or infirm it because later on, maybe a year or two after his mother passed, the little boy left the reservation."

"How did he do that?" I asked, haunted by the powerful image of a new *lost son*... One more. I had the feeling that my whole life was orbiting around the image of a *lost child*.

The old Indian leaned forward, making his short silhouette even tinier. He was having trouble breathing. He took a few seconds to get his breath back and continued.

"Missy, I'm getting tired. But I wanna finish telling you everything I know about what happened. So, a little later, when the boy was growing up surrounded by all our squaws, another lady came to the gates of our reservation. She came to get the little boy and told us that she was the late mother's best friend. That no one could take better care of the child than her. That she had the moral duty to do that."

"Who was she? Did you accept?"

"I couldn't say no."

"Why not?"

"Because when they let her into the reservation, it was like a shock. She was an African-American, just like the mother of the child. But what was even more unsettling – at that time my view was still excellent –

was that I thought I was seeing the ghost of the first woman..."

"The ghost?"

"You know, us Paiutes-Shoshones, we believe in reincarnation."

I didn't say anything, but I had to stop myself from saying that I personally didn't believe in things like that.

"Shondra's reincarnation," I then whispered.

"Anyway, that second black lady was the spitting image of the first one, and if it wasn't the mother who'd come back to get her own child, it must have been her sosie, or her twin sister..."

CHAPTER 53
A revelation

Countdown - 12 hours

It was midnight when Inspector Crimson called me again. Since I'd left the Paiutes-Shoshones Indian Reservation, thoughts kept swirling around in my head while driving back to Los Angeles, up to the point where I'd forgotten to call the inspector back.

"Hello, Inspector Crimson," I said with a sleep-filled voice.

I was having trouble keeping my eyes open and was tightly clutching the steering wheel to stay awake.

"Karen, what the hell? I've been trying to reach you for hours."

"You think I'm having fun? Inspector, weren't you the one who told me I had to step on it to progress in my investigation? Well, that's exactly what I did today in Lone Pine."

"Okay, sorry. You think I like being at the office at

midnight, knowing that in exactly twelve hours, if we can't find a solution to that riddle, Jabaree's kidnappers are going to cut one of his fingers off?"

I sighed, exhausted.

"That's all I'm thinking of too. All I can see is Jabaree's innocent little face and I feel guilty that I can't go any faster. But I've made progress, lots of it!"

"Well step on it then!"

"Sure Inspector, if you say so."

"What? I didn't mean that literally. Be careful, you're driving."

"Just let me talk, the line isn't very good, it's cutting off, and I've got things you should know. So I'll give you the Cliff Notes version. When I was at the Lone Pine Indian Reservation, I met an old man who was the chief of their tribe when Shondra Wallace went missing. He told me that on one night in summer, which maybe was June 2nd, 1988, a black woman requested asylum in their reservation, and it was granted. That lady was pregnant, and she stayed with them, incognito, for several months. In the fall, she delivered her baby there, a little boy. A few weeks or months later, she died, and the Paiutes buried her someplace in the desert, according to their own rites, and that the coyotes howled that whole night before she passed."

"That's fantastic! I don't mean Shondra's death. But that does tell us what happened to her, and we can rule out the hypothesis that she was kidnapped or murdered. So we don't have to look for the actress anymore, now we can concentrate on her child, who's now a man. Unless you already found him in Lone Pine?"

"Well, that's where things get even more complicated, because a couple of months after his mother had died, the child also disappeared..."

"Shit," the policeman said, cutting me off, "another disappearance? I'm tired of them! It's an obsession with those people!"

"Calm down. Maybe I wasn't clear. The child didn't go missing, someone came to claim him from the Paiutes."

"Claim him?"

"An African-American woman who said she had the right to do that. A lady who, and sit down here, was Shondra Wallace's spitting image, up to the point that the Indians thought she was the reincarnation of the late actress. Or her twin sister."

"Jesus Christ! Wait a sec! Her twin sister? That's incredible."

"What's incredible?"

"Believe it or not, after I had the bit of 35 mm film analyzed that I pinched from Ruppert Magloire's house, the one I'm convinced is from *The Coyote-Woman of the Desert*, it turns out that the lady riding the horse has a 95% probability of being Shondra Wallace, or at least her sosie or 'twin sister'... See what I mean?"

"That's impossible!"

"How come?"

"I mean that it's impossible that the film is from *The Coyote-Woman*, because Apfenstein, who had the rushes, assured me that all the reels of film perished in an arson fire in the studios where they had been stored, with all the others."

"Hmm, it's either one or the other. Either Apfenstein is mistaken or he's lying. Anyway that tiny snippet of film was really enlightening! See where I'm going here?"

"Meaning?"

"The way both investigations are meeting in the middle! This story of a twin sister or a sosie. Maybe we got the missing link here. We absolutely have to find that woman and/or her thirty-five-year-old son. Tomorrow bright and early, I'll organize a federal call for witnesses. Set up a press conference."

"I sure hope that will bear fruit, Inspector."

"You're preaching to the choir! Be careful driving back. Accidents happen all too quickly, especially when you're tired."

"Ah! One last thing. Could you send me those six images?"

"Consider it done."

An hour later, I was in my hotel in downtown L.A.

Exhausted, I couldn't seem to fall asleep, submerged by questions and fears. Hours were going by, days too, unstoppable, and I could see that deadline rushing up, without being able to do anything about it. Moreover, my stay here in Los Angeles wasn't helping my personal quest to progress and that also made me furious.

Struggling against fatigue, but incapable of sleeping, I opened my computer and with my red eyes, killed a couple of minutes trying to find the information I needed, meaning an email account.

I finally opened my voicemail and decided to write an email.

Blocked

My dear Luke Virgil,

You'll be – please allow me to call you my dear – extremely astonished when you open this email. If you receive it, if it's not lost in your spams, if you decide to read it.

To the end.

I would have liked to tell you things face to face, but that's something that's not easy and I'm not brave enough.

I tried several times since I set foot in Los Angeles, but never found the strength to actually do it.

I usually have no problem daring to do things, especially in a professional framework. Yet, in our case, with you and me, I've got a sort of psychological blockage, the closer I get to you.

The last couple of days, did you feel my presence? I wasn't far from you, following you, nearly in your footsteps.

Please don't be afraid – I certainly don't want to hurt you –, but I saw you leave your home. I followed you on the bus. Up to the entrance of UCLA where I know that you're studying medicine. How was your comparative anatomy course?

At that instant, we were just a snap of the fingers of being in contact. What am I saying? We were in contact. Do you remember a lady who wasn't paying attention who ran into you while you had stopped and were looking through your backpack? You probably thought it was a professor.

I was that lady.

We exchanged a couple of words, well, I asked you to excuse me, and you said it was no problem. I would have liked to tell you, right then, who I was, who you were for me.

I didn't know how. I couldn't.

Sheltered behind the virtual screen of my emails, I now dare to tell you how happy I am to have found you.

You must be thinking that I'm a crazy old lady, someone completely unbalanced, when reading this. And wondering about my intentions. Are they bad?

Quite the opposite.

I know almost everything about you. You were born at the Cambridge Massachusetts Birth Center, on February 28, 1999.

On that winter's night, already in the last century, a young girl gave birth to a magnificent little boy. But fate, cruel fate, had wanted both beings, though united by the most powerful link, an umbilical cord, where one gives life to the other, to be separated violently and cruelly.

The child was taken from his mother and disappeared.

A lost son... A grieving mother.

Your biological mother was me!

I know that you're having your finals at UCLA, but you must have seen the news. I'm sure you heard about Jabaree Smith, the young actor, who was kidnapped. Another lost son, another set of grieving parents.

I'd like you to know that I'm an investigative journalist specialized in missing persons and am involved in the investigation to try to find Jabaree. That's why I'm in L.A.

One of the reasons.

The other one, the one that has been eating away at me for years, was to find you, to get to know you. And speak to you.

I'm now taking this first virtual step, praying that you accept my request, that you believe me. Then that you give that mother the possibility to meet her child, who has now become a handsome young man.

We will never be able to make up for all the years we've lost.

But we can make the upcoming years better.

My heart is breaking, I'm signing off in the hope that you'll respond positively to this message.

Karen Blackstone.

CHAPTER 54
Cameras and mics

Los Angeles, June 10, 2024

Countdown - 3 hours

THE CLOCK WAS MERCILESSLY TICKING.

The cameras and mikes of the journalists facing Jonas Crimson and federal agent Lawrence McCormick looked like a hedge of people eagerly seeking scoops and information.

The inspector wanted Janice Lovelace and Ruppert Magloire to be present at the meeting with the media so viewers would understand that they were merely grieving parents, not stars in this case.

Right before going into the room where the journalists were noisily waiting, Crimson told Ruppert he had a couple of words to say to him, in no uncertain terms.

"Magloire, you think I'm an idiot? Whose side are you on, dammit? For us or against us? Ever since the beginning I've had the feeling that you haven't come clean with me."

"Inspector, I don't understand a word of what you're saying. What are you talking about? Of course I'm on your side. I'd do anything, I'd give up my life to get Jabaree back."

"So why did you lie to me about Shondra Wallace? Ah! You didn't know who she was! You never heard of a movie called *The Coyote-Woman of the Desert*? When we were in your projection and editing room in Vegas, the one you finally allowed me to visit, you had and were working on 35 mm reels of film that could be those that she starred in... Remember, your favorite hobby was fooling around with old reels of film, what were you doing?"

"Inspector, sorry but I still don't know what you're talking about? What reels of film? I didn't show you anything. I said I would when I'd finished editing them."

Crimson bided his time. He felt cornered to have to admit that he'd taken a bit of a reel. Tough luck though, he didn't have the choice if he wanted to force Ruppert to react. He took the snippet out of his pocket and put it in front of the movie director's eyes.

"Recognize this?"

Magloire took it and peered at it, holding it up to the neon lights. He hesitated a bit, visibly shaken up, before answering.

"It is one of the pieces I didn't use when editing. A useless excerpt for my project. You got it illegally..."

"That I did. But it was to advance the investigation."

"Okay. Use it then if it can help. On the other hand Inspector, I have no idea who the lady was riding the horse nor what movie it came from. That's stuff I bought on the internet from a specialist in vintage objects, like old postcards, daguerreotype photos, vinyl albums or 35 mm film. He was selling a package of a hundred or so B-series reels of film from the 80s – no idea how he got them – and I snapped it up. The price was right. I knew that most of them wouldn't be keepers, like this bit. They're miscellaneous rushes and not edited and mixed reels of film. Preliminary takes."

"Could you give me his name and address?"

Magloire, who had never stopped looking at what time it was on his Rolex, nodded.

"I'll look that up for you, Inspector."

"Okay then. Well, let's get going then, I think they're in a hurry."

∾

CRIMSON WAS the first one to speak to the journalists.

"Ladies and Gentlemen, I'd like to thank you for your presence aimed at broadcasting the latest events on our investigation about Jabaree Smith's kidnapping. I'd like to remind you that we are doing everything possible to prevent a tragedy from happening."

He then glanced at Lawrence McCormick.

"Agent McCormick has been sent here by the FBI to help us find and free Jabaree as soon as possible. As you know, the kidnappers made a threat in their last video and it will expire in three hours, at noon."

At his left, Ruppert Magloire was checking his gold Rolex nervously. Crimson said to himself that he understood him completely. He continued.

"That is why we organized this press conference. To try and speed things up, I'd like to ask any witnesses who think they may have even a tiny lead of where Jabaree is being held to contact either the local or federal authorities. The kidnappers have also made it clear that there is a link between the disappearance of Jabaree on June 1st, 2024 and that of an actress named Shondra Wallace that took place on June 1st, 1988. We now know that she died in 1988 in Lone Pine, California, in the Paiute-Shoshone Indian Reservation. But before she passed away, she had a baby boy and a few months later, a lady who looked nearly exactly like his late mother came to recover that child. Was she her twin sister? Just a sosie? We currently don't have answers to these questions. On the other hand, we hope that this child – who, if he's still alive, a thirty-five-year-old man now –, of African-American origine, will recognize himself in this story. The same is true for the lady who came to fetch him in 1989, and should she be Shondra's twin sister, would now be sixty-four years old. As Jabaree's survival potentially is linked to finding answers to these problems, the authorities and Jabaree's parents, who are with me today," he said, once again glancing at Magloire's golden watch that he was looking at with apprehension, "would please ask these persons or person to contact us if they think they are concerned by this, as soon as possible. Here on the screen, you can see Shondra Wallace when she was twenty-eight, in 1988, as well as a digital simulation of how she would look today. These photos will be broadcast throughout the United States and relayed internationally by our Interpol colleagues. Perhaps the solution is on the other side of our borders. Thank you for listening."

Countdown - 2 hours

CRIMSON, McCormick, Magloire and Lovelace went their separate ways after the press conference.

The next time they'd be together, the horsehair holding the sword of Damocles over their heads would have been broken.

CHAPTER 55
On air

Los Angeles, June 10, 2024, at noon

Countdown - 0

Bells in churches were ringing, the needles of watches met together at the top, digital clocks displayed a double zero after twelve, and the double sliding door of the non-stop news channel opened with a muffled little noise.

Just as had taken place several times during the day, a deliveryman came in, a motorcycle helmet on his head, and sunglasses protecting his eyes from the blinding light in L.A.'s streets.

He had an electronic handset in one hand, and in the other, wearing a glove, a little cardboard package just a tad larger than one that could have contained a mug.

The man walked up to the front desk. The receptionist, a young blond lady with doe-like eyes, smiled at him while taking the tiny package that the deliveryman had beeped using its barcode.

She glanced down at it. "To be given, upon reception and hand-delivered to Jodie Poelstra. She was the anchor on the noon news for the NoonLive program.

"Is there anything for me to sign?"

"Nothing," replied the deliveryman in a blasé manner, turning around and adjusting the visor of his helmet before leaving.

The "thanks and have a good day," of the receptionist were lost as the young man, always in a hurry to deliver his packages or mail to finish as quickly as possible, left without replying to her.

Following instructions, Maleeva, the receptionist, walked to the elevators that went upstairs where the news was being filmed. On the fifth floor, the doors opened with a *ding* that made the young lady jump each time she heard it. She strode down the long hall with its offices for journalists on each side in the various departments (sports, law, economy, entertainment, cinema, weather, etc.), all leading to the film set.

There she saw the imposing Shaun Livingstone, a six-foot three-hundred-pound black mass in front of the door, like a vigilant watchdog.

There was a sign that was lit up in red above his

head. Only two words on the screen: *ON AIR*. The news was live at noon.

That signal everyone in their line of work knew and respected: no one was to come in during shooting.

"Hey, Maleeva. Whatcha want?" he asked, pointing at the On Air sign.

"Hey Shaun. Yeah, I know they're live, but look, I've got a package to give to Jodie and I think it's really important."

The black giant took the package that disappeared in his huge palm, read the instructions, and sighed.

"Okay. Two seconds, I'll call Nino."

The Nino in question was the stage manager, in charge of everything that took place behind the door when it was live. The two men rapidly spoke in their headsets and then Shaun indicated that Maleeva should wait a minute.

On the other side of the soundproof wall, Nino motioned to Jodie, who had just finished her intro on the subject the TV spectators were now seeing on their televisions. She also had a wireless headset to communicate with the television control room, including when she was presenting news, something that often was quite unnerving to her and could be noticed by those watching.

"Jodie, just a couple of seconds. I got a package for you."

Nino read what was on the box. As soon as the news subject had started, she answered.

"Bring it here right now, I've got two minutes."

"Go in Shaun," Nino told him.

"Maleeva, give it to me."

The little box went from hand to hand. Maleeva, Shaun, Nino and finally Jodie Poelstra.

Jodie, sitting in her anchor armchair behind a round table with the shooting schedule* on it, behind a prompter with her text on it, opened the box.

WHEN SHE DISCOVERED THE CONTENT, she couldn't repress a scream that everyone heard as the live news had just begun...

---

* A shooting schedule on TV is a document that technically describes the sequence of a show, whether it is live or recorded. It is like a scenario for movies. The antenna shooting schedule describes the sequences of shows of a channel throughout the day.

CHAPTER 56
Breaking news

INSPECTOR JONAS CRIMSON, his head bowed and stomach jittery, though used to disgusting things like that, could only admit his helplessness.

He'd failed.

He felt responsible.

THE BLOODY FINGER, three phalanges of a little index finger from a mixed-race child resting in a soft bed of white cotton.

Its blood had coagulated and was now brownish, forming dark scabs on the skin and nauseating spatters on the cotton.

"Those bastards! They did it, those sons of bitches! Jesus, that is despicable! They have to be the scum of the earth to mutilate a little kid like that…"

THE LOST SON

Escorted by the FBI agents, Inspector Crimson rushed over to the studios of the news channel as soon as Jodie Poelstra had opened the box and seen its macabre and ill-smelling content. Upon seeing Jabaree's finger – she immediately understood that the kidnappers had kept their disgusting promise – and was sick to her stomach and couldn't help herself.

The red *On Air* light had just lit up again and all of America saw images of the news anchor bending over to vomit in a bin under the table. Irony with the situation, this news channel that boasted it was always there, always at the right place, at the right time, to cover live content of the smallest event, was right in the heart of it... No way could it have been more live than on the *Breaking News* set, handed to them on a silver platter!

Nino, the set manager, had immediately shouted out "Cut!" and the technicians interrupted the live news to broadcast a commercial presenting documentaries to be shown during the week.

"Don't touch anything," he ordered.

Something not necessary, as each cameraman, script, light technician, sound man, grip, electrician, or makeup artist required for the direct news program were immobile. You could read disgust on each of their faces.

They contacted the police and Crimson came, accompanied by the federal agents a quarter of an hour later.

"Those bastards!" repeated Jonas, clenching his fists with rage, ready to pound the table. Had it not been a glass one, he wouldn't have repressed his gesture.

"The inevitable happened," said McCormick, philosophically. "Too late... You fucked up!"

Crimson turned around to face the Fed, wanting to clock him to shut him up. He barely could contain himself.

"Dammit, McCormick, you really think this is the time to rub salt in the wound? You weren't any more efficient than we were that I know of. You can consider yourself as being responsible for this disaster too, the one that my team and especially myself assume totally. But now is not the time to rehash what went wrong. We have to speed things up. Now we know that the kidnappers will do anything."

The federal agent raised his hands in apology.

"Okay. Okay! Forget what I said. I also assume our failure. Now the first thing to do is to analyze this finger. Same thing for the box. Look for any residual fingerprints, crosscheck things with our federal data, state data, plus anything local. With a bit of luck, the kidnappers are already in our books for similar crimes or misdemeanors elsewhere than in California."

"I'll bring all that to the Los Angeles Forensics Lab to look for any DNA on the finger, analyze the tissues, skin and bones, all that. And don't touch anything without gloves!"

Agent Diane Payton, Crimson's partner, took the finger in the cardboard box with all the necessary precautions.

THE INSPECTOR also wanted to see Janice Lovelace and Ruppert Magloire again. They were both sitting in their home in Los Angeles, now even more despondent and desperate.

Both the movie director and actress were in tears. Crimson could nearly feel their despair, like acidity that had saturated the air in the room where all three of them were.

Jabaree's mother couldn't contain her tears whereas the stepfather's eyes were dry, but red, with swollen and heavy eyelids.

"They're going to kill him if you don't do anything," lamented Janice between two sobs.

"Miss Lovelace, you know, we are making progress, in particular in the Wallace case. Undoubtedly not as rapidly as we'd like and certainly not as quickly as you'd like it, but we *will* solve this case. Do you trust me?"

"Trust?" Magloire asked. "With what just happened? I don't know if we can trust anyone anymore, even our friends. Because I'm sure that the kidnappers, or at least the ones heading them, are people we know."

"Are you thinking of anyone in particular?"

"No, I don't know. I don't know anything anymore. Maybe it's just an intuition, but I have the feeling that those sons of bitches doing that to us aren't just strangers trying to make a quick buck. I can feel that they're close to us. I have no idea why though, sorry."

"Please, hurry up, Inspector," begged Janice before rushing off to the bathroom where they could hear the actress retching before vomiting.

When he left the couple's home, Crimson saw he'd missed several calls.

CHAPTER 57
Zooming in

My phone vibrated. Crimson had finally called me back. I was aware that he – just like I did – had his work cut out for him since America discovered that horror on the news, but I did think I had a scoop that he would appreciate.

"Thanks for calling me back, Inspector. You have no idea how sorry I am to have seen that on the news at noon. It was completely heinous and I'm partially responsible for it."

"Cut it out, Karen. Nothing's your fault. Not your fault and not mine if there are crazy people in this lowly world."

"Crazy people and... failures, like us."

"No, Karen. Our job just consists in preventing the majority of those idiots from hurting others. But we can't catch them all before it's too late. Cops are like a dip net: you pick up a lot of shit with it, but there are always those who get away."

"I'll have to try and remember that saying, Inspector. In the meanwhile though, I discovered something that could interest you."

"I'm all ears."

"So, it's about those six images from the reel of film that you sent me in a digital format. I studied them closely, because there was a detail that really bugged me right away, though I couldn't put my finger on it. I don't know if it means something that could help us in our investigation, but I have to mention it to you."

"Karen, why don't you get straight to the point? We'd gain time."

"You're right, Inspector, sorry. I just wanted to put everything in its context. I'm so overwhelmed by everything that sometimes I think I can't even think straight anymore. So, to make sure, I zoomed into the images of the girl riding the horse and scrutinized the actress's body. And bingo, there it was. A detail was missing!"

"What?"

"That woman, just like the Amazons, was only wearing a tunic that covered one of her shoulders. That meant that we saw her right shoulder on the images. But, on that right shoulder, the bunny was missing."

"The bunny? What bunny?"

"The bunny tattoo! Sort of like *Playboy*'s logo, if you remember back when you were a teenager…"

"You think this is the time to be cracking jokes?" the inspector asked, though I thought my remark must have really hit home.

"Sorry. Maybe I'm trying to relax using humor."

"It's okay, we do the same things in the police to avoid getting depressed."

"Are you in front of a computer?"

"No. I just left the Magloire-Lovelace-Smith family."

"Well, just use your phone and put in 'Shondra Wallace bunny tattoo' on it."

"Two seconds."

I waited for him to do that and have a look at the results.

"You're right, Karen," he replied. "You can see that Shondra had a bunny tattoo on her right shoulder from the photos. Except for the six of them that I found at Magloire's place."

"Exactly. On most of them, except for what I found on these bits of film. Inspector, what can we conclude?"

Outside of his silence, I could hear him coming and going on the street. He finally answered a couple of seconds later.

"A slew of hypotheses! The first one is that it wasn't her on that horse."

"Okay. But what else?"

"That the images in this little snippet, must date back to before her tattoo, as is the case in some photos at the beginning of her career."

"That could be possible. In which case the photos would not have been from her last movie, *The Coyote-Woman*. And incidentally, nothing really tells us that these images were from that movie, am I right?"

"That's true. Or maybe it was just a temporary tattoo, and that she removed it before her last movie," Crimson proposed. "To sum it up Karen, by giving me a new element here, at the same time you gave me a nice headache..."

I sighed.

"I'm quite contrite, Inspector" (it was hard for me to call him Jonas, though he'd asked me to do so – it felt like centuries ago). "But maybe we can look at things from a different angle and say that this detail points to an eventual twin sister or a sosie? What do you think?"

"I think that if such a person exists and is still alive, I sure hope she contacts us and sooner rather than later."

MAYBE JONAS CRIMSON WAS A MIND-READER, as a bit later in the evening we'd receive an astonishing response to all our questions...

CHAPTER 58
Close shot

THE JOURNALIST who was replacing Jodie Poelstra, who'd taken a few days off after what happened at noon, appeared on the screen after the six o'clock news credits.

She knew all of America was watching her and was visibly perturbed. Used to replacing Jodie during the day when there were fewer spectators, it was the first time she was on the news during primetime, on the West Coast's largest news channel.

She was hesitant as she began.

"*Breaking News* for... Jabaree Smith's... kidnapping. We have just received a new video from the kidnappers... of Hollywood's most famous kid-star. Here is the complete document, the one we anonymously received just a few minutes ago."

. . .

Video of Jabaree Smith, received on June 10, 2024 at 5:35 pm PST.

Jabaree is sitting on the same stool as the first time. He however is wearing different clothes. The stuffed rabbit, mascot of the *Daddy, Mommy, etc.* series, is on his knees.

One detail though, also different, that all the TV spectators must have immediately noticed: Jabaree's right hand is mutilated, his index finger cut off after the third phalange.

In the first seconds of the video, the person filming it zooms in and does a close shot of the child. The child raises his hand up to his face.

"Look," he says with a broken voice and muffled sobs, "they did what they said they'd do. Because no one was able to find me and free me before their deadline. Neither the police, nor my parents, nor anyone else. Nobody cares about me. Nobody cares about me just like nobody cared about Shondra Wallace. And her even more than me! Never forget Shondra Wallace…"

Right then the child breaks down. He interrupts himself, tears falling from his eyes, having trouble breathing and swallowing and his head drops just like that of a dead puppet. For long and difficult seconds, he cries noisily, his chest rising with repeated gulps. He finally regains control, looks back up to the camera and recites the text they ordered him to say, with a lump in his throat and at an irregular speed.

"Now, you have to speed up. Bring... justice... to Shondra Wallace. If not... in forty-eight hours... this hand will only have three fingers..."

He raises his hand again, spreading his fingers apart, showing the four remaining ones, and a reddish and swollen stub on his index.

"Hurry up, please!" he concludes before the video ends.

CHAPTER 59
In a loop

I THOUGHT I recognized the voice on my phone.

"Miss Blackstone?"

A feminine voice, an older woman, I was sure I'd already heard it.

"Speaking."

"You gave me your card so I could call you back if my uncle happened to have a stroke of genius."

I remembered!

"Mrs. Bannister! Nice to hear from you."

"Oh, I'm sorry, I didn't even give you my name. So, you saw and spoke to my uncle, and I'm sure you well understood that at his age, he'd lost some of his marbles."

I well-remembered when the old Bannister, ninety-five, imitated the Indians by tapping on his toothless mouth. "*Whouwouwouwouw, wouwouwouwou.*" I let her continue.

"Every once in a while he has a stroke of lucidity

and that's what happened when he was watching television, that's about all he does nowadays, and he saw the photos that the Los Angeles police had broadcast."

"And?" I asked, all excited. "What did he say?"

"Here's what happened when he saw those images..."

∽

FELICITY BANNISTER WAS PREPARING supper for herself and her uncle Paul while half listening to the news on TV. She was horribly sad because of the events that the media had been broadcasting in a loop for the past few hours. Firstly the police and federal agents' press conference, then the video of that poor kid and now the images of the finally famous Shondra Wallace galloping away on her horse.

While deftly stirred the chopped chicken and chorizo she was preparing jambalaya style, a recipe from Louisiana she loved, she suddenly heard movement from the veranda where Paul had begun shouting.

"It ain't her! It ain't her! It ain't her!" he kept on repeating.

"What are you talking about Uncle Paul? Stop getting all flustered like that. I'm going to turn the TV off if you keep on."

"It ain't her!" he insisted with his rocky voice.

"Who ain't her?"

"It ain't the one they're saying there. That whatchamacallit Wallace. That ain't her on that horse."

"You're sure of that? How do you know?"

The old former stuntman muttered for a while. He seemed to be brooding, digesting, and sorting his thoughts.

"'Cuz I know that she never rode a horse. I worked with her on several movies, and I never saw her get on a horse. She didn't want to get hurt! Ah! Them starlets!"

"So who was it then?"

"It was her standby for stunts. One of my colleagues! A lady who knew how to gallop as well as me. Or almost I should say, 'cuz no one was as good as me when they had to play cowboys or Indians riding horses. Yeah, I recognize that kid. It's her. The stuntwoman."

"You remember her name?" asked Felicity, now interested while turning down the heat on her stove.

"Ah! My poor Felicity, you're asking me too much. How do you want me to remember her name? It was so darn long ago. On the other hand, I never forgot her tight little black ass when she was standing on the stirrups and that she moved just right, nice and plump, like her people know..."

Felicity raised her eyebrows.

"That's enough! I don't want to hear any vulgarity or racist remarks under my roof, is that clear? You're just a dirty old man!"

"Hell's bells! She knew how to swing it, and not just her butt!"

The old man's eyes squinted like he was reliving that scene, looking at the young horseback rider, the actress's standby. His lips were moving over his toothless gums, his chin was trembling, he was nearly drooling.

"Stop it! You're sure? You're sure she's the stuntwoman?"

"I'm sure. Ah! I can see us side by side in the dust in Lone Pine, urging our horses on till they were exhausted, disguised as Indians with the Confederate army on our tails, between the director's 'Quiet please!' and 'Cut!' '*Whouwouwouwouw, wouwouwouwou.*"

His niece sighed and went back into the kitchen, nodding her head with chagrin in front of the sad show of her half senile uncle.

When the jambalaya was done, before setting the table, she took out that card that the journalist who had come to ask her uncle some questions a couple of days ago had left her.

~

"He seemed really sure of himself," I resumed. "Too bad he couldn't remember the name of that stuntwoman."

"Sorry to bring more grist to your mill."

"Not in the least, I think what you just told me will be useful, even though the source isn't a hundred percent sure, of course. Thank you so much for having called me, Felicity."

When I hung up, I had more calls to make.

I started, obviously, by informing Inspector Crimson about that useful information, which seemed to shore up our deductions about the "twin horseback rider" without the bunny tattoo. Just like me, he was sorry Felicity didn't have the name of that person, but he'd start investigations into her identity. As would I.

To do that, I tried to reach Brad Purcell, Peter Lundgren and David Apfenstein, the two directors and producer who had necessarily worked with the stuntwoman in their movies to replace Shondra Wallace, as she didn't ride herself.

None of them picked up and I left them all a message asking them to call me back as soon as possible.

I'd just finished writing that when I had a notification that I'd received an email.

A message that really shook me up.

Disinformation

Karen,

I hesitated before answering your message.

At first, I didn't know what to think of it.

Info? Disinformation? A contemporary question that journalists sometimes like to ask, and if I understood correctly, you are part of that professional category.

But what I especially understood is that it was a very personal and intimate initiative to contact me, one that required a lot of courage.

You were wondering if I would think you were crazy. And I must say that when I read your email for the first time, that is exactly what I thought. There are so many strange people nowadays. Especially through the uninhibited filter of virtual social networks.

Are you one of those "strange" people?

I didn't think so when I reread your message.

Karen, your words touched me, whether they were sincerely authentic or cynically false.

They were words of a grieving mother.

I must add that when I read your email, I was also as shaken up as you must have been when you wrote it. Everything it implied in so few words made me afraid to assimilate its content.

There were things that I knew. Including that I was born, like you said, in Boston, Massachusetts, on that date. All of that is written on my ID papers.

I can't deny that.

And my parents also told me that I was adopted just a couple of days after I was born. I'll tell you more about them later.

On the other hand though, they had told me that my biological mother died giving birth to me.

So Karen, you can well imagine how surprised I was and still am, to get your email!

Please understand me! You turn up in Los Angeles and then in my email inbox like a ghost who came back from the dead!

That was a lot all at the same time. Too much data, too suddenly, too many contrary emotions, too much fear, too many unknowns in the equation.

You used the words 'the lost son.' And what about me, could I use the words 'the lost mother?'

I don't know if I should delete this last sentence.

Because no, I never lost my mother. I still have a mother. A loving one, a considerate one, who did everything for the little baby that I was and that she couldn't have. For the child who grew up in a home with two loving, tender and united parents, ready to sacrifice themselves for him. For the often-rebellious teen that I was, just like all my fellow teens, who are searching for their own identity at that age.

Now I better understand that search for identity. And I'm not just talking about my skin color, which is chocolate, while my parents are both as white as whole milk.

Who am I?

Where did I really come from?

What are my true roots? An existential question between birth and experience, between who I am and what I learned.

Who are you? Where are you from?

From nowhere in my genealogical history?

Karen, I still don't know what to think. I write, I write, I explain myself little by little though yesterday I knew nothing at all about you, and today I still don't know you. And tomorrow?

Tomorrow?

Should I give an affirmative answer to your moving request?

Meet each other?

In flesh and blood.

I'm sure you understand that we're having our finals here at UCLA. Speaking of which, did you hear the Midnight Yell? Quite picturesque, wasn't it? And I must admit I also took part in yelling that midnight, it was so liberating!

And you haven't yet seen the Midnight Run, which will take place on Wednesday.

I'm surprising myself, asking you trivial questions, talking to you about this and that in my life. Maybe I'm freeing myself from the strangleholds that would block my decision?

After all, what's there to be afraid of? What have I got to lose? Nothing, I imagine.

Okay Karen let's meet.

I don't have a lot of free time this week because I've still got two more days of finals.

Nonetheless, I also have to relax, and I love basketball, and my favorite team, the Los Angeles Lakers, is playing in the NBA finals against... you'll never believe it... the Boston Celtics!

Do you like basketball?

If so, I've got two tickets for match 7 of the series that takes place at Staples Center – whoops, now it's called the Crypto.com Arena, I'll never get used to that – for Sunday at three. If you want, we could meet there, in a place full of people, which will save me – and maybe you too – from the anxiety of having nothing to say to each other and not even finding the strength to look the other in the eye, over a silent cup of coffee.

If you're free, let me know quickly. Here's my phone number.

CHAPTER 60
Special effects

LOS ANGELES, June 11, 2024

STUPEFACTION.

There was no other word to qualify what Jonas Crimson felt after what the agent from the Los Angeles Forensics Lab had told him.

Stupefaction meaning astonishment, plunging the inspector into a state of complete inertia and bewilderment.

"What the hell?" he grumbled to himself in his kitchen lit up by the lights below the cabinets.

The sun hadn't yet risen in California, but he had told the laboratory that they could – and should – call him at any time on his cell. He'd been lacking sleep for days, but that wasn't important to him; solving the Jabaree case meant that he'd have to give a two hundred percent effort. An effort where he felt he'd been running around in circles.

If he could, he'd scream with wrath for having been tricked by the kidnappers. Scum of the earth! But in the room next to the kitchen, his wife was still sleeping, and he didn't want to disturb her by taking his work home with him. He thus internally boiled over and got ready to go to the Hollywood Police Station where he'd meet with McCormick and Payton.

Hollywood Crisis Unit.

"What the hell?" repeated the federal agent, nearly the same words that Crimson had uttered when learning the lab's conclusions.

"Cinema, it's all fake, McCormick. We were royally screwed. The expert was formal, and it wasn't hard to check. Jabaree Smith's index finger, the one sent to Jodie Poelstra, wasn't human at all. A fake. Not a bit of skin or bones, no blood! Just plastic, silicone, paint, varnish and some synthetic odors."

"Like in B-series horror films?"

"Yup, exactly. No digital special effects like you see in today's blockbusters. More like movies shot back in the 80s, like the ones that Shondra Wallace could have starred in. A bit of cheap raw material, a good professional make-up artist, a bit of patience, a few camera filters to create an anxiogenic atmosphere, and *voilà*!

Maybe a bit of pig's blood to imitate human blood and there you go..."

"Same thing for the cops", the Federal agent scoffed.

Crimson seemingly accepted that insult.

"But when you say 'the cops,' you also mean the FBI, I imagine."

McCormick looked him in the face and finally nodded.

"Okay, let's not play good cops bad cops. What's important is that the kid still has his ten fingers."

"Plus, in that video they sent right after," Payton added, "we can hope that his mutilated hand was also just for looks."

"Probably so. So, what can we learn from that artificial finger?"

"That the kidnappers are screwing with us," the inspector said.

"What else?"

"That maybe they're not as dangerous as we thought? Or at least they're not going to maim or kill the kid."

"For now... What else?"

"That they're close to the world of movies and cinema," Payton added.

"Probably," agreed Crimson. "Right from the beginning, this whole story has been revolving around the universe of cinema and illusions, don't you agree? Jabaree is an actor. He was kidnapped during a party celebrating the end of his last movie, a party that all kinds of people working with movies - other actors, producers, critics, etc., were attending. And Shondra Wallace was also an actress. And now? Now we've got make-up artists! Someone working in special effects and illusions! What else can we find? Got it! Karen Blackstone told me that her investigation was now leading her towards one of Shondra Wallace's standbys, a stuntwoman who rode horses for her."

"That does seem pretty complete," agreed McCormick. "What's missing?"

"The sound man, the Foley artist, the editor, the composer, the scenarist, the cameramen, perch man, grip, script, costumes, distributor, and those are just a few," replied Diane Payton.

"Guess we got our work cut out for us," Crimson deplored. "Let's cross our fingers in hopes that we close this case before we have to include all the members of the profession in the equation."

The three investigators thought that over for a while. The federal agent was the first one to speak.

"What's next?"

"I'm going to put my guys on the professional make-up artists in Hollywood," Jonas suggested. "See if they can find the studio or freelancer who designed that realistic little finger. From there, maybe we'll find the kidnappers."

CHAPTER 61
Final credits

MY SLEEP IS OFTEN INTERRUPTED by my investigations that generate dreams or nightmares.

So I wasn't surprised to find my eyes wide open at five in the morning on June 11th.

Luke's letter had really impacted me. The outlook of finally meeting him and speaking with him still seemed unrealistic, yet I of course accepted by SMS to meet him at the Staples Center – whoopsie, at the Crypto.com Arena! – next Sunday, as I didn't think I was capable of phoning him. Twenty-five years had separated our first meeting from this one. Twenty-five interminable years during which I'd thought of him each and every day.

BESIDES MY PERSONAL CONCERNS, the Wallace case was also adversely affecting my sleep.

I grabbed my laptop that I'd put on the shelf above

my headboard and started looking in the large field of possibles on the web.

How could I find the trace – and especially the name – of Shondra Wallace's stuntwoman for *The Coyote-Woman of the Desert*? And if I did find her, would she still be alive? In which case, would she be able to give me some info or would it just be another shot in the dark?

I had an idea and quickly checked it. Most movie spectators, or even those at home watching TV, leave the theater once the movie has finished or zap with their remote controls, to avoid watching the final credits. Others, of which I'm a part, remain seated in their chair or slumped in their couch, watching all the names go by, with the tiny hope that the producer had slipped in a little goodie, just for the heck of it, a wink to his spectators, a small additional scene to reward all those who remained watching right to the end. I was often disappointed, as there was nothing. But in the meanwhile, I'd inattentively read the long litany of names of all those who worked on that movie. And that's where you really understand how many professionals it took to make one! Hundreds of people! Without even citing the extras who weren't listed, and in some cases, there were hundreds or even thousands of them in blockbusters such as peplums. Hmm, speaking of extras, I wondered if there were any in *The Coyote-Woman*. If so, what did they know about Shondra Wallace's disappearance? Maybe one of them was involved in it? Incognito…

In a nutshell, this habit of reading the final credits reminded me that in the list of staff members always mentioned, there were the stuntmen! Or in my case, a stuntwoman. So, as I didn't have *The Coyote-Woman*, I started looking for the last feature-length movies in which Shondra starred, available in streaming, and that could possibly have scenes where she rode a horse. I found a couple of westerns, launched the videos and moved the cursor to the final credits. The producer, list of actors, associated filmmakers, and finally the names of the stunt men or women.

There weren't loads of them, some of them probably doubled for several actors or actresses in the movie, if of course their physiognomies corresponded even a bit. If the actor was a tall blond man, there weren't too many chances that he'd be replaced in dangerous scenes, by a brunette lady who looked like Roseanne Barr in the 90s.

I spent roughly an hour combing through the final credits where I seemed to systematically find the same names:

~~Patrick Flanaghan~~
Maureen O'Hara
Melissa Westbrook
~~Paul Bannister~~ (hey look who's back!)
~~Raoul Culvert~~
Jennifer Sandgren
~~Victor Cramer~~

. . .

I LOGICALLY CROSSED out the names of the men, thinking they wouldn't have a feminine silhouette and wear wigs, and only kept three of them: Maureen, Melissa, and Jennifer.

Was one of those women Shondra Wallace's official standby or had all three replaced her?

Now a regular customer, I logged into IMDb, put their names in the search bar, but didn't find anything interesting that I didn't already know, meaning that they'd worked on several movies with Shondra. Plus they didn't have any contact details.

I luckily though found some information I could use.

It was from a phone call Peter Lundgren had made from Sweden, where he was still on vacation and who couldn't have cared less about the time difference with California nor waking me up. The old Stockholm Bear only cared about himself.

"Miss Blackstone, you're lucky my memory isn't too bad," he greeted me without even saying hello, making me think of my dear Big Boss, Myrtille Fairbanks.

"Mr. Lundgren, nice to hear from you. You must have received my message then."

"That's right. And I've got the answer to your question. I remember the name of the stuntwoman who replaced Shondra in scenes where she was riding a horse."

CHAPTER 62
Scenario

When Crimson, his team and the federal agents had nearly finished their meeting with the goal of finding out who had ordered and designed that artificial finger, one of the inspector's staff members rushed in, all excited to be bringing something new into the case.

"Jonas? We just finished contacting all the dealerships about the different ways all the cars parked in the underground lot blinked."

The inspector stopped for a moment, disoriented. There'd been so many elements, often without satisfactory answers, surrounding that double disappearance, that he'd forgotten about the warning lights. The police officer continued.

"Remember, you asked me to check all the license plates of the cars parked in the lot where the gala party was being held and to compare how each model beeped or lit up when it was unlocked. It took a while, but I'm done. So here we go, each model does have its own 'music,' even though most brands are the same. But usually a Ford won't have the same music as a Chevrolet or a Toyota. And we found out that the 'one long, two shorts' that we heard twice in half an hour is typical of Ruppert Magloire's Chevrolet Corvette."

"Thanks, John. That confirms that someone went down to the parking lot, opened the Chevrolet, but didn't start the car, as the same beep was heard a few seconds later but the car was still in the lot. Then a second time, half an hour later, about 1:15 am if I remember correctly, when Ruppert Magloire left to look for Jabaree, taking the same trip as us a couple of days ago. To conclude, I'd say that Magloire probably went down to his car about a quarter to one to get something. What though?"

McCormick seemed to be thinking aloud.

"In thrillers and cop series, that's when you try to have the reader or TV spectator believe that you're getting the weapon out from the trunk of your car. No?"

"Except we're not in a book or a police series," Crimson replied. "We're not starring in *NCIS*, or *Without a Trace*..."

"Stop being cute," grumbled the Fed.

"Seriously though, what did Magloire go down to get?" Crimson wondered. "Let me remind you of how things went down that evening. At that time, he'd just put Jabaree to bed upstairs in the place the gala was being held."

"Maybe we should just ask him," suggested Diane Payton.

"It'll be my pleasure to do it personally," the inspector said, taking his phone out of his pocket. "This guy is starting to get my goat..."

THE PHONE RANG four times before the movie director picked up.

"Magloire? Crimson here. Listen, how long are you gonna continue giving me in dribs and drabs about that gala party?" he said, without any explications.

"Excuse me, Inspector, you woke me up, last night was pretty awful as you can imagine, I'm sure. What are you talking about?"

"Ruppert, I can understand that. It's comprehensible. What you and your wife are going through is atrocious. But if you don't help me, Jabaree is going to be the one paying the consequences. So please, tell me why you went down to your car that evening about a quarter to one after having put Jabaree to bed upstairs. Why didn't you tell me that during the two auditions?"

"You didn't ask."

"Quit fucking with me Ruppert. I'm not in the mood."

After a few seconds, during which Crimson only heard Magloire breathing, he finally answered.

"Excuse me, Inspector. The truth is I didn't tell

you that because for me it wasn't important. It's true, now I remember having gone down to my car then. I needed some documents that I wanted to show my production manager."

"What documents?"

"A scenario that one of my friends sent me the week before and that I totally loved. I wanted to submit it to my producer that evening, so he could read it and hopefully put some money into the pot because I wanted to direct it next year. Except now, there's no projects with Jabaree miss…"

The movie director's voice broke thinking of the future without his stepson. Without his wife's son. Without his favorite actor. Or without his goose that laid golden eggs?

"It's astonishing that a document like that was just printed out, and wasn't on a flash drive," doubted the policeman.

"My producer is old-school. He likes to read things on a paper format."

"Okay. Could I see that document, Mr. Magloire?"

"Yes, of course, I'll go get it today from my producer."

"Don't bother, I'll do it. What's his name and where does he live?"

After having raised his shoulder to wedge the phone between it and his ear, the inspector grabbed a sheet of paper and wrote down the info.

CHAPTER 63
Script

"Mr. Lundgren, what was the name of that stuntwoman?"

The movie producer seemed to thrive when making me wait on the line.

"If I remember correctly, it was a gal named Melissa. Last name, Melbrooks, or Westbrook, something like that."

"Westbrook! I saw that name in the credits in movies starring Shondra."

"She was the one who generally was her stuntwoman. However, I can't remember her working on the last movie. I can't be categorical though about that because it's been such a long while and the scenes that are shot with standbys aren't necessarily done with the main director, but usually by an assistant."

"Would you have his or her name?" I asked with an ounce of hope.

"Sorry, no. I completely forgot. But you could ask

the script, she might have it. If there was one in that movie, which I doubt, now that I think about it."

"How come?"

"By definition, the work done by a script girl, and I'm saying girl because it's a feminine job, consists in making sure each full-screen shot is a link shot to the preceding one and the following one, to ensure a continuity, should I say, something realistic. This is true for details like objects, positions and postures actors have, decors, all that. Like, if an actor picks up a glass with his right hand on shot X and then on the next one, shot Y, he's drinking using his left hand, spectators notice stuff like that."

"Okay."

"So let's imagine a scene that involves riding. You see the actress mount on the rump of a horse and then in the next shot, the stuntwoman is galloping away, but she's not wearing the same clothing or her hair isn't done like the actress's, and then you go back to a tight close-up of the actress – who's actually straddling a chair pretending to hold the reins – and after that during editing, nothing goes together. Because during editing, all the shooting is finished and it's too late! So that's what the script-girl does, Miss Blackstone. She makes sure everything goes together. But all those avid B-series fans often find delicious little tidbits. A boom in the camera's range, a picture that's not on the same wall, an actress wearing a dress and a second later the same one wearing a blouse, an actor who leaves on the right and comes back from the left, things like that."

"I see," I replied, smiling.

"The problem was that Apfenstein, that cheapskate movie producer, was always trying to cut down on costs and had no problems not using that type of employee. Because a good script-girl will always be there to say that this detail or that has to be changed, that the scene has to be shot again. And that costs dozens of yards of silver print film. Remember, all this was before digital technology! Plus it takes time. And time is money! So, knowing Apfenstein, he considered something like that to be wasted money and didn't employ a script girl in a lot of his movies. Forget about her! The easiest thing to do would be to contact that old fart directly... If he doesn't remember, maybe he's got pay slips for technicians, extras and stuntmen in his archives. And could perhaps even tell you if that Melissa Westbrook was working the day that Shondra disappeared. Good luck, bye."

And the former filmmaker hung up without any further ado.

I IMMEDIATELY DIALED APFENSTEIN, as he hadn't bothered to call me back. This time, he paid me the ultimate compliment of answering, with his synthetic and moaning voice.

"Miss Blackstone! What can I do for you?"

I don't know why, but I felt like punching him, though of course I was my usual friendly self.

"I left you a message yesterday about a stuntwoman who you often employed to replace Shondra Wallace. I now know that her name was Melissa Westbrook. Would you be able to tell me if she was part of the team starring in *The Coyote-Woman of the Desert*?"

"That again? It's running in a loop..."

"Mr. Apfenstein, has your old age made you insensitive? You do realize that young Jabaree Smith's life depends on my investigation about Shondra? The little protected bubble where you live doesn't make you blind to that point?"

A shrill crackling sound ripped through my tympan, making me pull the phone away from my ear.

"How could I remember something like that?"

"You didn't store the archives for the accounts of your company that would have the information?"

"Remember, I told you I'd had a fire in my warehouse. Well, that's where all the files were stored. Up in smoke! But though I can't give you her name nor do I have access to my archives, I can categorically affirm that no, she wasn't working for me that time."

"You're sure about that?"

"Totally! Simply because my production company was going to the dogs. I didn't have enough money to cover my cashflow. My income was plunging. So I had to drastically make cuts in expenses, understand? That meant no more script-girls, no production assistants, standbys that I paid just with lunch and no more stuntmen either! It was up to the actors to move their asses and ride the horses... Or else they were fired! Out the door! That's it!"

"Apfenstein, you're despicable! A rat! Shondra Wallace was pregnant when you were shooting the movie, and you made her do her own stunts? You're crazy!"

"Like I told you, I didn't know she had a bun in the oven. Now, that's enough, you're royally pissing me off, Miss Blackstone."

And he hung up on me. Guess it just wasn't my day. All that was missing now was that Myrtille would call me and do the same thing.

I WAS SEETHING, my head was full of all those questions that were overturning the scenario that I had been building brick by brick in my mind.

Melissa Westbrook, Shondra's standby and stuntwoman, wasn't in Lone Pine in June of 1988.

Did Shondra, because she was pregnant, desert the movie because she was forced to do her own riding stunts?

Was Apfenstein, the ruthless producer, when he saw his movie turning into a fiasco, responsible for the sequence of tragic events that followed?

I immediately called Inspector Crimson.

CHAPTER 64
Visual artists

"Okay, Karen, I'll put out an APB for that Melissa Westbrook. If she's still alive, she could be one of the missing links here. It's surprising with all the media coverage in this double case though that she hasn't contacted us. Sometimes people don't make our jobs easy, do they?"

Inspector Crimson hung up after having thanked the journalist for having informed him of her latest discoveries. Then he asked Diane Payton, his deputy, to prepare a press release with a recent photo of that Melissa Westbrook. He asked her to add the contact details of the team leading the investigation as well as the phone number of the hotline that the Lovelace-Magloire couple had set up when Jabaree went missing.

"We gotta try to stack the deck in our favor," said Crimson as Payton left his office.

His small office where he worked way too long didn't remain silent for long though. Just a few minutes after Payton had left, Officer Starck came in, looking smug.

"Inspector, I've got a good lead on that fake finger."

"Tell me."

"Like you asked me to, I contacted several professionals or suppliers who were capable of creating an object like that, with that degree of perfection. And there's not too many of them in Los Angeles. I didn't even bother with costume and trick stores: all they sell is junk made in China or India that doesn't look more like a real finger than a raw hotdog!"

"I see what you're getting at, though I don't work in cold cuts. And?"

"So I focused on professionals who work in the movie industry and identified ten of them. Amongst those ten, there are two huge studios specialized in making things like that, the others are much smaller structures or independent visual artists."

"Did you contact them all?"

"Most of them. Those I talked to told me that they hadn't had an order like that recently. That it was something they would have remembered, and they would have contacted us."

"Ouch. And that was your great lead? Not a burning hot one."

"Wait a sec, Inspector. I'm not done. Most of them insinuated that there was a second-hand market for these types of objects used in movies. Lotsa little Hollywood studios, because they don't have many resources, acquire stock from major studios like Warner, MGM, Paramount, Colombia, Universal, etc. They purchase stage sets, costumes, reels of film or other accessories that were initially created for larger studios. And that's where things get interesting for us."

"You're gonna regret keeping me waiting, I'm warning you. So just spit it out!"

The officer smiled at his boss's fake anger. He knew when Jonas was really mad or when he was just messing with him.

"Okay. One person I talked to, an old-timer like the saying goes, an independent guy on the point of retiring, said he remembered an order that had been given to him ages ago by Warner, in the 70s or 80s. An order for a horror film. And the order included a whole list of parts of the human body. An eye, a foot, a nose, an ear, a heart, a hand and its fingers, one by one, including an index finger of course. After that, he thought that his silicone body parts circulated from studio to studio because of their quality and rather than having them gather dust in some closet or be thrown out, it was better if others could use them. The artist said he saw his works in several B-series movies. And especially in one of them, shot around 1982, entitled *The Collector*..."

"Charming," Crimson said.

"That's one way of seeing things. This movie is about a psychopath who lived in the northern United States and took one and only one body part from his many female victims: a nose, lips, etc. with the ultimate goal of recreating, part by part, a body that matched that of his mother... who'd died in childbirth! As it was impossible for him to find a perfect match, meaning the sosie of his mother at the age when she gave life to him and lost hers, he was putting it together part by part, just like a puzzle."

"There are really crazy authors and screenwriters," Crimson said philosophically. "I wouldn't like to be in their heads. And did you watch *The Collector*?"

"Not all of it as it wasn't my cup of tea, but if you want, I'll lend you the DVD."

"I'm good. So what did you learn from it?"

"Nothing much from the scenario itself. On the other hand, the final credits were interesting. Believe it or not, the guy who produced that dud back in the 80s was a certain David Apfenstein!"

"Jesus Christ!... I wonder why I'm not surprised. This whole thing has been orbiting around him ever since we began our investigation."

"And that's not all. You'll never guess the name of the actress who had a tiny role – that of the final victim who had one of her body parts cut off, more precisely her index finger..."

"I've got an idea. Wouldn't her name be... Shondra Wallace?"

CHAPTER 65
The public

THE KIDNAPPERS CONTINUED their diabolical little game. As if they were reading the investigators' minds, both those of Jonas Crimson and of Karen Blackstone. They were constantly one step ahead, just like what do when you play chess.

The general public began to mock the police, saying they were incapable of freeing Jabaree Smith. The kidnappers seemed to have the advantage.

Once again, on that 11th of July, a video would confirm the detractors in their negative opinion they had towards cops.

Crimson couldn't help swearing at the flat-screen television on the wall of the office.

The video was short but scathing. There was one of the kidnappers – or perhaps the kidnapper, as his physiognomy, though he was wearing a mask, seemed identical to that in the first video, the one released a couple of days ago, making Crimson think he was acting alone. The man – or woman, as the voice was transformed and the gender unrecognizable, let's call him or her *the person* – was standing. Their eyes gleaming with contentment shone through the thin spaces cut into the head mask.

"I HOPE you appreciated our little joke, ladies and gentlemen of the police force.

A bit of humor is always appreciated, isn't it? My little finger told me that it wasn't too hard for you to realize that the tiny object in the package was factitious. Factitious like movies! Oh! It wasn't too hard, was it? Let's just say that the goal here was to create a situation of urgency, to put some pressure on you.

Same thing with Jabaree's video. Bet that shook you up too. Discovering his little mutilated hand... Fake! Pure fiction! People love what's virtual, don't they?

Ah! No, actually what they prefer above all is fiction based on true stories, isn't that right?

Spectators adore that.

So, let's get back to reality now. Just to say that this time, our threat is serious and if tomorrow, June 12th at noon, you haven't put your finger on what took place in the Shondra Wallace case, Jabaree will really lose a bit of himself.

We got a finger in every pie here, something you are now sure of. I'm sure you can nearly lay your finger on the solution now. So if you don't want the authorities to give you a wrap on your knuckles, if you don't want to be fingered as total police dummies, if you're afraid we're going to slip through your fingers, shake a leg and let's all cross our fingers so tomorrow you'll find out the truth!

Doesn't it do a world of good to laugh in circumstances like these?

So, my dear investigators, take your fingers out of your a...!"

Crimson felt like throwing the TV out the window. He personally felt he was the target. If something should happen to the kid, he'd have, maybe not the responsibility but at least the burden of it on his conscience. Probably for his whole life. When you're a cop, there are some cases you can never forget.

Because before you're a cop, you're a human being.

So he ardently hoped he wouldn't fail.

He had to make headway, step by step, slowly but surely.

Crimson mentally made a list of all the tips he still had to check out and chose the one that seemed to be in the middle of them all: he was going to surprise David Apfenstein with a little visit to his Bel-Air residence.

CHAPTER 66
Preview

I WAS surprised by the notification I had in my inbox. I didn't think I'd ever hear from that person again, yet here was *meganoc1970* sending me another message on the MovieGeeks site.

```
Hey Karen.
Did you see the info? It was crazy,
I tell you! Who would have thought
that a document like that could come
out today when the case is, could I
say, closed and buried? Except you, of
course, the expert in cold cases. You
can believe me, this video is starting
to circulate on all the specialized
sites, and then social media will be
sharing it just as fast as that horse
can gallop! If you haven't seen it
yet, here's the link so you can see the
```

```
YouTube trailer. Call me if you want
to talk about it! That'll be easier
and more fun. Here's my number, we can
do a WhatsApp video if you want.
   Ciao. Megan O'C.
```

I IMMEDIATELY OPENED the link Megan had given me and the YouTube app on my phone opened. *Preview: The truth about the Shondra Wallace case.*

The audiovisual document only lasted thirty-three seconds. The trailer, on a powerful and anxiety-ridden musical background, opened, with several short sequences of archived movies. They were clips from feature-length movies starring Shondra. It was easy to recognize her in their clips. I even thought I remembered a bit of *The Bloody Machete 2*, the movie I'd watched till the end a couple of days ago, in my motel in Lone Pine. It was the scene when the character played by Shondra, alias Nikki LaToya, was trying to escape from a psychopath who was pursuing her in the Amazonian jungle after he'd killed her boyfriend in their cabin.

The preview also showed a couple of seconds of a wild horseback ride, a western shot in Alabama Hills, that I also recognized.

Another was focused on Shondra's index finger being cut off in *The Collector*. It was terrifying how that assembly joined what was now happening!

Lastly, between the various scenes or as an overprint, the preview also proclaimed:

*"Prepare...
... to discover...
the unique truth...
... about the disappearance...
... of Shondra Wallace!
On June 15, 2024...
... on all streaming platforms.
The only cinéma-vérité!
Signed...
Alan Smithee..."*

What really attracted my eyes though was the final sequence, inserted between "*The only cinéma-vérité,*" meaning it would be a true documentary, and "*Signed... Alan Smithee.*" This was a closeup of Jabaree articulating the words "Never Forget," just as he had with the video filmed by his kidnappers.

"Shit," I said, out of breath after having looked at the preview in apnea.

Alan Smithee? Why did I have the strange impression of having seen that name someplace without being able to put my finger on the where, when and why?

I entered Megan's phone number into my WhatsApp directory and sent her out a quick message.

> Megan, this is Karen Blackstone.
> Can we chat now?

I looked at my screen and saw the following words: *Someone is writing to you*.

> I was sure you wouldn't last long!
> I'm available. Meg'.

With my right index finger, I pressed the WhatsApp camera icon, and a few seconds later, saw Megan's face on my screen.

I HAD to admit I was quite surprised. I wasn't expecting that Megan, you could say. I have no idea why I'd imagined a young red-haired lady with freckles, but instead of that I had a sixty or so year old lady with white curly short hair framing a plump face and a large jaw. She made me think of John Goodman, in a feminine version.

"Hey, Karen!

I was surprised by her voice too. A throaty raw one that must have been broken by years of smoking, as there was a butt hanging out of her mouth as we spoke.

"Lovely to see you, Megan."

"Likewise, though the circumstances aren't really pleasant. What's the weather like in L.A.?"

"We're roasting! And what about yours? Where are you actually?"

"In Ireland, my fair lady. Well, let's just say that the weather here is... Irish! So enough of our weather reports. How's your investigation going?"

"Let me start by thanking you for your help, it was priceless."

"No problem. Just spit it out!"

"After our last exchange of emails, I was able to identify the person who was Shondra's stuntwoman. A lady named Melissa Westbrook, does that ring a bell?"

"I already heard or probably saw that name in credits at the end of movies, yes. But I don't know a thing about her. Have you found her? Met her?"

"Not yet, but I'm dying to. The cops put out an APB – that's an All-Points Bulletin, if you don't know the term, on her hoping she'd contact them quickly. The countdown is accelerating, it's totally freaking me out!"

"I can believe that. So you watched the preview?"

"As soon as I opened your message, yes. That was incredible! And that's why I called you straightaway. I'm sure you'll be able to tell me who that Alan Smithee is. I think I've heard of him but can't remember where."

On the other side of the screen, Megan broke out laughing, a deep and throaty laugh, followed by a cough.

"Sorry," she said after having put her butt out. "Fecking cigarettes, never should have started. Now it's too late to stop, I'll end up coughing my lungs out in front of a dud from the 80s, a good way to go! Anyway, enough about my health problems. Alan Smithee? Honey, you're disappointing me!"

"How come?"

"Really, everyone knows Alan Smithee! Well, maybe not everyone. Let's say, all the cinephiles or movie fans like me know him."

"So when are you going to tell me who he is, next year?" I joked.

"No, in a year I don't know if I'll still have my vocal cords left to talk to you. What can I say about him? Except that it's going to be hard to meet him..."

I seethed internally.

"How come? He's dead?"

"Dead? No! Worse than that!"

CHAPTER 67
An alias

I HAD to say there that Megan O'Conner's speech was totally incomprehensible.

"Worse than being dead? How can anything be worse?"

Once again, the Irish lady's loud guffaw filled my phone's speaker.

"That guy can't be dead for the pure and simple reason that he was never born!"

"Never born?"

"In reality, he never existed. Physically I mean. Alan Smithee is a pseudonym! An alias. You could say that he 'unofficially was born' in 1955 in a TV film and then in 1969 for a feature-length movie. To make things simple, this sort of became a way of contesting, one that some American movie producers who weren't happy with the end result used, often when they weren't satisfied with what their director and editor did, the infamous *director's cut* that was so popular back then. Now it's not as popular though. But in Hollywood, directors are kings you know. Did you ever hear of the DGA?"

"I don't think so," I admitted.

"The Directors Guild of America. Producers who think their movie was poorly edited and want to disown it could contact this guild and ask for their names to be taken from the final credits and replaced by Alan Smithee! Ya want me to tell you that story?"

"Please do."

"Okay. The first feature movie signed Alan Smithee was *Death of a Gunfighter* that Don Siegal and Robert Totten directed in 1969. The film began under the direction of Robert Totten, but after clashes with the star Widmark, and almost a year of work, he was dropped and replaced by Siegel; so both had worked on the movie for roughly the same length of time and neither wanted to be credited as being the movie's director. The DGA decided that the end result didn't reflect the vision of either of them and exceptionally suggested using a pseudonym. And that's how Alan Smithee was born! After that, he was credited in about thirty other movies, but also as a pseudonym for actors, producers, editors, composers, photo directors, you name it. There was also a movie Alan Smithee signed entitled *An Alan Smithee Film*: *Burn, Hollywood, Burn**. They came the full circle!"

---

* An Alan Smithee movie: *Burn, Hollywood, Burn*. 1997. With Eric Idle playing Alan Smithee. Also starring Whoopi Goldberg, Sylvester

I thought what Megan just told me over for a couple of seconds.

"Almost like the Wallace case," I said. "*The Coyote-Woman of the Desert* began with Lundgren, then Purcell continued it, and both directors didn't agree with Apfenstein, the producer... You think it's just a mere coincidence?"

"Not at all," retorted Megan. "In my opinion, using that alias was intentional."

"But who's behind that Alan Smithee today and his *cinéma-vérité* preview?"

Megan thought that over, biting her cheek. She finally replied.

"If there really is a *cinéma-vérité* movie and not just a teaser. I sort of feel like saying that it could be anyone who's a bit talented in editing. A filmmaker, an editor, a geek. Anyone who has access to Shondra Wallace's movie archives. Or even one of us MovieGeeks!"

"What about Jabaree Smith's kidnappers?"

"Why not? Everything's possible, sweetie! Nowadays, with digital technology and all the software out there, editing a video like that is child's play for lots of people. We just have to wait till June 15th when the movie will be released! Sooner or later that Alan Smithee will shed his mask."

I sighed, disheartened.

Stallone, Jackie Chan, Harvey Weinstein, Naomi Campbell, as well as the English soccer star, Alan Smith!

"Megan, we don't have time like that. I'd prefer sooner rather than later..."

We hung up and I sat down in the armchair in my hotel room. I was dreading tomorrow's noon deadline. I had the impression that hours were going by like seconds.

CHAPTER 68
The curtain closes

As the sun was slowly setting over the Pacific, the police vehicle stopped in front of the gates of David Apfenstein's luxurious property. Though the former producer had proclaimed loudly and clearly that his business had gone belly up years ago, he must have earned enough money during his career with hundreds of B-series movies he'd financed to pay for this little bit of heaven on the Bel-Air hillside.

The policeman pressed the interphone button.

"Yes?"

"Inspector Jonas Crimson, from the Hollywood station. I'd like to see Mr. Apfenstein."

"Inspector, I'm afraid that won't be possible."

"Excuse me for insisting Ma'am, but it wasn't a request. Open up, please."

"That's not going to help you much. Mr. Apfenstein isn't here. He was rushed to the hospital this morning."

Crimson clenched his fist, wanting to smash the interphone in, not from anger, but from frustration.

"What happened?"

"The rescue squad said he was in respiratory failure. They thought it might be an infection linked to his artificial larynx. That's awful at his age," said the lady with an emotion-filled voice.

"I'm sorry," the policeman said. "Which hospital was he taken to?"

"To the Cedars-Sinai Medical Center in West Hollywood, on Beverly Boulevard."

"Thanks, I know where it is," Crimson said.

WITHOUT WAITING for any objections from that lady who could have been either the producer's assistant, or a nurse, or even one of his descendants, the inspector jumped into his car, turned on the siren and headed to West Hollywood with his assistant at the wheel.

In just fifteen minutes, the duo had reached the hospital, asking for directions at the front desk and in the halls, before reaching the ICU's locked doors.

"The patient certainly can't have any visitors," the doctor told them. "He's suffering from a pulmonary embolism and been sedated with oxygen therapy. I'm sorry, Inspector."

"Your prognostic, Doctor?"

"Not too good, I'm afraid. Mr. Apfenstein is almost ninety and it's evident that he didn't take care of his body or his heart for his whole life. Just like many others in Hollywood, he was burning the candle at both ends. Plus, the comorbidity of several factors isn't helping."

"Meaning?"

"Despite what we're doing for him, I don't think he's going to make it. To use a metaphor, his curtain will soon be closing..."

Crimson sighed, resigned. One of his leads seemed to have gone up in smoke when he perhaps would have been close to touching its resolution with his fingertips.

HE GOT BACK into the car and his phone rang: Karen Blackstone.

"I hope you got good news, Karen," he said without greeting her. "Otherwise I'm going to hang up on you."

"Well, hello to you too," the journalist said ironically. "I've got news Inspector, if you want to listen. I just learned something completely crazy. Believe it or not, there's a video going around on social networking sites and specialized ones. One of my cinephile contacts, an Irish woman, told me about it. It's a teaser saying a *cinéma-vérité* movie, that's something based on a true story, will be released on streaming platforms on June 15th. You want to know the title?"

"I haven't hung up, have I?"

"*The truth about the Shondra Wallace case...*"

...

"Crimson, are you still there?"

"Yeah, yeah, I heard you Karen. It's just... unexpected. The truth and nothing but the truth? Wow! And the good Samaritan who produced the movie didn't think of releasing it before June 15th? Or contacting the police? Like does the guy live in a cave or something not to know about tomorrow's deadline?"

"No, I don't think he lives like a Neanderthal. You have to have a load of equipment and software to shoot and edit a movie. So, in a cave..."

"You got a name?" the inspector asked impatiently.

"I do, but that's not going to help much. The movie was produced by a certain Alan Smithee. And he's someone you'll never arrest."

"How come?"

"Because he doesn't exist, it's an alias used in the world of American cinema. And we don't know who's hiding behind that pseudonym."

"You got an idea?"

"A small composite drawing you could say. Though this is vague, without making too many mistakes we could say it's a person who's skilled in editing videos, who has specialized software, and all the equipment needed to do it, and who would be able to access archives of movies from the 80s as well as Jabaree's videos. All that's left to do is to assemble all that and upload it onto the networks and platforms."

"Jesus Christ!"

"What's going on?"

Crimson, ignoring Karen's question, turned to the driver of the police car.

"Diane, make a U-turn! We're going back to Bel-Air..."

CHAPTER 69
Enlightenment

LAST TIME CRIMSON WENT THERE, night had already fallen over Los Angeles and the Bel-Air hillside was sleeping soundly. Lights were turned off one by one when each inhabitant of the villas went to join Morphea. It had still been lit up at the Lovelace-Magloire's main house that evening, when the inspector and Ruppert, his assistant, had come back from visiting his various homes in Pasadena, Malibu, and then Las Vegas. When Crimson had discovered Janice walking back and forth in front of that huge picture window.

THIS TIME THOUGH, it was high noon when he parked his car in front of the villa. They were hit by a hot flash of air when they left the car.

The inspector and his assistant ran up to the front door with its marble columns. Crimson pressed the doorbell furiously and without waiting for an answer, began to pound on the door.

"Open up, Magloire! Police! Inspector Crimson. Open this door immediately, Miss Lovelace. Open up!"

He suddenly heard some noise through the door, like someone was dragging a chair on the tiles. The policeman quit knocking and a few seconds later, he heard the door being unlocked.

They could see Janice Lovelace's pale, nearly lunar face, though the door as it opened. Her red eyes, with bags under them, still seemed to be moist though she'd wiped them, making her mascara run.

"Please, stop pounding, Inspector. My head is killing me. My ophthalmic migraines, you know. I can't stand this light anymore."

"Please excuse my interruption, but I absolutely have to talk to your husband."

"Oh," she murmured. "Why didn't you call him?"

"I prefer to speak to him face to face. Is he home?"

"Unfortunately, not now."

"When's he coming back?"

The actress put a hand in front of her eyes to protect them from the glaring sunlight and began crying again.

"I don't know," she lamented.

"Can you at least tell me where he is?"

She shook her head.

"I have no idea. Ruppert left last night right before I went to bed. He just told me he had a meeting."

"With whom?"

THE LOST SON

"I asked him of course, but he didn't answer. He just put a jacket on and rushed downstairs to the garage. I ran after him and asked him again where the heck he was going, but he just got into his Corvette. Right before he closed the car door, he said, 'Now it's high time all this is over.' That's all. Since then he hasn't even answered my phone calls. I hope he didn't do anything stupid."

Crimson was startled.

"Excuse me? Like what? You think that maybe..."

Janice Lovelace sobbed, interrupting the policeman. She took a deep breath before answering.

"The last couple of days Ruppert has been really tense. It's understandable. All this horror surrounding our little Jabaree. My baby! I thought that Ruppert would be stronger than me, but now I realize that he's not. I can tell he's really affected, broken. I know that psychologically speaking, my husband isn't always stable. Sometimes he has crises. I hope he didn't do anything that can't be undone, Inspector. Good Lord! If after having lost Jabaree, I would also lose Ruppert, I don't think I could survive."

The policeman calmly tried to console her.

"Miss Lovelace, everything will be okay. We'll find both of them safe and sound. Believe me."

"Please, bring them back home."

"I hope so," murmured Crimson walking away. "I hope so."

CHAPTER 70
A role to play

FOR THE FIFTH time straight I watched Alan Smithee's teaser. I tried to detect the tiniest hint that could lead me to its author. To no avail.

My recent conversation with Crimson, though it was abruptly interrupted, made me think that he was heading towards the Bel-Air district, where Ruppert Magloire, Janice Lovelace, and Jabaree lived, as well as old Apfenstein who I'd met at the Country Club.

Was Magloire, an experienced and successful director, the one who produced the preview? Was he the one hiding behind the pseudonym of Alan Smithee?

If so though, if he knew the truth about Shondra Wallace's disappearance, why didn't he just trumpet it out immediately? Wasn't that what the kidnappers of Jabaree wanted, wasn't that in their demand to free Jabaree?

I couldn't believe that the kid-star's stepfather, Jabaree's mother's second husband, could keep key information that could lead to freeing the young actor from us. That would be heartless.

Or maybe he couldn't tell us.

That was my theory after I'd spoken with Crimson who had updated me with some interesting information.

He told me first of all that Magloire was missing again too. I concluded, – and it was a possibility – that the director, if he was that Alan Smithee, could have himself been kidnapped or eliminated by Jabaree's kidnappers. Maybe he was ambushed after he left his house last night. To keep him from speaking? Prohibit him from releasing the *cinéma-vérité* movie announced for June 15th?

On the first point, I couldn't help the inspector much.

But when the phone rang again and I saw Crimson's name, I wanted to say that things were starting to finally fall into place.

"Karen. We're almost there. I just left Magloire's place. I'm gonna put all my men onto finding him. He's the key player in this case. Ever since the beginning I thought there was something fishy about him. I'm sure that he's playing a role here, whatever it is. Leading player, extra, witness, victim ? That's the ball of yarn I have to unravel now. On the other hand, I can't be everywhere, and there's another new element that just came in. We just got a call after we broadcast a call for witnesses about Melissa Westbrook. There's a lady who says she's her neighbor. If it is her, we have to pay her a little visit. And I was sort of counting on you for that. As you're heading the Shondra case, you'd be the most qualified person to interview her."

"Of course! That's great news. Where does she live?"

"We got lucky here, she's not on another continent. Even not too far from us. She lives in Las Vegas, 2345, Cheyenne Avenue."

I glanced at my phone. It was nearly three. Crimson continued, as if reading my thoughts.

"It'll take you four or five hours. Faster by plane of course, but first you have to go to LAX, wait for the flight, it's an hour and a half, then rent a car in Vegas, etc."

I stopped him as I'm not a fan of flying.

"I'll drive there. I can leave now. Just text me the address please."

THE MONOTONOUS ROUTE between L.A. and Vegas reminded me of the one I'd often taken to and from Lone Pine. Though the scenery was beautiful between Victorville and Barstow, the drive itself through the desert was long and boring. Its beauty though overwhelmed me when I saw the sun setting in my rear-view mirror, an unequaled natural blaze of light.

It was dark out when I reached Nevada though I saw a nebulous halo in the sky announcing the countless lights shining in Sin City.

THE LOST SON

What sins would I be discovering in Vegas? Capital sins or venial sins?

I reached the outskirts of Las Vegas, Nevada's largest city. I was subjugated by the lighting and gigantic palaces, casinos, the wide Strip that I'd only seen in movies such as *Showgirls, Casino, Very Bad Trip, Sister Act,* or *Ocean's Eleven* and *Ocean's Thirteen*. And more recently, the fantastic biographical drama film, *Elvis*.

But tonight, Vegas wasn't fictional for me!

Karen, welcome into the reality of human sins.

I finally arrived at Cheyenne Avenue with its three-lane streets surrounded by empty lots between condominiums with their ocher walls and two-story homes, all exactly the same. My GPS took me to the number that Crimson had given me, and I parked, exhausted by the five-hour drive only interrupted by a few necessary pit stops.

It was nine pm, but a blast of hot air clobbered me as soon as I got out of the car. Dry, stifling air full of tiny particles of sand from the desert surrounding the city that never sleeps.

I COULD SEE that lights were still on in the living room downstairs. I read the name of Melissa Westbrook on the mailbox. While walking up to the door, I made out a silhouette behind its frosted glass.

I didn't even have time to ring the bell before the door slowly and silently opened.

I distinguished a hand with parchment-like black fingers on it. The door opened wider, unveiling half of a body then finally a peaceful and affable face topped with curly gray hair.

The voice that greeted me before I said a word was both soft, relaxed, and enigmatic.

"You took your time, Miss Blackstone… Come in."

CHAPTER 71
Fiction versus reality

I WAS STANDING THERE, on Melissa Westbrook's front porch, stupefied by her first sentence.

The lady, who must have been at least sixty-five, showed me into her small condo, identical to all the others in the street.

I finally was able to get a few words out.

"Excuse me? You know who I am? You were expecting me? That's crazy, I..."

My words were lost in my throat and Melissa smiled.

"Come in. Miss Blackstone, we've got a lot of things to say to each other. I'm sure that you've got tons of questions for me. Would you like something cool to drink? It's so darn hot right now. I nearly never leave my air-conditioned home. I've got a good thirst-quenching lemonade that I make myself if that could interest you."

I thanked her, accepted her offer of a cold drink

and we both went to her living room where there were two armchairs on both sides of a coffee table with a doily on it, that perhaps she'd crocheted herself. The air conditioning felt good, even a bit cold and I shivered. I noticed that Melissa, used to staying inside, had a shawl over her shoulders. I nearly asked her to lend me one too.

When she went into what I thought was the only other room on the ground floor, the kitchen, I looked around, and curiously felt uneasy. Like a sensation of *déjà-vu*, without being able to put my finger on the when nor the why of it.

When she returned with a tray with a carafe and two glasses on it, that feeling had already gone away. She put it down on the table, filled the two glasses and handed one to me before sitting down in the armchair across from me.

"What a story!" she said with a deep sigh. "Where should I begin?"

"Why didn't you contact the police earlier, knowing that little Jabaree was in danger? There's no way you couldn't have known about that. It was all over on TV, the radio and internet. Plus there are calls for witnesses all over the country! We had to launch a missing person's alert for you. Because you're a key witness for what happened to Shondra Wallace."

"That's true. A key witness. Shondra and I were as close as your five fingers in your hand. Inseparable."

What a horrible image, I thought about little Jabaree's five fingers... Melissa continued.

"I don't have a TV or a computer, you know. I sometimes listen to the radio when I'm cooking something in the kitchen, but not always. I like baking and making stews, things like that. All that to say that it took me a while to know what was going on."

"But once you knew…"

"Miss, you must know that in real life, things aren't always clear between what they really are, and the way people tell them to us… And that's even truer in the world of cinema and movies! Fiction versus reality. Or when they meet in the middle. So, Karen, where do you want to start? Can I call you Karen?"

"Of course, Mrs. Westbrook."

"Please call me Melissa. No 'Misses' between us. Maybe you can start by telling me what you know about this case and what you don't. I'll probably be able to fill in lots of things that are missing. Please, go ahead."

As I was used to conducting interviews, I welcomed Melissa's proposal. I was on the point of taking my notebook out of my bag, but decided I didn't need to. Everything was fresh and relatively clear in my mind. I summed up everything I knew or still didn't know for her.

"After all my cross-checking and verifications, I was able to draw up a chronology that seems realistic to me. On June 1st, 1988, Shondra disappeared in Lone Pine, while shooting a new movie, *The Coyote-Woman of the Desert*. It was produced by David Apfenstein, directed by Brad Purcell at first and then after by Peter Lundgren, after the producer and Purcell had a falling out, undoubtedly about Shondra. The shooting was halted. No one knew what happened to the actress. At that time she was pregnant. I was able to determine that in reality, she'd asked the Paiutes-Shoshones tribe to take her in and she stayed there for a couple of months and had her baby there, a male child, but I don't know his name. Then not too many months after she gave birth, Shondra died and was buried in accordance with their Indian rituals. The baby was raised and breastfed by other mothers in the tribe. Then, a woman, who was the spitting image of Shondra, came to the reservation and took the child. I concluded that this lady could have been Shondra's standby and stuntwoman in her movies, especially for riding. And that lady does seem to be you, Melissa."

She didn't reply to that straightaway.

"That's something I can't deny."

"So you're the one who took that little baby, Shondra's son."

"That also is true, Karen. You did some pretty good work reaching that conclusion."

The retired stuntwoman and standby smiled maliciously. She seemed delighted to be dilly-dallying and teasing me with her evasive answers. I was ready to explode!

"Melissa, are you going to tell me what came of the baby? The child that, you can say, was sort of yours, sort of your adoptive son. What's his name? What does he do? Where is he now?"

Melissa Westbrook nodded as I was reeling off my list of questions. She closed her eyes a few seconds before answering me.

"You're partially right: the child I took in Lone Pine is a bit mine. Or became it, you could say. I owed it to Shondra, we'd concluded a secret pact…"

CHAPTER 72
The background

Los Angeles, the same day

An hour after Karen Blackstone had set off for Las Vegas, there was an unexpected development in the media. Inspector Crimson was one of the first people to see the new video that Jabaree Smith's kidnappers had posted.

One that was quite similar to the previous ones, with the young boy sitting on a stool, clutching his stuffed animal, a little rabbit, against his chest.

There however was one difference and the investigators noticed it.

A masked man was standing behind the child. Probably the same one. He was standing behind Jabaree's back with his hands on Jabaree's shoulders, and the child, probably paralyzed by fear, didn't budge.

This time it wasn't the child who spoke. On the contrary, he was silent, his lips pursed till they were white, whereas the kidnapper spoke with a digitally transformed voice.

Video of Jabaree Smith, received on June 12, 2024 at 4:35 pm PST.

The man, with a gesture meant to be affectionate, pats the child's shoulders. During those interminable seconds, they are silent. As if the man is waiting until the camera begins to shoot. Or like an actor waiting for the assistant director's "Action," then the start signal "*The Kidnapping of Jabaree Smith, Scene 4, Take 1*" before reciting his text.

"This will be our last press release to the police authorities and of course, the general public.

Why the last? Simply because after this one, we won't need anymore. Everything will have been said, revealed, understood.

As everyone knows, a *cinéma-vérité* will be, released on June 15th at midnight to be exact, available on all streaming platforms. The entire world will finally discover the TRUTH about Shondra Wallace's disappearance, that unfortunate actress that everyone forgot, though she was so gifted, but who Hollywood didn't know how to promote. forcing her, undoubtedly, to have made the worst mistake.

Who's guilty in this case? Hollywood's tiny world? You must be aware that Hollywood is a machine that generates stars sometimes, but more often than not, one that crushes vocations. How many contenders for how few successful ones? How little glory for so many who drown?

Shondra was crushed by the system, you must know this! She died because she didn't succeed in twinkling amongst the other stars in Hollywood's skies, a meteor lost in the middle of a huge galaxy. A shooting star who burned out too quickly. Metaphors like that could go on for pages, but there's only one reality left: her disappearance, then her death.

Luckily, the lights didn't go out for everyone, and in the hearts and bodies of some people, she is still shining.

It's now time to bring her story to

THE WHOLE WORLD AND MAKE HER SHINE BRIGHTLY AGAIN.

THAT'S WHY I'M HERE. IT'S THE MISSION OF MY EXISTENCE.

THE SAME IS TRUE FOR JABAREE. THIS SMALL CHILD YOU SEE IN FRONT OF YOU (RIGHT THEN HIS HANDS TENDERLY CARESS THE BOY'S KINKY HAIR), IS THE EMBODIMENT, THE VECTOR EARMARKED TO FULFILL THIS NOBLE MISSION. CONTRARY TO SHONDRA, THIS YOUNG BOY IS FAMOUS, A STAR RECOGNIZED BY HIS PEERS AND THE GENERAL PUBLIC. THE ONLY ONES WHO REALLY COUNT!

SO, LADIES AND GENTLEMEN FROM THE MEDIA, THE POLICE AND THE FBI, FROM THE WORLD OF CINEMA, AND ALL OF YOU WATCHING THIS, ALL THAT'S LEFT IS TO DISCOVER ONE DETAIL TO UNDERSTAND ALL OF THIS. A MINUTE DETAIL, BUT ONE THAT WILL LEAD YOU TO US. OPEN YOUR EYES...

NOW. OTHERWISE..."

THAT WAS ALL the man said. He lowered his masked face towards Jabaree's and in a tender though unsettling gesture, kissed the child's cheek loudly.

Then the recording stopped though the frozen image remained on the screen.

Crimson mulled things over, seething, his brain cells pedaling as fast as possible.

He suddenly asked himself a question, nearly shouting.

"We recorded that video, right? Is there a replay?"

"What's going on, Jonas?" asked his colleague Payton, intrigued by his worried tone.

"I want to see it again. Can you find it quickly?"

After a few phone calls, especially to the news station, Crimson was finally able to watch the video again. He stood right next to the screen on the wall to observe it meticulously. A *minute detail*, the kidnapper had said, would allow them to localize them. Jonas knew that the devil hid in details, one of his instructor's favorite sentences when he was at police school. That man had taught him that often investigations were solved because of a tiny detail, a little nothing, something that generally is easily overlooked.

He suddenly jumped, pointing at the screen.

"Hit the pause button! There! Look! Out of the picture window, behind the man's left shoulder. In the background!"

"City lights at night."

"But not just any city," Crimson said. "Look, you guys don't recognize anything?"

"Well, it's not Los Angeles anyway," one of his officers tried.

"No. See that tower? Diane, you saw it with me too, the other day."

She suddenly understood.

"It's the Stratosphere Tower!"

"Right, Diane. A thousand one hundred and fifty

feet high! The tallest towner in the west of the States and..."

"Las Vegas!"

"Everyone get in your cars!" ordered Crimson, taking off first.

CHAPTER 73
One of them

It was now completely dark in Las Vegas. At night, the city seemed to be even more sensational than during the day, enshrouded in thousands of bright blinking lights of all colors.

Through Melissa Westbrook's window, while she was telling me about what happened in the 80s, my eyes were attracted to the palaces, the towers, one higher than the next one, including the famous Stratosphere Tower, the highest one in the city.

"You could say that Shondra and I sealed a pact," the former stuntwoman continued. "It was until we died. Don't believe that I was simply her standby, her stuntwoman in movies. We were like two sisters, two twin soul sisters."

I could feel how sincere she was!

"It's true that you look alike."

Melissa laughed softly, or was it ironically?

"Ah! How many times have I heard malicious

gossipers affirm that all Black people look alike, or all Asians look the same, or Indians look like other Redskins? As if Whites all look completely different! The color of your skin, what nonsense! How many dramas stem from this type of primary racism? Everyone's heart is the same color! The blood flowing through our veins is composed of the same cells! It's so tragic that humans only consider others through their appearance, without caring about what each person has inside of them... Anyway, pitying the human race is to no avail, no one's going to change. I'll continue."

"Yes, I totally agree with you. Tell me about your secret pact."

"Let's say it was more of a secret than a pact. Or that the pact consisted in never revealing the secret. About Shondra's pregnancy. You must be wondering who the father was."

"That would be useful for my research."

"I understand. First of all and despite the rumors that were spread at that time, the child was not David Apfenstein's. Even though he did take advantage of Shondra's candor, at the beginning, when she still accepted sleeping with famous people to penetrate the world of Hollywood cinema, one that's often a professional vacuum. Apfenstein wasn't the only sex blackmailer, unfortunately. But I'm a hundred percent sure that he wasn't the father."

"So what about Brad Purcell? He admitted that they were a couple for quite a while."

Melissa smiled.

"Good old Brad. A dreamer. He wasn't a bad guy. Easy to manipulate and under Apfenstein's control. It's true that they'd fought over my friend. Between Brad and her, I think they sincerely did love each other, though both knew that it was something that could never last. And in the world of cinema, there are very few couples that do last! They shoot movies with so many actors, they give each other fake kisses, pretend to make passionate love below the sheets, have to make their viewers think that all this is true, and finally end up believing it themselves. Fiction then becomes reality... up until the next movie when you change partners. Then it starts all over again. Hollywood is undoubtedly the most gigantic exchange club in the world," concluded Melissa, satisfied with her formula.

"So Brad wasn't the father's child either. Who was?"

Melissa briefly closed her eyes and then looked up at the ceiling, as to summon her souvenirs.

"We were friends, very good friends, you could say we were sisters, like I already told you. So you must think I know everything about her. And she knew everything about me. That's almost true. Yet, some things remained unsaid between us. Even though we did tell each other so many things. And I can affirm that no man was the father of her child back then."

"Why did you say 'back then?' What happened?"

"Of course, we weren't always in each other's hair, our respective movies took us right and left, either in Hollywood or Lone Pine, or all over the country actually, sometimes even abroad. I'm sure I missed some of her... her brief encounters, should I say. But there's one thing that I didn't miss, and that she admitted to me, and that's that she was fond of both sexes."

"You mean..."

"You understood me Karen. As years went by and she had more and more unhappy experiences with this guy or that one, little by little Shondra drew away from men. Meaning that at that time, she was more attracted by women – whether or not they were actresses – and more particularly by *one of them*..."

When she said that, Melissa lowered her head and sighed.

CHAPTER 74
Panorama

IN THE SCORCHING DESERT HEAT, the Los Angeles police cars cut through that black night, lit up only by a slim crescent of the moon and a myriad of bright stars. In the middle of the Californian desert, without any urban light pollution, it seemed to them that there were ten times as many stars. On the other hand though, Inspector Crimson's morale was far from twinkling as brightly as the stars above him. He hadn't stopped ranting against his own incompetence since they'd left the Hollywood station.

"What an asshole that Magloire is! He's been pulling the wool over our eyes – over my eyes – since the very beginning! Since the day that Jabaree vanished, he's been faking it, pretending we're spectators watching one of his stupid movies!"

"Relax, Jonas," said Diane Payton, who was driving. "We couldn't have known despite his inconsistencies and repeated lies. How could we have imagined even one second that he was a part of all that? Hells bells, he's almost his father!"

"Yup. And Janice, his mother, blindly trusted her husband... Jesus Christ, those Hollywood people in showbiz! Nutjobs! Step on it, we still got a ways to go."

Right then Crimson's phone rang.

"Shit! The Feds," muttered the policeman though he picked up. "Yeah, McCormick?"

"So very nice of you to have let us know you were leaving for Nevada, Crimson," said the FBI agent ironically. "Where you heading?"

"To kick Ruppert Magloire's ass, that son of a bitch who's been playing us for days. He's a part of this and I know where he is. Or at least I understood where Jabaree Smith is."

"Where?"

"On his last video, I recognized one of Las Vegas's iconic towers through the window behind the kid and the masked man. I had a flash and remembered having seen the same panorama from the room where the clip was shot. I'm nearly sure it was in Magloire's villa in Vegas. That's where we're headed, Jabaree must be there."

The voice on the other end of the line got harsher.

"Crimson, don't fuck things up. Vegas isn't your jurisdiction. You don't have any right to intervene there. You have to alert your colleagues in that zone. Moreover, as a hostage has been taken, you'll also have to contact a SWAT squad. We still don't know the kidnappers' true intentions nor revindications, if they're armed, if they're thinking of blowing up the house and the kid with it. And the FBI has to be present too, this is clearly now a federal case. We'll be taking a jet. Got it? You don't do a thing without us!"

"Sure."

Jonas hung up in a poorly disguised movement of anger.

"Fuck 'em all!"

Though he wasn't happy about it, Crimson had no other options than to obey the federal agent's orders and comply with the legal procedures. If not, he could have been accused of irresponsibility, or procedural errors, or even worse than anything else, risk Jabaree's life in the case of a poorly coordinated assault without the support of specialists in a dangerous situation like this one was. He thus made a few calls.

While he was on his phone, he texted Karen, knowing that she was also in Vegas, with Melissa Westbrook.

> Karen, I think everything took place and will end in Vegas. I'm heading to Sin City. Take care. Jonas.

CHAPTER 75
A groupie

No one said a word in Melissa Westbrook's living room. She seemed to be thinking about the past, thinking about Shondra's liaison with a woman.

I was also quite dumbfounded by her revelations and needed a couple of seconds to formulate my next question.

"The woman that Shondra was in love with. Was it you?"

The former stuntwoman slowly shook her head, several times.

"I told you, Shondra and I were like two sisters, two soulmates. I'm not gonna hide the fact that yes, I was attracted by her, just as were other men and women who gravitated around her like flies with a hunk of meat. But in most cases, once love invites itself into friendship and two friends become lovers, that's when the problems start, and there's no more friendship. Just to say that despite the many temptations, we never spoiled our beautiful relationship for a few moments of carnal passion. No, the woman that Shondra was in love with was Lauren, and she was one of Apfenstein's makeup artists. They'd met at a party when we were shooting a movie. Lauren was agog with delight to see her favorite actress in real life and Shondra was stupefied to discover that someone was interested in her as an actress. Something happened between those two, a look, a few words, a couple of minutes in the makeup trailer. They met like that, on the sly, one following the other's career while standing back in the shadows. A true groupie, a fan. Little by little, they became lovers."

I jumped. There was a noise, like something had fallen on the floor, upstairs. Melissa raised her head quickly.

"My cat. He always jumps on the shelves. I can't even count the number of knickknacks he's broken."

She cleared her throat and took a sip of her homemade lemonade. I took advantage of her pause to glance at my phone, as I'd felt it vibrate a couple of minutes ago. A text message from Inspector Crimson saying that he was heading to Vegas. Unsettling.

"Was that their secret?" I asked Melissa Westbrook. "Your secret?"

"Partially. But you'll see that there's more to it. You have to understand though that a lesbian couple, though it wasn't that rare at that time, was something that would have hurt Shondra's career. Remember, we were back in the 80s, and that meant that it was just a few years after AIDS. And I'm not telling you anything new when I say that the gay community was harshly stigmatized."

"Mostly men though, right?"

"That's a popular misconception, Karen. Homosexual women were also targeted, as were drug addicts. The seventies with their sexual freedom were long gone. In 1985, when Shondra and Lauren met, Rock Hudson, one of the mythical stars of American western movies, the embodiment of a dominant male, also had a totally improbable coming out! A man. So just imagine a woman. Only Billie Jean King, the tennis player, made her bisexual preferences known back in 1981. So that was the situation back in the day."

I mentally assimilated little by little what Shondra Wallace's life must have been. Especially, besides a romantic idyll with another woman, there was another detail – and a big one you could say – that had to be taken into consideration. Which is what I said to Melissa.

"Plus there was the baby. But technically, I mean, two women..."

Melissa laughed.

"Ah! Karen, I see that you were a good student in your biology classes. It's true that for human beings and for the vast majority of most species here on earth, you need a male and a female to perpetuate the race. So, at first sight, for two women, it's just not gonna work. Unless?"

"Unless there's a gametes donation?"

"Exactly! A donor... Anonymous or not... and a partner who accepted that."

CHAPTER 76
Giant screens

A FEW MINUTES ago the jet turned off its two motors. On the runway, Agents McCormick and Gomez joined the men from the Las Vegas Metropolitan Police Department SWAT division, headed by Lieutenant Lance Fraser.

Crimson, Payton and their team hadn't yet arrived, but they'd all decided to meet directly near Ruppert Magloire's home, there where the inspector had snitched a bit of film in the projection room.

The local and federal teams were thus headed towards the outskirts of Sin City, one of them in an FBI car and the other in an armored vehicle, the SWAT's Lenco BearCat. The first SWAT teams were formed around 1965 to handle riot control and violent confrontations with criminals during the Watts riots in Los Angeles, as well as the North Hollywood shootout in 1997. How ironic could that be!

"You don't wanna wait for Inspector Crimson

before going in?" asked Lieutenant Fraser to Federal Agent McCormick.

"He'll catch up with us."

"But isn't he the one heading this investigation? And..."

"And nothing at all! As a federal agency, the FBI I'm representing is legitimately able to take the lead in this affair. Ever since the beginning Crimson has been lagging behind, losing precious time that could have allowed us to arrest the guilty parties before it was too late. We don't got enough time to wait for His Hollywood Highness! Go!"

AFTER HAVING DRIVEN for a couple of minutes in the artificial light-filled night – streetlights, neon lighting, strings of light, giant screens, flashing lights and lasers – just like Crimson a few days ago, the men discovered a hacienda type house in the middle of a large yard planted with palm trees, banana trees and other tropical plants. Here the desert had been taken over by a tropical environment, a debauchery of vegetation, undoubtedly costing a fortune in upkeep. They could see the Stratosphere Tower in Vegas's skyline.

The villa, however, was sleeping at the end of a long driveway, surrounded by impenetrable gates and walls, unless you used an armored vehicle to bust through them.

But that wouldn't have been the most discreet way of proceeding and would also tip off Jabaree's kidnappers, who they believed were in the hacienda. Light was coming through some of the windows upstairs. You could tell the hacienda was inhabited, though apparently calm.

"Out of your vehicles," Fraser ordered to his men. "We're going to try to sneak in. If we break the gate down with our BearCat, our little birdie might fly from his gilded cage."

One of the SWAT officers checked the gate to see if it was locked. It was, but that wasn't a problem for this elite squad used to overcoming more important pitfalls. Using their vast experience and skill sets, they quickly disabled the electronic lock and just had to push the gates towards the inside and continue on foot to the villa. Hidden by the nocturnal sky, the commando progressed silently. In a mere three minutes they were in front of the hacienda's porch.

"Three men behind, all the others go in through the front door."

They were all carrying advanced weaponry. One had a Colt M4A1 gun with a holographic view and a SureFire light system, another had a 12-gauge pump action shotgun that could break any recalcitrant door down, others had HK416 assault rifles, asphyxiant gas grenades, or just simple Tasers to electrically neutralize their targets. Dressed in black, wearing helmets, rangers, bulletproof vests, and above all, they all had irreproachable team coordination.

Much to their surprise, the front door wasn't

locked. One of the team members just turned the gilded doorknob and they were in.

Silent despite their equipment, the SWAT team members entered the huge modern house and spread out in the living room, their guns armed, scrutinizing each corner of the room. It was dark, but they had a bit of light coming from the stairwell.

Fraser made a gesture with his hand signaling the men to go upstairs.

One behind the other, each one covering their teammate, the ten men walked carefully up, step by step. It was completely silent upstairs. Though they'd seen lights, was the hacienda deserted?

At the end of the hall, there was another door, different from the others that were made from glass and wood. This one was upholstered with a type of brilliant black leather coating. Fraser immediately thought of an armored door or a soundproof one, like the ones used in psychiatric hospitals. An eerie silence reigned behind him. Was it the lull before the storm?

The SWAT lieutenant put the palm of his hand against the leather upholstered door. It didn't have a doorknob, just a simple lock dissimulated in a leather hem. Would they be needing a shotgun or a ramrod to get in? If so, they had to be ready to attack in less than a second, as soon as the door opened. Without knowing what they'd discover inside. How many men? Just Ruppert Magloire? Or had he also been kidnapped? And what about Jabaree in the middle of all that? There would certainly be shouts, noise, orders yelled out, stress, threats... and maybe shots fired. Blood?

But that door wasn't locked either and Fraser just pushed it open to enter the dark den.

The lieutenant only had a couple of seconds to understand the room, decor, those in it and the situation. Four stages: analyze, understand, decide, act.

Firstly, the surprise he hadn't been expecting. The commando saw a movie theater with several rows of leather seats, and in the middle of them, the back of a man. Only one man, watching the giant screen on the wall in front of him, without even jumping up with the sudden intrusion of the SWAT teams. There was a movie running, filling the room with background music that was supposed to generate fear in those watching it. The images, twenty-four per second, showed a young African-American lady running in the Amazonian jungle, followed by a masked man carrying a bloody machete...

"Ruppert Magloire, hands up!" shouted Agent McCormick, with his Glock 22 aimed directly at the movie director.

CHAPTER 77
Glamorous

THE PICTURE WAS BECOMING CLEARER in my mind as Melissa continued her story. Shondra was having a homosexual liaison in the midst of the AIDS health crisis and was also pregnant. Did that give her two good reasons to want to disappear? I summed things up.

"So she necessarily used in vitro fertilization then. Unless she had sexual intercourse with a man, voluntarily or not, and became pregnant?"

Those words sent me back to my own experience and I felt some painful cramps in my lower abdomen. I tried to concentrate on the actress's case.

"Who was the mysterious donor? Someone well known? Someone working with Shondra? A convenient biological father?"

There were several cases in point running through my mind. Melissa seemed to find it amusing to let me think about all the possibilities.

"It would have been a beautiful story, wouldn't it have, had the father been Brad or Peter! Or even better, Russel Eubanks..."

I'd already heard that name someplace! I needed a couple of seconds before my memory kicked in. I then recognized the face of that man I'd met in Watts a couple of days ago.

"Her first love, the one she left to try to break into Hollywood?"

"Himself. A beautiful fairy tale, right? But no, reality is rarely as romantic. She simply used medically assisted procreation with anonymous male gametes. Not quite as glamorous, right? But that's life. Shondra and Lauren, the lesbian couple, didn't have any other choices than being assisted by science. Medically assisted procreation was still in its baby steps at that time. Just imagine that situation... inseminating a homosexual woman? Never! Yet, that was what happened, but they had to be imaginative, hide, camouflage. When you knew the position that American legislators had, meaning that just mentioning two women in a couple, that was something that made the few hairs still remaining on the heads of the Republican senators stand on end. The Ronald Reagan era. Another ironic situation, right?"

I didn't immediately get what she was referring to.

"What do you mean?"

"Remember that before becoming president of the United States, Reagan also had a career that wasn't often fantastic as an actor. He mostly starred in pitiful westerns, just like Shondra Wallace! But I'm digressing here Karen. Finally, after several unsuccessful attempts, my friend got pregnant in 1988, just a couple of weeks before *The Coyote-Woman of the Desert* was to begin. You can easily imagine all her emotions. From an immense joy to becoming a mother, to forging a bond with Lauren by having a child, up until the fear of what others would say. A judgement that was biased by preconceived ideas about homosexuals. It was impossible for them to reveal what had taken place, to come out publicly. Even though Shondra wasn't as well-known as she would have liked to have been, she still was in the limelight."

"True!" I butted in. "But she still could have used the bit of a reputation she had to claim her preferences, her differences! Demonstrate for women's rights, for the gay community, things like that."

"We were in the 80s, Karen! Not in 2024. Back in 1981, when Billie Jean King was publicly outed, she was shamed, pointed at. Her sponsors threw her out. She had a depression and thought of quitting her job. It was only much later that she could fight for women's rights and LGBT rights as well. And in 2009, Barack Obama awarded her the Presidential Medal of Freedom for what she did for women and homosexuals! And I even learned that recently in France, President Macron gave her the Legion of Honor... It's a whole different world today. But back in the day, the only alternative Shondra could think of was disappearing. Hiding to have her baby without being hassled. In

Lone Pine, at the Paiutes-Shoshones Reservation. You know what comes next."

"I do," I said, pensive and full of compassion for the former actress who passed away in the Indian reservation.

Melissa got up, groaning, a hand on her lower back and walked to the window where she looked out over Sin City's luminous skyline.

Was she thinking about the sins Shondra and Lauren committed?

She surprised me though.

"That's not all though," she said with a tired voice. "Added to the double shame of their not quite legal pregnancy and their homosexual relationship, my friend and her lover had another problem..."

CHAPTER 78
That's all, Folks

"Turn that fucking projector off!" shouted Lieutenant Fraser in Magloire's private cinema.

Between those shouting out orders and the movie that was being projected with its horribly loud soundtrack, there was a stressful auditive maelstrom.

One of the men in the commando team rushed to the projection room as soon as he saw where it was, behind the opening on the wall where the luminous beams were coming from.

During that time, downstairs, Magloire didn't budge, his face riveted to the screen where he was devouring Nikki LaToya's frightened face in *The Bloody Machete 2*, starring Shondra Wallace. The movie director was now the target of the men surrounding him, some on the leather armchairs, others in the aisles. The cyclopic eyes of a dozen arms were blinking at him.

IN THE ROOM filled with rolls of film on the floor, the SWAT team member found the projector running, with yards of cellulose films exposed. How can I turn this thing off? he must have said to himself. He finally found a large red button and slammed his fist on it. Emergency shutdown. That's all, Folks!

IN THE PRIVATE THEATER, the screen was now black.

A churchlike silence replaced the noise.

Magloire seemed to be coming out of a daydream.

"Where's Jabaree?" barked Agent McCormick.

No reaction. A haggard look.

"You hear me Magloire? What did you do with the kid? Where is he? Where are your accomplices?"

The man, suddenly concerned about what was going on around him, turned his head from right to left, looked at the rifles aimed at him, at the furious eyes of the elite police officers and seemed to realize that he was being questioned.

"Jabaree? I don't know. I don't know anymore."

McCormick was furious, ready to crack.

"You think we're idiots Magloire? Quit playing

with us. The life of a kid is at stake! Your wife's child, Jesus Christ! So move your ass and spit it out. You were the one behind this little game, weren't you? You're the one hiding behind the name of Alan Smithee, right? You got stuff you wanna tell us. Why wait until June 15th? Tell us! And now! Where did you hide Jabaree?"

Ruppert's lips trembled, his eyes filled with tears. He mumbled, shook his head with weariness and fatigue.

"Jabaree's not here. Don't bother looking. I'm alone. This is my sanctuary here."

As he had finished his last sentence, they heard a muffled noise downstairs. A door was slammed, footsteps on the stairs.

The men turned around at the same time, looking at the movie theater's soundproof door.

Through the door's frame they saw a silhouette they all recognized.

CHAPTER 79
That eclectic cast

I DECIDED to let Melissa finish her story without interrupting. She turned from the window with its view of the Las Vegas skyline and looked at me.

"Besides what I told you earlier, Shondra and Lauren had something else going against them. When you're lesbian, you're soon to be parents of a child conceived in a test tube, plus you're an illegitimate and mixed couple..."

"Mixed?"

"That's right. Lauren was as white as a sheet, see the picture? Shondra and her, they were like yin and yang! Life-sized checker pieces. With that cocktail, and Karen, and I'm sure you'll understand, those two women were never able to live their lives in public and one of them had to disappear. First of all, voluntarily, then... then she died. That was a permanent disappearance, and eternal one."

She had trouble finishing her sentence. When she

raised her head, Melissa's red and moist eyes touched me. I could feel how she was still affected by the loss of her best friend.

"But that Lauren lady," I remarked, "why didn't she pick up the child – I could even say it was her son – in Lone Pine?"

"Because Lauren died in a car accident on Christmas Eve, in 1988. So, because of the promise I'd made to Shondra, I drove to the Indian reservation, and I raised her child."

"What ever happened to him? He must be thirty-five now, right? Where is he?"

Once again noise came from upstairs. The cat who must have been having a ball.

"Six feet under, him to, like they say in westerns. You could say I'm the last one standing from that eclectic cast." Melissa looked at me with a strained smile.

"What was his name? I don't think you ever told me."

"You're right, Karen. I did omit that detail, and you'll see, it's essential in the comprehension on the events that you're concerned with now. Shondra and Lauren called their son... Dwayne."

An electroshock. How one word, one first name, can be the missing link between those two June firsts, 1988 and 2024. I needed confirmation.

"Dwayne? Like Dwayne Smith, Janice Lovelace's first husband, and Jabaree Smith's biological father?"

"That's right," Melissa assured me. "One more missing person from that cast, may he rest in peace."

"So Jabaree is then Shondra Wallace's biological grandson…"

My head turned towards the stairs when I said that. Another noise. Smothered, delicate, yes, but enough to alert my ears.

I saw an object rolling down the stairs, step after step. A silky, furry object with two black marbles in the place of its eyes. But that seemed to be staring at me.

CHAPTER 80
The stage and its characters

JONAS CRIMSON and Diane Payton joined the Feds and the SWAT team, coming down from the hacienda's projection room.

Right then the inspector's phone rang, just before entering the room where a couple of seconds later, he wouldn't have had any network at all, as that room had been designed to be hermetic to any electronic interference.

"Karen?"

"Where are you, Inspector?"

"In Vegas, like you! At Magloire's place."

"Well then get yourself over to Melissa Westbrook's, and do it now! And if you can, bring Magloire with you, this is going to interest him too."

Then she hung up.

IN JUST A COUPLE OF MINUTES, a part of the police force, including the Feds and the SWAT team, headed out towards Cheyenne Avenue. Some of the SWAT team members stayed behind to make sure that there were no others in the hacienda. A meticulous investigation would subsequently prove that Magloire had been alone. His confession, obtained later, would explain why.

And in the meanwhile, in Inspector Crimson's backseat, Ruppert, carefully watched by Diane Payton and FBI agent Gomez, hung his head down, nodding with the potholes on the roads in the outskirts of Vegas, trying to ease the pain caused by the handcuffs on his hands behind his back.

The sirens were hurling at the moon like famished coyotes, their flashing lights adjusted to code three with their red, yellow and blue lights, allowing the policemen to rush through traffic and lights without even slowing down.

Crimson was hoping it would be a mere matter of minutes before they arrived.

~

THE TWO MARBLES from the stuffed little rabbit looked at me as if they wanted to speak, to tell me the truth about these two disappearances that I now understood better.

I was eager to hear Ruppert Magloire's version and hoped the inspector would soon arrive with him.

While waiting I looked at Melissa, who, like me, had followed the white rabbit's descent down the stairs. The little animal was now on the bottom step, disarticulated, its long ears hanging down onto the tile floor of the living room where we were.

On the landing at the top of the stairs, I saw two bare feet. Two little light brown feet.

∽

DOORS WERE SLAMMED in front of Melissa Westbrook's well-lit house, where three vehicles had parked, their sirens slashing through the tranquility of that night in Nevada's desert.

In just a few seconds, the policemen were at the doorstep. Without knocking, they opened the door. Lawrence McCormick was the first one in, immediately followed by Ruppert Magloire that Crimson was shoving, pushing on his handcuffs behind his back.

"Get going."

∽

THINGS WERE HAPPENING all over the place. Firstly, policemen from Hollywood, the FBI, the Vegas SWAT team and Ruppert Magloire had all rushed into the house. Plus, Jabaree Smith was slowly coming down the steps, barefoot and wearing his pajamas. His eyes were still half-closed.

"What's going on?" asked the young actor, with a

raspy, sleep-filled voice, looking down at all of those now in the house.

And Melissa and I were in the middle of the cast.

"Everything's fine, sweetie," Melissa assured him. "The nightmare is over."

Jabaree began to run towards Melissa, but Diane Payton stopped him.

"One minute!" she said. "We have to figure this all out. Understand who is who and who did what..."

Crimson then pushed the still handcuffed movie director onto an armchair.

"Now you have to explain, Magloire! Because this clusterfuck has gone too far. For what? And why?"

The movie director winced, his mouth twisted in a hateful smirk.

"Can't you take these things off my wrists? I'm not going to attack anyone. I'm not dangerous:"

"Not dangerous?" the inspector retorted. "Maybe not, but oblivious and inconscient, that's for sure. You don't even realize the consequences of your actions. You generated fear in the general public, in your public, as you like to call your fans. People could even have died because they were too affected by your fake kidnapping. And I'm not even talking about, as you can see here, about all the cops and intelligence services that were mobilized because of you during these two weeks. It's not pretty, Magloire. You know, you're gonna do time. I'm going to keep you handcuffed, that's going to help you think about what you did."

"But what? I didn't hurt anyone. All I wanted was to do some good!"

"You're nuts. What good could come from your stupid staging?"

"Ever since the very first day, all I wanted was to rehabilitate Shondra Wallace's memory, that's honorable, isn't it? This little boy's grandmother. It was for her, for both of them, that I imagined this stratagem."

"Jesus Christ!" said McCormick, "you had to set up a fake kidnapping? You didn't even think of making a movie, not even for a second? That movie that you were planning on showing on June 15th wouldn't have been enough?"

Magloire sniffed noisily, still haughty.

"Because you think that would have been enough, that people would have watched it? In 1988, when Shondra mysteriously disappeared, no one gave a damn! Just think, a common, second-rate actress, starring in pitiful B-series movies."

Melissa, sitting in one of the armchairs, nodded, agreeing with what Ruppert had just said. He continued.

"The poor girl was no one. When she was young, she dreamed of becoming the new Pam Grier, she'd given her entire life, her heart, her body and her soul to movies, and that was how she was thanked? She never had an Oscar, that's for sure! Or unless, a posthumous one: The Oscar of the Forgotten Actress! No, her career didn't impress anyone, her death didn't stir anyone. So how could a movie pay homage to her? No one would have been interested in it either. That's why I concocted that synopsis. Having Hollywood's kid-star go missing, the one the whole world knows and adores. A young ten-year-old star who's kidnapped, yeah, that would create a buzz. Even more so now, with social networking and the internet to spread news. I was sure that the whole world, headed by the United States, would be riveted to this event. That way, we'd make them pay attention, they'd tremble for Jabaree, they'd want to know the whys and wherefores of the June 1st mystery, someone would go back to dig up the past, would target this actress who was so unfairly forgotten! Shondra Wallace would be on everyone's lips, in everyone's mind, finally in everyone's hearts... Those were my good intentions."

"Yeah, sure," the inspector muttered, "we've already heard crap like that: the road to hell is paved with good intentions. Magloire, you're crazy. That was a despicable thing to do. You dragged Jabaree, an innocent kid, nearly your own son, into your delirium! Was your wife Janice part of the plan?

"No. She never would have agreed to something like that."

"And you didn't even stop to think for a single second that the kidnapping of her son could have killed her? Killed her from fright and affliction? You don't have a heart."

"All I thought about was what good I could do," admitted Ruppert with a sincerely sad voice.

A repenting one?

"And nothing, no remorse at all, could have stopped you in this insane act? Yet, I'd imagine that you spent days or even weeks preparing and designing your Machiavellian plan. Because yes, even Nicolas Machiavel wouldn't have imagined something as crazy as this. But I have to admit, but that doesn't make you any less guilty, that the scenario was well planned. Meticulously thought out and diabolically put in place. Tell us about that, Ruppert."

"Where should I start?

"Explain to us how the *fake* kidnapping of Jabaree took place on June 1st. I'm sure we're gonna learn a lot..."

CHAPTER 81
Synopsis

EVERYONE IN MELISSA WESTBROOK'S living room, and especially me, was hanging on Ruppert Magloire's every word.

The little boy, sitting cross-legged on the floor, was also listening, though strangely absent and disconnected.

"We planned it all together, Jabaree and me," he began after a moment of silence. "Sort of like when we're shooting a movie. The actor follows what the director says, something he was used to doing. He'd learned his role by heart, repeating it dozens of times so it would seem real. You must admit that this kid is an exceptional actor! It's not for nothing that he fills theaters in the whole country and all over the civilized world. The staging concretely began on the gala party night. When it was drawing to an end, a bit before midnight, Jabaree played the role of an exhausted kid and pretended to fall asleep in an armchair, where everyone who was still there could see him."

I looked over at Crimson, who seemed to be confirming that this version of the facts explained how all the witnesses bought into the act and their misunderstanding. What followed was similar and left us dumbfounded.

"Then," continued Magloire in a neutral voice, as if he were reading a synopsis, "I delicately picked up Jabaree and carried him upstairs so he could sleep, and we also had several witnesses here, all useful for our little conspiracy. I put him to bed, tucked him in, and then went back downstairs. After that, luck would have it that someone actually walked into the room where he saw Jabaree sleeping peacefully. But he was mistaken, as Jabaree had already left."

"How?"

"Well, Jabaree followed the next scenario in our little plan right to the letter. I'm repeating myself, this kid was born an actor, it's in his blood. When I left the bedroom upstairs, I looked around to make sure no one was in the hall, and then he left, after having dissimilated some pillows under the sheets and covers so that it would look like he was sleeping. Then he walked to the emergency exit in the building, one that we'd used before and that led directly to the underground parking lot. He had a double of my Corvette keys in his pocket."

"Damn it!" the inspector said, his jaws clenched, "the lights blinking half an hour before you left. One more of your lies, right? You weren't the one who went down to your car to get a scenario for your producer. It was Jabaree!"

"Yes, it was him, right Jabaree?"

The child merely nodded. Magloire continued.

"He opened the car, made sure he hadn't been detected by the CCTV cameras and hid in the trunk with his little stuffed rabbit. He closed the trunk, then waited a couple of seconds as I'd told him to, then locked the car with the electronic key, which was what caused the lights to blink and that's what you saw, Inspector. He is a brave kid. Being locked in a trunk over half an hour, in complete darkness, in a deserted parking lot, at midnight. He's already bold, our Jabaree."

"You could have given him a flashlight," said Agent McCormick, ironically. "Your plan wasn't that well prepared."

"Really? Not well prepared? All of you fell for it. You, the Feds, you, Crimson, and you Miss Investigative Journalist. The whole lot!" said Magloire triumphantly, happy to have fooled all of them. "You only saw smoke and mirrors. Cinema's fine art of illusions!"

I could tell the inspector was biding his time, on the brink of strangling Ruppert. He forced him to get back on track.

"Magloire, you better stop trying to pull the wool on us, that might help you not have any additional problems in court. Some friendly advice! Keep going!

Then you went down to the parking lot, you took your car, and after that – what you told us after we forced you and what we did that night together – is that also an illusion? More smoke and mirrors?"

The producer smirked with a mocking grin. He seemed to be thinking over the response.

"Sometimes, when you're shooting a movie, you have to modify your plans, adapt the scenario, shooting one scene rather than the one you'd planned on. An actor who's sick, a camera that broke down, rain when you needed sunshine, stuff like that. Let's just say that on the day we did our reconstitution, I did take you for a little ride... I tweaked the replay! To tell you the truth, Jabaree and I didn't go to Pasadena and Malibu that night, we went straight here to Sin City, here to our hacienda. That's where we were when I disappeared too, without informing anyone, even my wife."

"And that's where you shot all your videos that went on air after," Crimson said, understanding what had happened, as we all now did. "I recognized Vegas's skyline with the Strat Tower at the last minute."

"Because I wanted you to, Inspector! Ever since the beginning, I'm the one holding the reins, dealing the cards!"

I couldn't stand Magloire's megalomania and just like Jonas, was ready to get up and slap him in the face. Tell him how much I hated him. I couldn't admit to myself that he'd cooked up a scheme like that and dragged little Jabaree along in his diabolical wake. We let him continue his Machiavellian tale though and explain how they filmed each scene one after the other. Some of them had required several shots before validating the best one, the one who would make tears well up in the eyes of its viewers, the one that would generate the best buzz. Also the one that would cause the most problems for the investigators. Something that worked as all of us were worried sick about the mortal countdown he had set up.

"Once I was happy with each scene, I programmed their successive distribution on the days and times I wanted to, all of that using secure servers that were untraceable. Meaning you couldn't find me before I was ready, before I decided you would."

"Now you think you're the master of time? Soon the master of the world? Playing God, who knows?"

"All filmmakers, just like all authors, are the masters or gods of their characters."

CHAPTER 82
The pseudonym

"Magloire, you are completely insane," Crimson ranted. "You can no longer distinguish fiction from reality. For you, Jabaree is just a character in a movie?"

"No! His character was just a way of making people aware of Shondra Wallace. He was my weapon! A powerful virtual weapon. A weapon that hit spectators right in their hearts. Him and his little stuffed rabbit, what a moving duo, don't you think?"

I looked over at the child with his stuffed animal. I had to admit that yes, he wasn't wrong there. Like you wanted to gobble them up, they were so cute.

"Magloire, you're making me want to barf," said the inspector. "You're saying that you spent three days in your hacienda, you shot all the video clips and also at that time you edited the *cinéma-vérité* movie that you slotted to be released on June 15th using Alan Smithee as a pseudonym. When my colleague and I visited your hacienda and I went into the projection room, where there were snippets of reels of film all over the floor, that was where you were working, right?"

The filmmaker raised his head, stuck his chin out in a stuck up pose that didn't do anything to raise the opinion I'd had about him. And I could see in Crimson's eyes that he was equally disgusted.

"A good job wasn't it! You'll see, the movie is sensational! My masterpiece, undoubtedly. And especially, it truly does pay homage – and finally does – to the late Shondra Wallace."

There was a detail that intrigued me. I butted in.

"According to my information and research, all the rushes from *The Coyote-Woman of the Desert* were destroyed in the fire in David Apfenstein's warehouses back in 1988. If so, how did you insert scenes from that movie into the one you said you made?"

"Where did you get that information from?"

"From Apfenstein himself, and it was confirmed by sources who love B-series movies, called MovieGeeks."

Much to my astonishment, Magloire burst out laughing.

"Apfenstein? But Miss, that old man was lying through his teeth! Just like most people like him, movie producers, lying is a sport and they're experts in it. If not, how could they make money? They're all opportunistic, cheaters, and con artists! The only thing they're interested in is profit. I'm persuaded that he sold the takes for *The Coyote-Woman* and got good money for them before his warehouse got burned up, and he probably even started the fire himself. As for me, I acquired the takes on – well let's call it – the black market or a specialized parallel market. You know, there's all sorts of stuff sold there, including some things you wouldn't want your kids to see, if you get where I'm going."

"We do, thank you," Crimson interrupted him, looking at Jabaree whose ears were hearing everything though he wasn't a part of the conversation.

The child had become a normal ten-year-old kid now, one who was tired, who was wearing pajamas and not an actor who had been employed for underhanded motives by his step-father and was now dozing off. The inspector noticed this.

"So, I think it's time for us to take Jabaree back to his mother. At this time of night she must really be fretting."

"Jabaree, you want to come with me?" said Diane Payton in a maternal voice.

The child opened his eyes, rubbed his hand on them while slowly getting up.

"I wanna stay with Granny Melissa," he stammered, running towards her open arms.

This scene, one that megalomanic Magloire hadn't written, moved everyone in the room. I understood how much that lady who, thirty-five years ago had adopted Dwayne Smith, you could say, Shondra Wallace's son, could love the kid that she considered as her adoptive grandson, and rightly so. They hugged each other for a long moment while the policemen took Ruppert Magloire out to drive him to the police station and have him give an official audition.

Finally Jabaree and Melissa let each other go and Diane Payton took the child by the hand. Tears were slowly falling from the old lady's eyes.

"Don't worry, sweetie," she said to him tenderly, "you know you can come back whenever you want with your mom. My door will always be wide open for you. So go now, it's late."

In just a few minutes, Melissa Westbrook's house emptied out.

The SWAT squad was the first to leave, as it was evident that Magloire didn't represent any clear and imminent danger. They'd only stayed till now because they were spectators and wanted to understand why the filmmaker had done all of this, his confessions and motivations.

Then Agents McCormick and Gomez said goodbye to Melissa and went to their car.

They were followed by Crimson who escorted Ruppert Magloire to the Fed's car, pushed him into the back seat and then sat next to him before they all set off to the local FBI station where his formal interview would be held.

After that, Agent Payton, Jabaree and his little rabbit left, followed by Melissa who waved him off.

. . .

I THEN WAS ALONE with Melissa in this now silent room. I was getting ready to leave too. I felt though that I'd forgotten something. A little detail that I wanted to shed light on but couldn't remember. Sometimes that's how the cookie crumbles. Or doesn't. Unless my memory would come back before departing from Sin City.

I was picking up my bag that I'd left in the living room, on the floor next to the coffee table where our glasses of lemonade were still half full, as we'd been interrupted by both Jabaree and the police.

What an evening!

I picked up my purse and walked to the door.

"Thank you for your cooperation, Melissa."

The lady went with me to the door, and then held out her hand.

Right then her shall slipped from her shoulders and fell to the ground.

My eyes were drawn to a detail, and I stopped, stupefied.

I knew I had to say something.

But it seemed that my brain refused to admit what my eyes saw.

How could that be possible?

CHAPTER 83
Rewind!

"That can't be possible," I stammered at last after a few seconds of stupor.

"It can," Melissa Westbrook simply replied.

Maybe I should have been calling her Shondra Wallace as I saw a bunny tattooed on her right shoulder...

"But... How? Why? Melissa, tell me that you had this tattoo done as a souvenir of your friend."

She slowly shook her head.

"No."

"Can you explain?"

"Of course. You deserve the right to know everything, Karen. Except, starting now, you can call me Shondra, it'll be easier. Come back in, we'll finish up our lemonade."

We went back into the living room with its coffee table and comfortable armchairs.

"So everything you told me tonight is completely false? You're a liar too?"

A contented smile barred Melissa-Shondra's face (mentally I can't decide what to call her). She affirmed the opposite though.

"No, Karen, I didn't lie at all. Each word I said tonight was strictly true. Everything happened exactly like I told you, whoever the persons were. To understand how every event took place, I can only give you this piece of advice, Karen: *Rewind*!"

"What?"

"It's simple. Just think back on our conversation tonight, turn the needles of the clock back and *replace Shondra by Melissa*. And vice-versa: replace 'she' by 'I,' etc. Then you press replay in your memory, and you *watch all the scenes again*!"

I didn't believe it. It was not only a mind-boggling bombshell for me, but besides that, I concluded that she (Shondra, the real one) and Melissa had also cobbled up a diabolical plan and fooled everyone for decades. I tried to recall the chronology out loud.

"So it was Melissa then, the lady who was in love with a young white woman named Lauren who formed a couple of mothers and who gave birth to a little boy named Dwayne. And Melissa was the one who died in Lone Pine and was buried by the Paiutes-Shoshones. That means it's you, Melissa's look-alike, who came to the Indian reservation to recover Dwayne and raise him here in Vegas with you. So when Jabaree calls you Granny Melissa, he's not really wrong... Does he know all this?"

"No. We didn't want to tell him. I'm Granny Melissa for him. For everyone I've been Melissa Westbrook since 1988. Shondra Wallace has been unofficially and virtually dead since then."

"I understand. More specifically though, how did you two proceed in fooling everyone when you 'changed identities,' changed your personalities?"

Shondra Wallace poured us some more lemonade before continuing.

"That idea seemed evident to us from the very beginning of *The Coyote-Woman*..."

CHAPTER 84
The makeup artist in love

"We both had very deep motivations" continued Shondra. "Melissa was pregnant, as I told you, with an in vitro fertilization, she was in a homosexual couple, and all this took place during the AIDS health crisis on a background of latent racism. She was starting to show though she did everything to hide her curves so people wouldn't talk, spread rumors about her. Of course, she no longer could be a stuntwoman in those conditions. So she wanted to disappear! She told me about that and both of us designed this plan, both of us agreed on it after long discussions. As for me, I was tired of a job where I no longer was fulfilled and happy. Had I ever been, actually? I'd never reached my dreams of stardom, or at least recognition. Never even come close. Instead of that, I'd been vegetating for nearly ten years in alternative cinema, B-series films, always with a shoestring budget and often duds, something that brought me no satisfaction at all. So, to help

– to save I should probably say – Melissa, my best friend, I also accepted to disappear. To conclude, we invented the *crossed disappearance* concept!"

"On paper, I do understand. But practically speaking, how did you accomplish that feat?"

Shondra cleared her throat and took another sip of lemonade.

"I have to say that the stakes were high, and it wasn't easy. The tiniest error, the smallest mistake could have been fatal to our dissimulation project. The *switch*, if I can call it that, took place the day before I disappeared, on May 31, 1988. After a day of shooting. You have to remember, but I think you already know this, that Melissa wasn't employed as a standby or stuntwoman in *The Coyote-Woman*. I didn't have any stunts in that movie. But she was in Lone Pine then, as that was a part of our plan. She had to be. Both of us had to be ready. As everyone knows, we were physically quite similar, and that's why she was my standby. People always said we looked like twins. Soul sisters, too. To understand how we deceived everyone, including our closest friends, you have to know that Melissa had short hair, because it was easier in her job. So it wasn't a big deal for her to look just like me by simply wearing a wig that looked like my hair. That's how fans never noticed a thing in the closeups where she was appearing in my place. And that's how we proceeded."

Another sip of lemonade, I could tell Shondra was getting tired. I let her continue without interrupting.

"The day before then, once the shooting of the day was over, we used an accomplice. The only other one who knew about this and who respected our choices. You heard of her, of course."

Once again, I rewound that strange movie in my head and gave her a name.

"Lauren?"

"Correct. Lauren, the makeup artist who was in love with Melissa. Dwayne's 'second mother' in their couple. So that night, when everyone was sleeping, Lauren cut my hair, sacrificing all my magnificent long hair I'd grown for years. But it was obviously part of our plan. My new hairdo was now the same as Melissa's. So all she had to do was put on her wig, the one she used when she was playing me riding a horse or doing another difficult scene. And to top it all off, that night we also exchanged our ID cards. I had officially become Melissa, and she had become Shondra. That night, I left Lone Pine, and I never went back to making movies again. The next morning, on June 1st, 1988, Melissa was the one starring in my place in *The Coyote-Woman of the Desert*."

"And then she also disappeared the following night, asking the Paiutes-Shoshones Indians for asylum, and then giving birth to Dwayne Smith. That little baby that you, Shondra Wallace, who had become Melissa Westbrook, would recover a few months later. Speaking of which, that last name, *Smith*..."

Shondra smiled.

"And not *Smithee*," she pointed out, smiling.

"Though I could have named him that. More seriously though, when I declared his birth, as his mother had died and there was only a biological and anonymous father, I decided to use one of the most common last names for children born anonymously, Smith. But, as luck would have it, that was also the last name of his 'second mother,' Lauren Smith! Fate must have been smiling at us that day, don't you agree, Karen?"

"Like a loop coming around in a circle, yes."

"Or the words

THE END

on the screen..."

Epilogue

Los Angeles, June 15, 2024

Though the Crypto.com Arena logo was displayed over the stadium's main doors, for me it was still the Staples Center.

My legs were wobbling, my heart was pounding in my chest like Notre Dame's largest bell, and my mouth was as dry as the Sonora Desert. I arrived early for my appointment with Luke.

Luke, my *lost son*.

I'd waited twenty-five years for that moment and was quivering like a teenaged girl hoping for her first kiss.

Now that I'd wound my investigation up, now that the *cinéma-vérité* movie about Shondra Wallace had been released, I was granting myself a few more hours here in California to try to get closer to my son.

. . .

WHILE I WAS CHOMPING at the bit in front of Magic Johnson's statue, I saw Luke walking towards me with a tiny smile. What could that mean? Probably the same thing as mine, which was having trouble showing itself: fear.

"Karen?"

"Luke!"

Then there were a few seconds of an embarrassed silence between us, with the iconic basketball player as an impassible witness to that scene between two people separated by twenty-five years. We didn't know what to do. Hug? Shake hands? Nothing at all, except look at each other and finally smile?

"Thank you for coming," I said gently.

He nodded.

"I got the tickets," he proclaimed, raising his hand. "Should we get going? The match starts in half an hour and there's already a line. Game 7 at home, it's not surprising! Us fans have been waiting for that for ages. And it'll probably be LeBron's last one too."

We followed the line of fans and little by little went into one of the historical sanctuaries of American basketball. During the twenty or so minutes it took us to reach our seats, we talked about trivial subjects. The atmosphere was heating up while the players were warming up on the court. LeBron James and his teammates such as Anthony Davis or Austin Reaves were applauded triumphantly. Luke was the one who told me that, I personally don't know a thing about basketball. Just sitting next to my son made me happy.

The game began and the first quarter started slowly for the Lakers, but in the second quarter they stepped on it, taking the lead against the Boston Celtics, 45 to 43. When the referee blew the halftime whistle, Luke and I went to one of the stadium restaurants to get something to eat and drink.

"Luke, I'm really happy to be here with you today. I wanted you to know that," I told him while taking a bite out of my vegetarian "downtown dog.".

"It's really strange. I'm having trouble believing this. All of a sudden a mother who comes out of nowhere, unexpectedly, you gotta understand me."

"I do, and don't worry, I'm not expecting anything in return. I have no pretentions of being loved by you. I'd never ask you to refer to me as *mom*."

"Especially as I already have a mom. And a dad. Parents who raised me, took care of me, loved me and allowed me to study at UCLA, who made me the person I am today. I owe them everything. I don't need a second mother."

I NODDED, powerless, faced with his merciless line of thought. He loved his adoptive parents. They were all he knew! As for me, his biological mother, it was as if I was born today for him!

"Luke, I never wanted to abandon you. I was so

young. My parents forced me to do so. I'm still so sorry about that. If I could do it over…"

"You can't do anything about the past," replied my son philosophically. "That's life. You have to live with it, go with the flow."

The bell rang in the stadium announcing the second half. Luke and I watched the spectators go back to their seats, but we didn't budge. We continued our conversation for the whole second half of the game.

Those twenty-four minutes of regulation game time would never be enough to catch up on twenty-five years of separation.

Every once in a while the spectators began to shout, making us think that the Lakers were doing pretty well.

When, forty minutes later, the spectators and the anchor both shouted at the same time, we understood that the Los Angeles team had won its eighteenth NBA final, putting its Boston competition in second place!

The stadium slowly emptied out and we followed the movement in L.A.'s cool nighttime weather.

We looked at each other in front of the stadium filled with joyful fans, without really knowing what to add. I decided to ask a direct question.

"Would you like to come and see me in Portland?"

"I don't know. I need time."

"We could maybe call each other then."

"Like I said, I need time."

I didn't say anything else. I respected his choice,

albeit with a lump in my throat. With those words we went our separate ways. I was heartbroken, almost as much as I'd been twenty-five years ago. As if I'd lost my child for the second time.

How could I recreate a link between us, especially as it had never really existed?

Except perhaps, the link of the flesh, that umbilical cord that was cut at birth...

The lost link.

My lost son.

THE END
(in real life, not in the movies)

Acknowledgments
AND JUST FOR YOU!

Just for info!

And just for you!

Dear Readers, this is your section, this is where I can never say "thank you" too many times to you. Without you, I'd be nothing at all. Because of your unwavering support, each time I finish a book, I can't wait to start the next one to entertain you, intrigue you, plus destabilize you too. I love inventing stories, illustrating them with words... but most of all, I love it when you love them!

Please take a moment or two to rate this book on the platform you purchased it from and comment on it. That's something that means so much to me and as I'm not well known in the United States, helps me generate sales. Thanks in advance!

Thanks also to my beta-readers, my graphic artist Ludovic Metzer, my editor (me, myself and I), my favorite translator, Jacquie Bridonneau, without whom you wouldn't have read this book in English, as well as Germain, my cat, who spent numerous hours behind my desk and chair, and with whom I often fought (and lost) for the most comfortable place.

See you all soon, Nino S.

Bibliography

THE KAREN BLACKSTONE SERIES
Sugar Island (2022) *(Winner of the Cuxac d'Aude Favorite Novel, 2023 / Finalist in the Loiret Crime Award, 2023)*
I Want Mommy (2023) *(N°1 in Amazon Storyteller France sales 2023)*
The Lost Son (2023)
Alone (2024)
Volume 5 to be published in 2025

THE BASTERO SERIES
French Riviera (2017) *(Winner of the Indie Ilestbiencelivre Award 2017)*
Perfect crime (2020)
Bloody Bonds (2022)

OTHER NOVELS
True Blood Never Lies (2022)
Thirty Seconds Before Dying (2021)
Eight more Minutes of Sunshine (2020)

About the Author

Nino S. Theveny is one of France's leading indie authors. He's married and has two children. In 2019 he was laid off from a multinational publishing company and decided to make the most of his newly found liberty, turning to writing, his passion, which is now his day job.

With 14 books published to date, Nino S. Theveny has over 250,000 readers. Translated into English, Spanish, Italian, and German, his thrillers are appreciated throughout the entire world.

With his fourteen-year-old son, he has also co-authored a thriller for young adults which came out in March, 2024.

Printed in Dunstable, United Kingdom